A MOTHER'S TOUCH

Holding Joshua's right wrist with one hand, Susannah spread the ointment with the other, working it into the skin on his palm. Recapping the jar, she said, "Does it feel better yet?"

"It would if you kissed me," Joshua said with an edge to his voice.

Susannah's heart skipped a beat. She picked up the jar and placed it back into the cabinet. Turning toward Joshua, she deliberately stepped to a spot where the table would be between them.

"Only six- or seven-year-olds in short coats are entitled to kisses as part of my doctoring," she said.

His presence in the small room seemed overwhelming. Her eyes lost in his, Susannah waited for Joshua to speak. She ought not to feel so many warm emotions toward a man whose length of acquaintance could be counted in hours.

"Pretend I am Ethan," Joshua said, his voice husky.

Susannah's pulse quickened because she knew that he was not joking. Joshua Cameron wanted to kiss her.

—From "A Mother's Heart" by Alice Holden

BOOK YOUR PLACE ON OUR WEBSITE AND MAKE THE READING CONNECTION!

We've created a customized website just for our very special readers, where you can get the inside scoop on everything that's going on with Zebra, Pinnacle and Kensington books.

When you come online, you'll have the exciting opportunity to:

- View covers of upcoming books
- Read sample chapters
- Learn about our future publishing schedule (listed by publication month *and author*)
- Find out when your favorite authors will be visiting a city near you
- Search for and order backlist books from our online catalog
- Check out author bios and background information
- Send e-mail to your favorite authors
- Meet the Kensington staff online
- Join us in weekly chats with authors, readers and other guests
- Get writing guidelines
- AND MUCH MORE!

**Visit our website at
http://www.zebrabooks.com**

MAMA'S LITTLE MATCHMAKER

ALICE HOLDEN
JULIETTE LEIGH
BESS WILLINGHAM

Zebra Books
Kensington Publishing Corp.

http://www.zebrabooks.com

ZEBRA BOOKS are published by

Kensington Publishing Corp.
850 Third Avenue
New York, NY 10022

First Printing: April, 2000
10 9 8 7 6 5 4 3 2 1

Printed in the United States of America

CONTENTS

A MOTHER'S HEART

by
Alice Holden

ONE

"And, tell me, Mrs. Bixby, is this Joshua Cameron a typical lawyer? Shifty-eyed, sly, stooped, and ancient?" Lady Susannah Taylor asked her housekeeper, who had handed her the solicitor's business card across the large mahogany man's desk spread with sketches for a sawmill.

Mrs. Bixby smiled merrily. "Hardly, Mrs. Susannah. Mr. Cameron is not much over thirty, quite attractive, and comes close to Mr. Stark in height, although not in girth, being much more slender," she said, measuring the lawyer against Berryhill's own burly bailiff.

Susannah rolled up the plans for the sawmill she intended to build for her tenants, turned in her chair, and placed the sketches on the lowest shelf of the open bookcase behind her.

"Looks can be deceiving," she said offhandedly with a small smile. "All lawyers are crafty."

The gray-haired matron, who had served the household long before Susannah had become the mistress of Berryhill eleven years before, put a finger to her rosy cheek and said, "Not this one. He has honest eyes."

Susannah chuckled. "Honest eyes? Really? Let's have a look at him, then, and discover what has brought him all the way from Chelsea to see me."

While Susannah waited for Mrs. Bixby to show the lawyer in, she gazed through the twelve-paned window to where a stone fountain bubbled in the courtyard. The afternoon sun streamed through the clear glass into the well-appointed library. Why would a solicitor from a village near London have come to see her? No matter how strenuously she plumbed her brain for a sensible reason, nothing even remotely logical sprang to mind.

The door opened, and Mrs. Bixby preceded the tall man attired in severe black into the room. Susannah came from behind her late husband's desk where she customarily pored over the account books and enacted estate business. Mrs. Bixby unobtrusively vacated the room, closing the door quietly behind her.

From the short distance between them, Susannah saw that the lawyer was indeed good-looking with thick, dark hair and compelling eyes as black as the coal in the copper bucket on the hearth where a significant fire had been laid to chase off the chill of the cool spring day.

Susannah moved forward across the predominantly red Persian rug which covered the parquet floor. At close range Mr. Cameron's eyes did have an intelligent warmth that engendered trust. As his large, strong fingers grasped her extended hand, his smile melted gradually, and his black eyes swept over Susannah with a new expression that gave her the definite feeling she had surprised him in some way.

"Please be seated," Susannah said when he released the hand he had kept a moment too long and indicated a man's oxblood leather chair which had been her husband's favorite place to relax with a book.

"After you, Lady Taylor," the solicitor said in a deep, self-assured baritone which Susannah thought must be an asset in a court of law.

She took a straight-backed chair and waited for him to sit down before saying, "You have come a long distance, sir. What brings you to Berryhill?"

He braced the elbows of his black wool coat on the chair's padded arms, clasped his long fingers together, and rested his strong chin on them. "My mission has to do with your brother, Benedict Kearny," he said.

"Benedict?" Susannah's voice climbed a notch before her face became grim. "I have not spoken with my brother in more than eight years. Don't tell me after all this time Benedict has decided to sue me for the money that my father left me in his will."

Joshua Cameron gazed at her in bewilderment. "No, ma'am. Benedict Kearny died last month."

"Oh, my." Susannah fell back in her chair and clutched her hands to her breast. She had stopped liking Benedict long ago, but still he had been her brother. "Of what illness? He was not so old, thirty-two, a mere four years older than I."

"Mr. Kearny did not die in his bed. He was thrown from a horse and broke his neck."

"Lord," Susannah said, bereft of words. How could she say anything without appearing insensitive? She could think of nothing but the afternoon when the man of business had finished reading her father's will in which she shared equally the inheritance with her brother. Benedict had cursed her and accused her of poisoning their parent's mind against him. As the male heir, he claimed, he should have inherited everything. His conduct and unjustified rude words had been degrading and disgusting and unforgivable.

Susannah gathered her wits. "You have not come simply to inform me of Benedict's demise, Mr. Cameron," she said. "I am not *his* heir, of that I am certain."

"Not in the normal sense."

She stared at him, confused by the enigmatic pronouncement.

"Were you aware, Lady Taylor, that your brother had wed and fathered two children since you last saw him?"

Susannah shook her head. "No, Mr. Cameron, I was not."

"When he died, Mr. Benedict Kearny left behind two orphaned boys," the lawyer said. "Ethan is seven and David is five."

"Orphaned? What of his wife?" Susannah asked. A strong premonition that Mr. Cameron's visit spelled trouble rushed into Susannah's consciousness. Whatever the lawyer had to say to her was not going to be in her best interest.

"Mrs. Kearny died giving birth to her younger son five years ago," he said. "The family resided a few streets from my law office; so when no one came forward to claim the children after their father's death, the rector of the local parish asked me to find the next of kin, which is why I am here. I know, Lady Taylor, you will want to become the boys' guardian."

Susannah's eyes widened. "I?" She nearly choked on the word. "I want no such thing. No, no, Mr. Cameron," she said, shaking her head slowly from side to side. "I cannot take on the care of two young children."

The solicitor's dark eyes chilled noticeably. "You are not too poor to feed a couple of small mouths?"

"Don't be impertinent, sir. I am not accustomed to being addressed in snide tones." Susannah speared him with a haughty look. "Anyone with eyes in his head can see for himself that Berryhill Manor is one of the most profitable estates in the county."

"Exactly," he declared. Susannah was aware that his patent sneer mocked her autocratic scold. "You are the boys' closest living relative, a woman of means who can well afford to raise them. Ethan and Davey need a surrogate mother, and as their aunt you are the logical choice."

"Surrogate mother?" she echoed. She opened her eyes wide. "My good man, you definitely have the wrong person. I do not have the time nor the will nor the temperament to raise children."

The lawyer's dark countenance became even darker. His stare seemed focused on a Spode vase in the Imari pattern near the window. But Susannah knew he was not really seeing the expensive blue and red, gold-edged jar. Clearly, Mr. Cameron had never expected her to refuse to take in her nephews. He was put off for a moment, but she had no illusions that he would easily give up on his mission. Stalwart determination was on his face.

Yet, being at loggerheads with him and prolonging their

fruitless discussion would solve nothing. Since Benedict had died without providing for the disposition of his sons, Susannah decided that she would do what she could for her nephews, short of making them her legal dependents.

"Mr. Cameron," she said, drawing his attention from the vase and back to her, "I do have money as you have so aptly pointed out. And, while Benedict and I were estranged, he was family. I am perfectly willing to contribute to the children's bed and board and other necessities, even their education, if it comes to that. Moreover, I have a number of cousins who have families and will, I am sure, happily add Benedict's progeny to their own if you apply to them."

Susannah congratulated herself on being fair-minded, generous, and pragmatic, but Mr. Cameron looked at her as if he would like to box her ears. For a moment he seemed disposed to argue, but then he rose from his comfortable chair and walked to a teak bookcase with a cabinet below on which mythological scenes were etched into the glass doors. He stared for a long time at the eye-level titles, all relating to agriculture, on the spines of the books on the upper shelves before he turned back toward Susannah.

His voice became cool and correct. "Surely you don't want to foist Ethan and Davey on just anyone as paid boarders. These unfortunate little boys are your own flesh and blood."

Susannah tightened her lips into a stubborn line at his presumptuous reprimand. "Don't think to play your May game on me, sir. I owe Benedict nothing, so do not expect me to wallow in guilt. Even so, I will do the best I can for his children." She got up from her chair and walked behind her desk and sat down.

Susannah opened the top drawer and removed a black leather address book. The lawyer's rebukes were like stinging chinks piercing her not so invulnerable armor. She was sympathetic to the children's situation, but she would not be goaded into agreeing to an imprudent decision by this uncivil, meddlesome dogooder which would be detrimental to both her and Benedict's sons. She would be doing the children a great disservice if she took them in rather than making certain they would be housed in the bosom of a caring family.

"I will compile a list of relatives who would make excellent foster parents, much better than I, I assure you," she said to the solicitor without looking at him.

Susannah turned the pages of the seldom-used book which contained the directions of distant kin, most of whom she had not seen in years, if ever, and began searching for a few likely names.

Idly, Joshua played with a large globe on a mahogany stand with clawed brass feet which stood beside the bookcase, sending the world spinning before he gave in to the impulse to gaze at Lady Taylor in silence. He moved to a location very near to the fireplace, where he could watch her head-on.

She dipped her quill pen into the inkwell she had uncorked a moment before and transcribed something onto the sheet of paper in front of her on the desk. She had stunned him when he had first walked into the room because she was radiant and blooming like a spring flower. The words *country widow* had not prepared him for this pretty woman with full, pink lips, lustrous, deep green eyes, and winsome, soft red curls that could only have been cut into that gamine style by a talented London barber. He had felt the unmistakable tug of attraction between them, palpable on both sides, the moment they had set eyes on each other. But now, with the disinterested expression of one who was privy to the outcome, he watched her complete what he knew was a useless task.

Pleased with herself, Susannah returned the pen to its holder and put away her address book. The four families she had chosen had sent birth announcements within the last ten years. There was no need to inform the solicitor that she had little personal knowledge of them. Fortunately, she had kept detailed records. Beside each family name she had written the date of birth, the sex of the newborn, and the gift she had sent. The cousins she had chosen had boys close in age to her nephews.

She looked up to find the solicitor regarding her in a preoccupied manner. She stood up and held out her list of names across the desk to him. "Each and every person, therein, is a solid citizen of excellent character," she said glibly.

Once the list was in Mr. Cameron's hands, he stared at the names with knitted brows. "As I suspected," he growled, balled up the paper, and with cool composure, pitched the list into the fire. Susannah's mouth flew open as she watched her written exercise turn into ash.

Before she could condemn his audacious conduct, he said, "I contacted every *esteemed* name on your list. Their first concern was the size of the remuneration in his will that Mr. Kearny had set aside for his children's expenses. Since the sale of Benedict's house was barely enough to pay for a decent burial for him and to clear his outstanding debts, the penniless children quickly became unwanted and unwelcome by those *good* people."

Susannah fingered the lace on the neck of her primrose pink morning gown before becoming absorbed with the ivory-handled letter opener on the desk. When Joshua Cameron said, "Ethan and Davey have been living with me, but mine is a bachelor's establishment without a wife to see to the welfare of children," Susannah answered, "I do not think I would be very good at raising little boys."

Joshua detected a wistful note in her voice which gave him hope and emboldened him. His lips relaxed into a sympathetic smile. "Every woman has a mother's heart deep within her," he said. "Women are born with the natural instincts for mothering; the trait is strong, particularly in well-bred females."

Suddenly, Susannah had to laugh. "What rubbish," she said. She had admired the solicitor's iron control. Except for the single lapse when he had figuratively counted to ten while pretending to examine her book titles, he had kept his temper inside. His arguments until now had been rational, but this was pure pandering. Even though she was weakening in their contest of wills, she could not let this puffery pass unchallenged.

"You know as well as I do that mothers come in good, bad,

and indifferent, among both the rich and the poor," she said. "Neglect of children is not unknown in any class. And as for the well-bred being superior parents, I can point you to a dozen bad mothers who are venerated by the cream of the *ton.*"

Joshua's color mounted with the realization that he had unthinkingly blabbed some ridiculous cliché and been caught out by his lovely adversary. "Pretty stupid on my part. You are right, of course." Their smiles meshed, his sheepish, hers teasing.

"But that does not mean that you lack maternal instincts. You simply have not been tested," he said. "I'll bring Ethan and Davey inside now, and you can see how it goes."

"You have the children with you?"

Joshua was daunted, for Lady Taylor's aspect lost all look of capitulation. "My coachman is watching them," he said warily as he kept a vigilant eye on her.

"You never mentioned that the children were already here." Her green eyes accused him. "You should have said so from the beginning."

"I assumed you knew." Joshua stuffed his hands into his trouser pockets. He decided that before she came up with another objection, he would deal up one more card. His ace, really.

"Look, my lady," he said, in his most suave and persuasive voice, "at least meet Ethan and Davey. I donate funds to a home for destitute children which is a shade better than the norm for those places. If after you have been introduced to your brother's sons, you still cannot find it in your heart to take them in, I shall enroll your nephews in the Chelsea Orphanage."

Susannah looked at him as if he had lost his mind. "Have your wits gone begging?" she said. "You could have saved us both all this meritless dueling. Did you honestly believe that I could send the children away when they were already on my doorstep? Bring my nephews to me."

TWO

"Make your bows to Lady Taylor," Joshua Cameron prompted. Susannah watched with amusement as the solicitor forced a bow from each child by simultaneously placing two large hands on two small necks and compelling each boy's head into a bob. When the boys arighted themselves, the older child whispered something to the younger, but before anything else passed between them, Mr. Cameron prodded the taller boy toward Susannah and said, "This is Ethan."

She leaned forward. "I am pleased to meet you, Ethan," she said to the blond-haired youngster dressed in a short brown coat and dusty black breeches. The seven-year-old stared at her with stony blue eyes which, as Susannah remembered, were the color of his father's. He had the look of Benedict about him, except for the fair hair which must have come from his mother. What disconcerted her was that the child seemed openly hostile. He moved closer to Joshua Cameron's side. Her smiles were answered with scowls.

At a loss, she made to greet the younger boy, who was attired in a dark blue coat and tan breeches, the knees of which were stained green from rolling in the grass, Susannah surmised. But before she could extend her hand, the youngster tugged on Joshua Cameron's black trouser leg and looked up the solicitor's long length. His upper lip trembled. "I want to go home, Mr. Josh," he said.

Susannah thought the lawyer looked as confused and flustered as she felt. He hunkered down and held the child's shoulders, balancing easily on the balls of his feet. "Berryhill is your home now, Davey. Lady Taylor is your papa's sister. You are to live with her."

"I don't like her," the child mumbled and sank his face into the lapel of Joshua Cameron's black coat. Susannah watched helplessly, uncertain what to do. The lawyer put the boy from him and stood up.

Before Joshua could say anything, Ethan grabbed hold of his arm. "Why can't we stay with you in your house by the river, Mr. Josh? I like it there."

"I'm not your guardian, Ethan. Lady Taylor is your closest relative. Your papa would want you to live with her."

"She don't want us," Ethan said. Susannah cringed inwardly as he pointed a small finger at her as if he were some vengeful preacher assaulting a sinner.

The solicitor's rattled expression hardened. "Now, why on earth would you say such a thing? Confound it, you have not met your aunt before."

"I just know, Mr. Josh. I know for sure," he said stubbornly.

"Gad," Joshua said and threw up his hands. The children's aversion to their aunt made no sense to him at all. Perhaps, he had not prepared them adequately for the change. But neither Ethan nor Davey had objected when he said he was taking them to the country to live with their aunt.

Susannah read the plea for patience in the solicitor's dark eyes. If he expected her to soothe the children with placating words, she would have to disappoint him. Instead she put voice to the first idea that came into her mind. One that would buy time.

"Are you returning to Chelsea today?" she asked him.

"No, ma'am," he replied. "I have already spoken for a room at the Inn of the White Hare in the village for the night. I will leave in the morning."

"Then, perhaps you would consent to remain with us for what's left of the afternoon and take supper with me and the children before you go to the inn for the night."

"Yes, I could do that, my lady," he said, following her thinking and welcoming the invitation. He had been troubled with the idea of leaving the boys abruptly when the two were so obviously unhappy. It seemed a heartless thing to do. He could only hope that by their bedtime, Lady Taylor would have won the children over.

Susannah stepped to the bell rope. Within a matter of seconds, Mrs. Bixby answered her summons.

Susannah made arrangements to have a bedroom prepared for the boys with a cot in the adjoining dressing room for a young maid who did all sorts of work inside the house.

"Although she is a girl of sixteen, Patsy comes from a large family and is accustomed to children," she explained to the solicitor. "She will take good care of Ethan and Davey."

"Come, lads," Mrs. Bixby said, her round, sunny face beaming maternally on the boys. "We might be able to talk Cook into letting you sample the raspberry tarts she baked this morning before Patsy takes you to the nursery to play."

Leery-eyed, Ethan looked at the solicitor. "Go on," Joshua said, harboring his impatience. "I will be here when you come back for supper."

"Are there toys in the nursery?" Davey asked Mrs. Bixby, plainly not the least overset to be going off with the comfortable woman.

"Indeed there are," the housekeeper said, "and you can play with every one of them."

Ethan still looked sullen, but he followed Davey and Mrs. Bixby from the room.

"I warned you, Mr. Cameron," Susannah said, steering the lawyer to the cozy chair he had occupied earlier. "I have no maternal instincts. Children sense those sorts of frailties in adults."

"Nonsense," the lawyer said, sitting down and crossing one long leg over the other. "Children need time to warm to strangers."

Susannah leaned her back against the library table. "Your

excuse won't wash. The boys' antagonism runs deeper. Look how readily Davey trotted after Mrs. Bixby."

"Wouldn't you if you were that age and someone offered you raspberry tarts and toys?"

Susannah broke into a wholehearted smile. "Perhaps," she said. He had a nice answering laugh, and Susannah found herself liking him.

"Would you care for some tea or wine, Mr. Cameron?"

"No, ma'am, thank you, but I would like to take a walk around the grounds before supper. You have a beautiful estate. I understand you manage Berryhill Manor on your own."

"I am in charge, but I have excellent help, particularly in my bailiff, Ezra Stark, who is an old family friend. When my husband, Sir Aaron Taylor, became ill in the second year of our marriage, Berryhill was a marginal venture. It was then I began running the estate. Aaron died the following year."

Joshua put a contemplative finger to his mouth. "I am no expert on agriculture, but you seem to have been remarkably successful—quite a feat for a woman."

Susannah made a sound of rueful exasperation. "Why is it that men never think women have good sense? Actually, Mr. Cameron, the profits have doubled under my management. I handle the estate accounts myself. I know where every penny goes, what each employee is paid, and what he does to earn his wages. Moreover, I try to keep up with everything published on modern farming."

The solicitor's eyebrows raised a fraction in just the faintest hint of amusement. "I had already discerned that you did not subscribe to the theory that reading anything more weighty than a popular novel is dangerous to the delicate brain of a female."

"Oh, and how did you come to that conclusion?"

Susannah waited for his elaboration with interest.

"I could see that the volumes on scientific farming in your bookcase there were too recent to have belonged to your husband. In truth, Lady Taylor, I am impressed with your accomplishments."

Their gazes locked in an intimate communion. A small voice in the back of Susannah's head told her that he was sincere. She was surprised how much the good opinion of this handsome stranger pleased her.

Joshua saw her as fresh and new and different from the society females his brother and sister-in-law pushed on him. Perhaps fate had brought him here to meet the kind of woman he had unknowingly waited for all his life. But he needed time to absorb this astounding idea which had come to him out of the blue.

He rose from his chair. "I will take that walk now," he said.

"Please do, Mr. Cameron. I have to get back to the task of working up some figures for a new sawmill."

Holding his gaze with her own, she said, "Would you have put the children in the Chelsea Orphanage?"

With a dismissive flourish of his hand, he said, "Pure fustian, ma'am. My infallible instincts told me the minute I laid eyes on you that you would never have allowed it. But had I been mistaken, I have excellent servants who are up to the task of looking after two small boys. In fact, I have enjoyed having the scamps around."

"Fraud," she said, dimpling.

He let their eyes tangle in mutual admiration before he spun on his heels, walked the length of the room in large strides, and vanished into the hall.

Susannah called after him, "Dinner is at six!"

He popped his dark head back inside the room. "Yes, ma'am," he said and was gone.

The first thing that came into Susannah's mind as she walked across the carpet and settled in her desk chair was that it had been a very long time since she had been in love. Why should the appearance of the Honorable Joshua Cameron have brought such an odd thought into her head? She shifted her shoulders as if throwing off something bothersome, reached down to the bottom shelf of the bookcase, lifted the sketches of the sawmill, and spread them out across the surface of the desk. But she did not look at the plans. Her elbows rested on the desk top. She steepled the fingers of her folded hands and stared into space. Benedict was dead. Until he went to university, he had been such a lively, funny boy with the sweetest disposition. Afterward, he was always short of money. While still a schoolgirl, countless times she had given him her quarterly allowance. "As a loan," he had said, but the loans had never been fully repaid. In time his mounting gambling debts had soured him. The end of their cordial relationship had come abruptly when he had tried to intimidate her into turning over her portion of the legacy from their father to him, but at the time Aaron was ill and Berryhill was on a downslide and badly needed the infusion of capital. Benedict had called her vile names when she refused to bend to his will. Yet, he was dead. Knowing this made her sad.

She could see that she was not going to get any work done, for she had developed a rare throbbing headache brought on by the tensions and emotions of the past hour. From experience she knew that the swiftest remedy for the malady was to take a headache powder and lie down. Leaving the sawmill sketches on the desk, Susannah left the room, her mind still crammed with distasteful memories of Benedict and worries about the unwelcome responsibilities thrust upon her with the guardianship of his orphaned sons.

THREE

Responding to the dinner gong, Susannah came downstairs at six o'clock in an elevated mood. Her headache and the shadows of Benedict had been dispatched during a restorative nap. She was dressed in an emerald shot-silk gown that was cut low across her bosom. Something in her had made her want to look her best tonight. She knew this up-to-date creation of a London modiste would ensure that she would be turned out in style.

Ezra Stark, her bailiff, and Joshua Cameron were sipping their predinner wine near the dining room window where the green brocade drapes had been drawn against the coming dark. Ethan and Davey stood before a walnut china cabinet in the corner. Their small noses were pressed upon the beveled glass, staring at the collection of porcelain circus animals on one shelf.

Susannah had invited Ezra Stark, who was a friend as well as a valued employee, to dine at the manor house tonight for the avowed purpose of meeting her nephews and the solicitor. Ezra was an amiable fellow and a good conversationalist. She hoped his presence would ease the strain of being in the company of the children, who seemed to hold her in contempt and dislike, and of Mr. Cameron, whom she was finding much too attractive. Looking at the two men, Susannah found that her bailiff and the lawyer had apparently found a mutual interest. Their conversation appeared to be particularly congenial, and somewhat animated, marked by man-to-man smiles and laughs more common between old friends than brand-new acquaintances.

Her approaching footsteps caused Joshua, who stood with his back to the room, to turn around. His discourse died in midsentence, and he looked at her a bit in awe. For a country widow who was supposed to be past her prime, she looked remarkably young and lovely in both face and form. Her skin was the delicate pale variety often found with red hair, but her cheeks had an attractive rosy glow, possibly from hours spent in the fresh air looking after the estate. Impetuously, Joshua raised his crystal wine goblet in a salute to her perfection.

Taking the encomium, at first, as no more than an homage to her fashionable gown, Susannah, nevertheless, flushed with pleasure. But when Joshua Cameron distractedly swirled the wine in his glass and prolonged his forthright stare, Susannah was left with the impression that his approval of her extended far beyond her dress.

Momentarily ruffled by this perception, she became as speechless as the solicitor. But when she saw Ezra Stark's lips crooked drolly with comical amusement at the romantic exchange, Susannah pulled herself together and quickly regained her aplomb. She said to her bull-shouldered bailiff, "I see that you and Mr. Cameron have introduced yourselves to one another."

Ezra's farcical look vanished. "Yes, and it seems we share common backgrounds," he said, stepping to a side table and helping himself to an hors d'oeuvre.

"Oh?" Susannah looked from one man to the other with curiosity while Ezra demolished the appetizing morsel in one bite.

"We are both younger sons who chose nontraditional occupations rather than appease our families and go into the military or the church," he said.

Joshua Cameron gave an acquiescent nod. "My brother is an earl who, in private, considers me something of a loose screw. He makes no bones about pointing out to me that as a solicitor, I am no better than a tradesman because I take fees." He winked at Susannah and broke into a knavish grin. "But outside the family, his lordship would defend me against critics with his last breath. We are, after all, in spite of our disagreement on this score, decidedly fond of one another."

That drew a laugh from Ezra Stark. "I see your kin are like mine in yet another way. My family, too, tightens the circle when one of its own is attacked."

The pool of shared experiences made for pleasant talk between the men until they were cut off when Susannah's man Collins appeared and forced them to the table. The butler informed his mistress that Cook had sent him to warn Mrs. Susannah that the joint of beef was roasted to a turn, but would be overdone if allowed to stand a moment longer.

Reminded of her hostess duties, Susannah seated her guests around the lace-covered Chippendale dining table from which several leaves had been removed to accommodate the small party into a more intimate grouping.

Ethan and Davey sat on high stools under the watchful eye of Patsy, who stood at their backs. The young maid was there to cut their meat and butter their bread, and repress any excessively noisy prattle which might interfere with the adults' enjoyment of the meal.

Collins wheeled in the dinner trolley, removed the covers from the dishes, and expertly served the roast beef, its accompaniments, the fresh-baked bread, and glasses of the best wine from Berryhill's excellent cellars.

Once the table talk commenced, both Ezra Stark and Joshua Cameron courted Susannah's views on the politics of the day. She was not shy in making her opinions known on the Prince Regent's extravagant spending or on any of the other ensuing topics which pertained to the state of the nation.

Through all of the meal, the children had been successfully kept from intruding on the grown-ups' dinner dialogue by Patsy's diligence. But Davey had forked the last bit of creamed potato on his plate into his mouth moments ago. He started to fidget. Collins, in the course of his duties, reached for the child's empty plate and unintentionally came between Patsy's

impeding hand and Davey's intentions. The boy leaned toward
the solicitor who sat next to him and nipped like a little crab at
the well-made sleeve of Mr. Cameron's fine black coat until he
captured the lawyer's complete attention.

"Mr. Josh, there is a wooden horsey upstairs in the nursery,"
he said, beaming.

Fueled by the delicious meal and the superior wine, Joshua
was in a mellow mood. Davey's cheerful smile caused him to
conclude that the boys had ceased their brooding and had become completely acclimated to their new surroundings. Smiling, he asked, "Did you ride the horse?"

Davey bobbed his head in the affirmative. "It was fun."

"The rocking horse is ancient," Susannah interjected, as up-
lifted as Mr. Cameron to find Davey so agreeable. "Everything
in the nursery is old. The books and toys belonged to my husband. Had he lived he would have been Mr. Stark's age."

Ezra Stark, who was past his fortieth year, laughed. "Very
old, indeed."

Susannah gave her bailiff a bright smile that did not last long,
for Ethan spoke up, his voice sullen and reproachful.

"Patsy said you would scold me, lady, if I bounced the ball
I found in the house."

The rude manner in which Ethan had said the word *lady*
rasped on Susannah's nerves as would a file over metal. The
child was becoming tiresome. Stern words shot from her
mouth. "Ethan, do me the courtesy of addressing me as Aunt
Susannah or Auntie, if the former is too much of a mouthful to
wrap around your tongue. As for the ball, it is a plaything for
outdoors. You could break an irreplaceable treasure in the house
should you throw it carelessly."

Susannah was immediately appalled at her own outburst.
When she saw how tightly her hand gripped her wineglass, she
realized how tense her nephew's pouting disapprobation had
made her. But he was only a child. She should be more tolerant.

Joshua Cameron said in a voice that was soft and nonthreatening, "Ethan, you will play with the ball only outside. Do you understand?"

Ethan said yes without arguing, but he pinned Susannah with a dark frown.

An uncomfortable aura fell upon the table while Collins removed the dinner plates.

Patsy stared miserably over her charges' fair heads at Susannah. The young maid, who at sixteen was little more than a child herself, was unsure of what to make of having her name brought into the unpleasantness.

"Patsy, you must be hungry," Susannah said, planting a buoying smile on her face in order to banish the innocent girl's apprehension. "Go have your supper now." Patsy bobbed a relieved curtsy and hurried from the room.

While Collins passed around the chocolate mousse on the china dessert plates, Ezra broke into the hush which had fallen over the diners. "Lads," he said, his usual booming voice sounding especially loud in the quiet room, "beside my cottage is an oak tree which has a perfect branch for a swing."

Ethan gave him a blank look. "What is a swing, Mr. Stark?"

"You have never been on a swing?" Ezra said in amazement.

Helpfully, Joshua explained, "Ethan lived in an area of Chelsea where the houses were close upon one another with few trees. Swings, Mr. Stark, are more familiar to country children."

"Just so," Ezra said. "Let me tell you, then." A new enthusiasm punctuated his words, and his gray eyes shone. "A swing, lad, makes it possible to soar high into the air."

"Can you fly like a birdy?" Davey asked, his head cocked to one side like a bright-eyed sparrow.

"Not quite, for one remains anchored to the ground, but the magic is in the imagination." Ezra's finger tapped the baldness below his receding brown hair. "If one keeps his eyes on the sky, he will feel very much as if he is flying."

Mr. Cameron's smile from across the table encompassed both

Susannah and her bailiff. But something in those dark eyes led Susannah to believe his smile was more for her than for Ezra.

"Can you make a swing, Mr. Stark?" Ethan asked eagerly.

"Indeed, I can and will," Ezra promised. "After supper I shall draw a picture for you so that you can see how the finished product will look."

When the meal was over, the rejuvenated party adjourned to the music room, which took its name from the unique piano-forte made from contrasting inlays of rare woods that occupied the space in front of the bow window hung with Honiton lace curtains.

Susannah directed Ezra to a tall, cherrywood lady's writing desk when he requested paper and a drawing pencil.

"You should find what you need in one of the drawers," she said and got comfortable in an antique walnut chair with embroidered covers from which she watched Joshua Cameron examine the Dutch seventeenth century paintings grouped on one wall. He was returning to Chelsea tomorrow. She would be left to cope with her nephews herself. Was that what bothered her? Or had she formed an incipient attachment to him that made her reluctant to see him disappear from her life for good? She could not take this thought further, for she was distracted when Collins came into the room and approached the lawyer and offered him a glass of brandy from the silver tray he carried.

Joshua took the welcome drink and sat down on a green silk sofa with carved mahogany legs. Ethan and Davey had crowded in on Ezra Stark and had become deeply absorbed in watching him sketch the swing. Collins placed a second glass of brandy on the end table near the bailiff and withdrew from the room.

Ezra finished the drawing, put down his pencil, handed the picture to Ethan, and picked up his drink.

"May I see?" Joshua asked from across the room. Ethan brought the illustration to him.

"Isn't it grand, Mr. Josh?" Ethan said in wonder. Joshua agreed, for the bailiff was a talented amateur artist and had captured a faithful rendition of a boy on a swing.

Davey had lost interest in the picture and had drifted toward the pianoforte unnoticed. The open keyboard proved an irresistible temptation. With full force, he brought his closed fists down again and again on the keys in discordant thumps.

"Davey, stop it!" Susannah cried, over the clamor. The keys went silent. She got up and went to stand beside the child. "The proper method is to press one key at a time," she said. "Let me show you how."

Davey brushed past her and fled to the sofa where he climbed up beside Joshua, rubbed his fist against his small nose, yawned, and cuddled into the solicitor's side.

Susannah's sense of injury mounted when Joshua's arm went around the small shoulders. She felt the lawyer was putting her in the wrong. She remained unplacated when he said, "Perhaps you would consent to play for us, ma'am, and show Davey how the instrument should sound," even though there was no mockery in his tone.

"Yes, do, Susannah," Ezra seconded from where he sat on the desk chair which strained under his considerable bulk.

Susannah paged through a book of music to gain time to calm herself. She was unhappy with what she saw as both her bailiff's and the lawyer's aligning themselves with the child. The instrument was old and fragile and easily put out of tune. She had volunteered to show Davey an acceptable alternative to his inappropriate pounding. How could anyone fault her when it was the child who was being rude? She selected a piece and began to play, immediately aware that she needed practice, but she carried on and managed to reach the final chord without making a serious mistake. Closing the piano, she turned toward Joshua. While she had performed, Ethan had joined Davey on the sofa. Both boys were asleep, one on each side of the lawyer, in the curvature of his arms.

Although the children had slept through her playing and would not likely awaken to the sound of her voice, Susannah said softly, "I will ring for Mrs. Bixby to get the boys' beds ready."

However, before she could cross the room, Collins came in to replenish the gentlemen's brandy snifters. Hearing her, he said, "No need, Mrs. Susannah. The laddies' beds have been turned down. Patsy is waiting for them to come upstairs."

"In that case," Joshua said, taking charge, "Collins, if you would be kind enough to carry Davey and lead the way, I will follow you with Ethan."

When Joshua and the butler had gone, Susannah returned to the chair in which she had been sitting before.

"More brandy, Ezra?" she asked.

The bailiff got up and placed his empty glass beside the decanter Collins had left on the wine table.

"No, I think I have indulged quite more than my norm in Mr. Cameron's excellent company. I will repair to my cottage in a minute." He crossed his arms over his broad chest and looked down at Susannah. "You are not taking to the youngsters, are you?"

"I?" she said defensively. "Ethan and Davey developed an aversion to me on sight that I have been unable to dispel. What am I supposed to do?"

"Come, come, Susannah. You are not normally so short-tempered. Those boys have recently lost their father. You need not poker up at every small slight."

"Oh, Ezra," she said on a sigh, suddenly all solicitude. "Do you really think I am proud that a seven-year-old can goad me into shrewlike behavior? I should have been more diplomatic with Ethan at the table. Mr. Cameron must think very badly of me."

Ezra let out a booming laugh. "My dear Susannah, from what I observed, Mr. Cameron would not think badly of you if you murdered his grandmother. The man is obviously besotted."

Joshua walked through the open door a split second after the tactless quip. Ezra's face colored into a deep scarlet.

"I was bidding Lady Taylor good night," he said sheepishly, for he was positive that Mr. Cameron had overheard him.

To his immense relief, Ezra was spared the set down he feared. The solicitor gave no indication by manner or tone that he was privy to Ezra's unfortunate remark or that he was offended by it.

Looking as guilty as a boy caught stealing apples from his neighbor's tree, Ezra made his escape.

Susannah and Joshua regarded one another without speaking. To comment on Ezra's faux pas, which was uppermost in both their minds, was unthinkable.

In the past, Joshua had scoffed at gentlemen who wore their hearts on their sleeves in company, and he was uncomfortable to find himself now among their ranks. He had chosen not to compound his embarrassment over the lampoon by admitting that he had heard Mr. Stark. He suspected that the bailiff was already conscience-smitten at having uttered his suppositions. Joshua did not require a public apology which, in his opinion, would only have made him appear an even greater fool.

"It has been a long day," he said, still vexed at himself for having behaved so openly like a lovesick pup. "I must be going as I plan to leave for Chelsea at dawn."

Susannah's heart went still. "Then, I shall not be seeing you again?"

"Do you wish to?" he asked. The hope that she might not want to end their budding relationship any more than he did rose within him.

"You will always be welcome at Berryhill," she answered evasively.

Never a slow-top in seizing the moment, Joshua said boldly, "Will I? Then, may I venture a suggestion?"

He took Susannah's silence as tacit permission to go on. "The children seem to have formed a strong attachment to me," he said. "Perhaps weaning them from that predilection would be preferable to an abrupt severance from me. Such a sudden parting could prove traumatic to them and add to your problems."

"What are you suggesting?" Susannah said, all ears.

"I could put up at the village inn and come to Berryhill on a daily basis until the children are settled in to your satisfaction."

"Whyever would you want to continue to help me," Susannah asked, "when you can now, in good conscience, forgo the responsibility for the children which you have shouldered since my brother's death?"

"Let us just say that I feel responsible for being the author of your predicament."

Susannah smiled faintly. "You are simply the messenger, Mr. Cameron. Benedict is the author of my predicament, not you. However, I would be an idiot to turn down your offer of help."

"Then, you accept?" His deep voice was incredulous.

"Why not?" she said. "I am very uncertain of myself where those children are concerned. You seem to have charmed them. Perhaps, I can learn a trick or two from you on how to get on with my nephews."

Having achieved his heart's desire with such little effort, Joshua's voice grew more emphatic as he made his plans known to her. "I must return to Chelsea to give instructions to my law clerks. But since I prefer to travel light and by horseback, I should be back here by the day after tomorrow."

He went on in that vein, informing her that he would leave his coach and driver at home and send his valet on a holiday. He could safely give her a week, he said, before he would be required to be in court again.

Susannah rose and extended a hand to him. "I look forward to your return," she said.

When Joshua had departed, Susannah became thoughtful. She decided that there was a kernel of truth in Ezra's outrageous eruption. The lawyer's willingness to spend some days at Berryhill had more to do with her than with the children. There had been clear signs all through dinner to that effect. But she had to sleep on it before she could come to a definite conclusion about what it all meant.

FOUR

Susannah sorted through her work-related correspondence and attempted to keep focused on estate business, but thoughts of Joshua Cameron came obstinately between her and the problems on her desk.

Last night when she had gone to bed, she had been impeded by the chaos of the day from thinking clearly. But, when she awoke this morning, she had been able to marshall her thoughts and come to some logical inferences about Joshua Cameron's motives.

Ezra's claim that the lawyer was besotted with her suggested that the solicitor might be marriage-minded. However, Susannah was not a virginal flower in the first bloom who was ripe for the Marriage Mart. The likelihood was that Mr. Cameron looked upon a twenty-eight-year-old widow as fair game for seduction.

On this repressive thought, Susannah closed the ledger and rang for her butler. When Collins appeared, she requested that he send word to the stables to have her horse Firefly saddled. She then gathered her papers into a neat pile on the desk. Mr. Cameron was an attractive man. There wasn't a woman born who wouldn't give him a second look, but being someone's mistress had no appeal for her.

In her bedroom, her maid, Prissy, buttoned Susannah into a dark blue habit which was pretty enough for a gallop in Hyde

Park at the fashionable hour and adjusted a navy hat with a slightly larger brim than current mode dictated over Susannah's short red curls. The riding hat was specially designed to protect her fair skin from the direct sunlight. She bent toward a mirror to overlook Prissy's work.

Her fallen face sprang out at her from the looking glass. The idea that the solicitor might be a rake had made her feel glum. She gave herself a mental shake. Why should she be miserable if Joshua Cameron turned out to be a womanizer? He would still honor his promise to help her win over the children. And wasn't that the chief reason that she had invited him to come back to Berryhill?

Susannah treated the question as rhetorical and managed to push Mr. Cameron from her mind after she left for the stables and mounted Firefly for a business tour of the estate. Forcing the state of her land to be her sole concern, she nodded with satisfaction as, in field after field, the weeds had been kept down as evidenced by the fresh hoe marks in the rich soil around the green sprouts. She noted the recent repairs and the bright paint on an old barn which had been brought back into mint condition. Area after area proved to be well-maintained. But, when she came to a tumbled down wall, she found reason to frown. She slid from the saddle and poked at the stones with her riding crop. Two weeks ago, Ezra was to contract with Fred Cunningham, a villager who did excellent stonework, to repair the damage. She would need to speak to her bailiff about the reason for the delay.

Back at the stables, Susannah decided to do just that when she heard Ethan's and Davey's laughter and Ezra's distinctive rumble coming from the direction of the bailiff's cottage. She handed Firefly's reins to a groom and set off on foot down a woodland path of birches, sturdy oaks, and sycamores. She passed in and out of patches of sun coming from above her where the branches failed to meet overhead.

When she stepped from the woods into her bailiff's yard where perennials grew around the stone cottage wherever the flowers took root, Susannah saw that the new swing was up. Ethan pushed Davey, who sat on the solid board seat and firmly gripped the strong new rope. "Higher! Higher!" the smaller boy egged on his taller brother as he flew through space.

Susannah called, "Hello, children," and gave them a friendly wave. Ethan and Davey ignored both her amiable verbal greeting and her raised hand as if she were invisible.

Color stung Susannah's cheeks. She had a churlish impulse to shake their rude little bodies to repay them for their calculated snub. She watched a minute as Ethan let the momentum of the swing die down. Davey came to rest, stopping himself by dragging his high black shoes in the long grass.

Ezra lumbered over to stand beside Susannah as the boys changed places, and Ethan took his turn on the swing. Facing her bailiff, Susannah asked, "Why hasn't the east wall been mended?" All of her frustration from her vain attempts to win over her nephews found its way into that one high-handed question.

Ezra's face went rigid, but his voice remained calm. "Fred Cunningham is laid up with a bad back. He will do the work when he is better."

"Sorry," Susannah said, avoiding her bailiff's eyes while digging distractedly at the cropped grass with the toe of her brown riding boot. "I wasn't angry with you."

"I know," Ezra said with real understanding. He had been annoyed, as well, with the children's provoking behavior toward her. Sympathetically, he said, "I didn't understand yesterday how entrenched the lads are against you. Do you think it might be because they want to live with Mr. Cameron in Chelsea? They mentioned to me that his house is on the river, and Mr. Josh has a boat."

Susannah watched Ethan on the swing, pumping his legs to propel himself higher. Davey leaned against a nearby tree, sucking his thumb. "What do I know of children's minds," she said peevishly. "You seem to be suggesting that my nephews think I am standing in the way of their going back to their village."

Ezra lifted his brown cap and scratched his head beneath the thinning hair. "The little lads are fond of Cameron. Perhaps they believe that it is your fault he won't take them home to live with him. Children often behave irrationally. Their odd behavior might be their way of punishing you."

"Ethan and Davey are succeeding," Susannah said acidly. "Maybe Mr. Cameron can sort things out. He comes back tomorrow."

"So I've heard," the bailiff said, stroking his stubbled chin. "He has the children's welfare in mind, I'm sure, but I won't recant what I said before. I still think he has a real interest in you." Ezra made an overdrawn show of looking behind him. "I trust he is not going to pop up like he did last evening. I was never so humiliated in my life."

Susannah laughed. "Your face was beet red."

"Too much wine and not enough discretion," he said. He shook his head in a sign of disgust with himself. But Susannah's light thrust was in such good humor that it permitted him to ask, "If I am not being too forward, do you like him?"

"You are being forward, but, yes, I do like him." Despite her recent dark thoughts about him, she realized that was true.

"I do, too," Ezra said. "Perhaps, he will succeed in bringing the children around and convincing them their happiness lies here with you at Berryhill."

"Yes, but, then again, his best intentions might ricochet. His presence could prolong the boys' animosity by keeping their hopes alive that he might adopt them; whereas, if he never comes back, Ethan and Davey, in time, will probably forget him and accept me."

Ezra kept his counsel, but he suspected that Susannah would be very unhappy if the solicitor failed to return to Berryhill. She was more powerfully attracted to Cameron, he believed, than she had yet admitted even to herself.

"Mr. Josh! It's Mr. Josh. He's here."

From the entryway, the children's eager voices announcing

the lawyer's arrival brought a spontaneous smile to Susannah's lips. She stored her quill pen in the ornate silver inkstand, removed the sander and blotted the small, precise handwriting on an unfinished letter.

Before she could rise from the desk chair where Ezra Stark days before had sat to draw the picture of the swing, Joshua Cameron strode through the open door with his long stride, flanked by Ethan and Davey. The lawyer was dressed for riding in comfortable cord breeches, a down-home country coat, and scuffed brown boots. Susannah found him impressive even in what must be his most casual clothes. Her heart sped up, and she gave him a glittery welcoming grin that would gladden any man's heart.

Joshua felt his chest tighten with desire when he looked down at her. He returned her amazing smile with a devastating one of his own. The magic she had worked on him before came flooding back in full force. Lovely in an eye-catching pale cream gown worked with blue and yellow beads, the sight of her left him slightly winded. Had he been alone with her, he would have taken a chance and kissed her. Instead, he was compelled to move to the green silk sofa and sit down facing her. Ethan and Davey bookended him and crowded against his sides as if they expected him to vanish.

When all the commonplace verbal exchanges had been exhausted, Joshua said, "I dined last evening with a friend of yours," and smiled in remembrance.

"Who, sir?"

"Lord Jansen."

"Then, we have a mutual friend indeed," she said. "His wife and I are bosom beaus. In fact, I was just this moment writing to her. I have stayed on several occasions with Lord Jansen and Lady Cecily at their town house during my sojourns in London."

"So he said. Carl Jansen and I have known one another since Oxford." His dark eyes took on an impish twinkle. "I understand that you are quite the belle and kick up your heels during your visits to Town."

Susannah laughed and candidly conceded, "I love to dance and cannot bring myself to forgo the balls and parties. But I travel to London for extended periods only twice a year."

From Lord Jansen, Joshua had learned all she had just said and more. Lady Taylor never lacked for partners, for she showed to advantage in the ballrooms, nor for invitations to the drawing rooms of the *ton,* for she conversed easily and made friends quickly. Joshua had wondered aloud to Lord Jansen why, given her popularity, Lady Taylor had never remarried. But his aristocratic friend had shrugged. "I suppose she has never fallen in love again," was the best he could offer.

Ethan and Davey with their endless interruptions made it impossible to carry on an intelligible conversation with Susannah. Over and over again, Joshua was reminded that he must see the swing. Finally he surrendered. "I brought you something special," he said to the boys. "The groom has taken it to the stables."

His broad hint allowed the children to ascertain in one guess that the surprise was a horse.

"Come, my lady," Joshua said. "I can see there will be no peace until we examine the animal."

Inside the stable, the horses stretched their long necks over the doors of their stalls to investigate the humans coming down the hard-packed dirt floor. The previous day, Ezra Stark had taken the children to see the stock. He had let them pet the horses and feed them chopped carrots from outstretched palms.

Ethan, therefore, was easily able to identify the new acquisition. "He wasn't here yesterday," he said perceptively. "What is his name, Mr. Josh?"

Joshua winked at Susannah as if sharing a private joke. "Nellie," he answered. "He is a she."

"I like the name Nellie for a lady horse," Davey piped up.

Susannah stroked the brown mare's nose. "She has such gentle eyes. You don't think she might be a little large for the children to ride, Mr. Cameron?"

"I would have preferred a pony, but the livery in the village had none available," Joshua said. "Nellie was the smallest horse I could find, and she should do for my purposes. You see, my idea, at least for the time being, is for Ethan and Davey to take turns in the saddle. While one rides, the other will lead the animal. You don't object, do you?"

"No, your plan is excellent. I wish I had thought of it."

His dark, masculine eyes showed his obvious pleasure at her sanction before he said to the boys, "Now, I would like to see the swing Mr. Stark put up for you."

"I know the way, Mr. Josh," Davey insisted, grabbing the lawyer's hand and pulling him toward the barn door.

"But when can we ride Nellie?" Ethan asked, his shoes firmly planted in front of the new horse's stall.

Joshua brought himself and Davey to a halt when it was apparent that Ethan was not about to move. Though Ethan had asked the question, it was Susannah, who had been walking beside him, whom he addressed. "Would you be free to go with us this afternoon, ma'am? I would like to find a flat stretch of meadow where the children can ride safely."

After a moment's reflection, Susannah replied, "Let us see the swing at Mr. Stark's house, have our tea, and then I will change into a riding habit and take you to a suitable field."

Joshua smiled widely. This was exactly what he had hoped to hear.

Susannah spoke to a groom who was repairing tack nearby. "Spacey, please have Firefly, the new mare, and Mr. Cameron's stallion saddled in an hour and brought to the front of the house."

Well satisfied, Joshua linked arms with her. This afternoon Ethan and Davey would be occupied with the new horse, and he would, at last, have the private moments with Susannah for which he hungered.

FIVE

Susannah and Joshua sat on a grassy rise overlooking a field sprinkled with dandelions, their backs propped against the trunk of an old apple tree from which in the fall the estate still harvested a half bushel of crisp, juicy pippins. The spring green grass around them was sprinkled with snowy petals, reminders of the white blossoms which in recent days had decorated the tree's ancient branches.

In the field below, Davey was in the saddle on Nellie's back while Ethan led the horse. His city boots flushed the hidden crickets in the high grass as he tramped over the meadow.

"I wonder what could have been in Benedict's mind," Susannah said to the solicitor as she looked down on the youngsters from her higher vantage point. "Patsy says that Ethan cannot read or write at all. At seven, he should at least know his letters and be able to print his name."

"I heard that your brother changed when his young wife died after giving birth to Davey," Joshua said, his tone more understanding than condemning. "He drank to excess and caroused with low females. He wasn't as attentive to his sons as he might have been, although he did engage a kindly, grandmotherly housekeeper to look after the children during the day. And to give him his due, he never left Ethan and Davey alone at night." Joshua rested his arm on one raised knee. "You know, Lady Taylor, it is not unheard of for a man to become unhinged at the death of his wife in childbirth. He sometimes feels responsible because it is he who got her with child."

"Call me Susannah, Mr. Cameron," she invited. The brown velvet hat with the broad brim which exactly matched her riding habit rested on her lap. She toyed with the tuft of decorative gray feathers in the band. "You have probably noticed that my people do not stand on ceremony. I am Mrs. Susannah to them—not exactly socially correct for the wife of a baronet, but far warmer than Lady Taylor."

Joshua brushed a petal from his sleeve and smiled. "Neither has it escaped me that your staff holds you in deep affection and respect."

"That stems from when I came to Berryhill as a very green seventeen-year-old," Susannah explained. "Aaron had already passed his thirtieth birthday, but we had less than two years in a normal marriage before he became ill with some wasting disease. I was forced into making take-charge decisions before I was twenty. All the employees, house and field, sympathized with my difficult task and formed a bulwark of support for me which has not diminished over time."

Joshua listened with only half an ear. He was conscious of how strikingly attractive she was. He traced her lips with covetous eyes and knew that what he really wanted to do was to kiss her.

"You must call me Joshua," he said to match her invitation to put them on a first-name basis and to have something to say that had nothing to do with his improper longings.

"Joshua, then," Susannah said with a slight inclination of her head before she returned to her earlier concerns.

"Regardless of the reason for Benedict's neglect, I suppose I will have to find a tutor for the children. The vicar takes on pupils, but perhaps it would be better to hire an educated governess. What do you think, Joshua?"

To Joshua his name was like music on Susannah's lips. He leaned over and cupped her chin in his leather-gloved hand and turned her pretty face toward him. "What I think is that you have the most gorgeous eyes I have ever seen. In the sunlight they are the color of the most precious of Chinese jades."

Susannah's heart beat fast when his overly warm eyes sought to hold hers, but with a calm she did not feel inside, she moved her chin from his light grip.

"While your practiced gallantry is flattering, sir, though a bit suspect, it is hardly an answer to my question."

Absently, Susannah stared at the tips of her boots, peeking from beneath the hem of her velvet skirt. In London society, it was all the rage for a gentleman to heap lavish praises on a lady and commonplace to tender extravagant compliments. Yet she was disappointed that Joshua Cameron had resorted to such an obvious gambit. It reinforced her suspicion that he was a seducer.

However, when his voice suddenly sounded disgruntled as he said, "Give the boys time to adjust before imprisoning them in the schoolroom; what difference does it make in the scheme of things if Ethan learns his ABCs now or in the fall?" her head came up in dismay.

A covert glance verified that something had caused his temper to simmer. His jaw had tensed visibly. Susannah suspected it had nothing to do with the children's education. Could he have taken offense at her mild chide about his tendering false compliments?

Susannah went on about the deferred lesson as if she had not noticed his altered mood, saying, "Waiting until autumn will do no harm, I suppose. But I think when the time comes it should be a governess. The vicar can appear quite stern and formidable and is better suited to the instruction of older pupils."

His next words left no doubt that Mr. Cameron, indeed, was smarting from her unintentional rebuke.

"Now that you have solved that dilemma," he said much too dryly to be mistaken for ordinary politeness, "answer me something, ma'am. Just how the devil can you tell the difference between shameless flattery and a sincere compliment?"

Susannah arched her brows, and her chin came up to meet his challenge. "Any woman worth her salt recognizes excessiveness in speech when she hears it."

"Really?" he said contemptuously. "Even though the counterfeit nonsense of a London popinjay is not all that dissimilar from a true admirer's bona fide compliments?"

"Fie! There is a difference," Susannah insisted. "A discerning woman can determine when a drawing room lothario is waxing poetic. Precious Chinese jade, indeed!"

A wounded look leapt into Joshua's eyes. He wrapped his arms around his raised knees and muttered, "You couldn't be more wrong, ma'am. I am anything but a practiced flirt." His voice was so low through gritted teeth that Susannah was about to ask him to repeat what he said when a swarm of Glory moths floated in the air near her face. As she swiped at the insects and turned her head to watch them scatter, she noticed a cloud of dust in the field below.

Susannah gaped for one heartbeat. Nellie galloped pell-mell across the meadow. Both boys were in the saddle of the runaway mare. Davey was fused to Ethan's waist, and Ethan was clutching the horse's mane. Susannah bound to her feet and slid down the hill, almost tumbling head over heels on the incline.

Belatedly, Joshua saw that the boys were in peril. He swore violently under his breath, sprang up, and hurled himself down into the meadow in one giant leap. He overtook Susannah with his much longer stride and passed her. Veering into the path of the fugitive horse, he flailed his arms and yelled, "Whoa, Nellie, whoa!"

Susannah covered her mouth with her fist. Her heart thumped wildly. Joshua lunged at the horse, grasped the reins with his gloved hands, and hung on. His boot heels upended the turf like a plow before he fought the horse to a standstill.

Susannah ran toward where the mare snorted and pawed the ground. Joshua plucked the children from the saddle and lifted them dually to the grass. Kneeling before them, he put an arm around each child. "It's all right. It's all right. You are safe now. Sh! Sh!" he purred, soothing their hiccupping sobs.

Seeing shades of Benedict's demise, Susannah's fear turned to anger. She pulled Ethan from Joshua's hold. Bending over nearly double, she put her hands on the child's shaking shoulders, looking into the fear-widened eyes in his tearstained face.

"What's wrong with you, Ethan?" Susannah scolded. "You disobeyed Mr. Josh. He told you the mare was to be led."

"I'm sorry, lady! I'm sorry!" Ethan's hands came up to his face as if to ward off a blow.

Startled, Susannah released him and stepped back. Ethan looked as if he had expected her to strike him.

Still on his knees, Joshua was calming Davey with circular motions on his back.

"Come here, Ethan," he said as he put the younger boy from him.

His head hanging, Ethan walked to the solicitor's side.

"What happened?"

"I got tired of leading Nellie, so I climbed onto her back with Davey; but a bird flew up from the grass and scared her, and she ran away."

Only snatches of what followed reached Susannah's ears, for the lawyer's voice was very quietly controlled. But she heard enough to discern that Joshua was not excusing Ethan's folly. But neither did he prolong his lecture.

The lawyer got to his feet, reached for Ethan, and hoisted him onto Nellie's back. He picked up the reins, smiling at Davey, who came to his side and thrust his small hand trustingly into Joshua's large one.

"Quite an adventure, my big boy," he said to the child. "You are very brave. Why, you hardly cried at all." Davey gave him a proud grin. Joshua smiled back. Leading the mare, he began to walk over the meadow back toward the hill, holding Davey's hand.

Feeling like an interloper, Susannah trailed behind, certain that she was in Joshua's black books for losing her temper with Ethan. She climbed up to where he waited for her with her abandoned riding hat in his hand. He handed it to her without a word, and she rammed it over her red curls. When he boosted her onto Firefly's back, Susannah saw that the palms of his leather gloves were in shreds and marveled that a man in such a sedentary occupation could summon the brute strength to stop a spooked horse.

Silently, the small party rode back to the stable in tandem as they had come to the meadow earlier. Susannah, once again, led Nellie with Ethan aboard while Joshua, on his horse Wizard, held Davey before him in the saddle.

In the stableyard, the groom Spacey lifted the children to the ground. Immediately, Ethan and Davey took off at a run toward the house.

Wordlessly, Susannah walked up the brick path side by side with Joshua. He surprised her by circling her shoulders with his arm and saying, "Are you all right?"

"Yes, of course," she answered, although she was still shaken by the whole incident and baffled by Ethan's violent reaction to her scold. "But you have hurt your hands."

"Yes, my palms sting like the very devil," he admitted.

"I think there is some burnet cream in the apothecary room."

"Burnet?" he said. "I don't know it."

"The herb grows wild on the estate. Cook uses the tender leaves in salads. The flavor is much like that of a cucumber. But Mrs. Bixby pulverizes the root into a cream and mixes it with some other things known only to her. The ointment is excellent for soothing scrapes."

Ethan and Davey had vanished upstairs by the time Susannah and Joshua came through the front door.

Susannah set her velvet hat, along with her riding gloves, on the hall table and said to Joshua, "This way." He followed her to the back of the house and into a small room where neatly labeled bottles with a variety of dried herbs were lined up on the white wooden shelves. Susannah opened an overhead cabinet and removed a ceramic jar. She placed the medicine on a well-scrubbed oak table and turned to Joshua.

"Let me have a look," she said. He extended his hands. She removed the tattered gloves carefully and turned his hands, palms up, aware that his eyes never left her face.

"The thick leather saved you from serious abrasions," she said, forcing herself to be all business to cover the fact that his stare made her want to fan herself in the small room. "You seem to have nothing more acute than this redness. The cream will soon alleviate the sting."

She removed the lid from the jar and dipped her fingers into the off-white cream. Holding Joshua's right wrist with one hand, Susannah spread the ointment with the other, working it into the inflamed skin on his palm. She repeated the treatment on his left hand. When she was finished, she rubbed the residual cream on her hands into her own palms and fingers. Recapping the jar, she said, "Does it feel better yet?"

"It would if you kissed me," Joshua said with an edge to his voice.

Susannah's heart skipped a beat. She picked up the jar and placed it back into the cabinet. Turning toward Joshua, she deliberately stepped to a spot where the table would be between them.

"Only six- or seven-year-olds in short coats are entitled to kisses as part of my doctoring," she said.

His presence in the small room seemed overwhelming. Her eyes lost in his, Susannah waited for Joshua to speak. She ought not to feel so many warm emotions toward a man whose length of acquaintance could be counted in hours.

"Pretend I am Ethan," Joshua said, his voice husky.

Susannah's pulse quickened because she knew that he was not joking. Joshua Cameron wanted to kiss her.

"Ethan is a bad choice," she said. "I am not in charity with that young man at the moment. It was a cork-brained thing for him to attempt to ride a horse without instruction."

"I gave him a good talking to. He won't do it again."

Susannah's tone softened. "He was afraid of me, Joshua. I could see it in his eyes."

"You were a little loud, and he was scared out of his wits. That is all," he said, dismissing her concern. "Ethan is very young. Don't be too hard on him. He will be doing a great many foolish things before he is grown. But, then, we all do henwitted things at one time or another, even when we are old enough to know better."

"Yes, and should I kiss you now, such an act would put me in that category," Susannah said, resting her hands on the edge of the table.

"Dashed unkind of you to say so, ma'am," Joshua countered. "But"—he shrugged without changing a line of expression on his face—"perchance you are not as astute as you claim in discerning a man's intentions, or you would not tar me with the same brush as you do the dandies of the *ton*. There is something you should know about me. I don't use pretty words unless I mean them." He spun around and marched from the room.

Susannah picked up the ruined gloves he had left on the table. Somewhere deep within her she wanted to believe him. There had been a strong attraction between them from that first day when he had walked into her library. Like it or not, that had not gone away. But that had nothing to do with love, she told herself. A seducer's stock in trade was to make a female believe that he was sincerely in love, she warned herself, and tossed the gloves into the dust bin.

SIX

Joshua recovered quickly from Susannah's rejection of his advances in the apothecary room. He had fallen in love . . . hard. But she was noticeably lacking in enthusiasm for his passionate overtures. As a lawyer, he was accustomed to planning alternate strategies. He decided to bide his time and change his tactics. He launched into a honey-and-cream courtship, apparently to good effect, for Susannah responded favorably to less obvious tenders of affection. For the time being, Joshua was reasonably satisfied with the results of his tepid wooing.

Five days into his sojourn at Berryhill, he was still in this accommodating frame of mind as he and Susannah rode into the stableyard after he had accompanied her while she visited tenants on estate business. He should have been bored listening to endless discussions of such agricultural matters as the amount of seed corn she had issued for sowing. Instead, he was fascinated to find that her friendly manner transcended class as she interacted with her workers, proving herself an excellent steward of her lands. Joshua saw for himself what he had long suspected. Estates did not run themselves, as a number of his absentee landlord acquaintances would have had him believe.

After dismounting, Susannah moved beside Wizard and looked up at Joshua, who had remained in the saddle.

"Won't you take some refreshment before you return to the inn?" she asked, a gloved hand on his horse's mane.

Joshua shook his head. "Regrettably, I can't even have supper with you since my law clerk, who is riding down from Chelsea this afternoon, should be arriving at any minute now. I shall be spending a boring evening going over briefs and signing papers."

She gave him a smile that was designed to tease. "Too bad. I heard from my spies in the kitchen that Cook has made a delicious gooseberry pie, especially with you in mind."

He chuckled, a distinctly masculine sound. "Save me a piece."

Youthful shouts and high-pitched laughter came across the woodland which lay between the stables and Ezra's house where the boys were playing on the swing. A small frown developed between Susannah's brows when her eyes were drawn in that direction.

Joshua knew what she was thinking. "Ethan and Davey will come around in time, my dear," he said equably. "The children are no longer hostile."

"No, just indifferent." Susannah pulled a face. "If something delights them, it's 'Mr. Josh, look at this'; if they are showing off, it's 'Mr. Josh, watch me.' When I attempt to engage them in small talk, their cheerless replies are curt and aloof."

Joshua leaned cross-armed on the pommel, his countenance a mixture of sympathy and his own frustration, for he had tried to reason with the children to no avail.

"I wish I could be of more help," he said. "But Ethan clams up when I bring up his coolness toward you, and Davey takes his cues from his brother. Yet I have this irrational inkling that their detachment might have something to do with Mr. Kearny's mistresses."

"In what way?"

Joshua shrugged. "I'm afraid it's a farfetched theory. But something as simple as associating you with those fallen women by virtue of your age and sex. Jealous lovers can resent their partners' children and have been known to take out their spite on vulnerable little ones."

Susannah sighed. "I'm at my wit's end. Even farfetched theories might give me hope. To have Ethan and Davey repel every kindness at every turn is most disheartening, especially when one does not know the reason for the animosity."

Joshua said no more on the subject, for, in truth, he was not at all certain that he was treading on solid ground and did not want to give her false hope that he had an answer to her plight.

Forced to take his leave by his pending appointment, Joshua bid her farewell until the morrow with a smile and a wave. Susannah watched him until no more could be seen of him and his horse than a trail of dust in the distance.

Only then did she walk back to the saffron stone house where the ivy climbed to the eaves. She stepped through the front door into the vestibule and paused before the hall mirror. Her high color was due more to Joshua than to the cool spring air. He went to her head like French champagne. Walking hand in hand with him was more exciting than dancing at Almack's with the handsomest man in the *ton*.

She ran up the stairs, realizing that she was no longer afraid that he wanted to seduce her. In fact, she was all but certain that he truly cared for her. Still, there always seemed to be some phantom chain that held her back from encouraging him to take his light flirtation to a more serious level.

After a bath in a copper tub before the fire, Susannah brushed her red curls dry, changed into a peach muslin gown, and ordered a supper tray to be brought to her at her desk in the library.

Having been deprived of Joshua's company for the evening, she set about catching up on the paperwork she had put off while she spent time with him and the children.

At ten o'clock, Susannah gave up on her figuring, stretched her aching shoulder muscles, and closed the ledger. She ignited a single taper to light her way upstairs and snuffed out the remaining library lights. She picked up the candlestick and set off for her bedroom. She had had an exceptionally long work day and craved nothing so much as a good night's uninterrupted sleep.

Once abed, her mind did not dwell, as usual, on either Joshua or the children. Exhausted, she sank into a deep sleep almost as soon as her head met her goosedown pillow.

Confused and disoriented, Susannah bolted upright as the long case clock downstairs chimed midnight. She peered into the darkness as though expecting something to materialize that would account for the scream that had awakened her. She listened to the frogs croaking in the garden pond beneath her window as her stomach calmed and reason took hold. Sinking back beneath the bed covers, she curled her fingers around the silk border of her quilt and wondered if she had dreamt the shriek. Before she could decide, a second scream removed all doubt.

Susannah pushed back the covers and swung her legs over the side of the bed and onto the cold floor. She lit the same candle that she had earlier carried from the library and which now rested on her night table. The harrowing cry had been a child's, made either by Ethan or Davey.

Swaddled in a woolen robe, Susannah rushed down the hall. Her cupped hand shielded the wick of the candle against the air currents her own rapid pace created.

She entered the children's firelit bedroom without knocking. Patsy stood in the doorway of the dressing room where she slept on a cot. Her unbound fair hair tumbled over her solid shoulders and down the bodice of her long flannel nightgown.

Ethan and Davey sat up in their separate beds, their small, bare white feet sticking out from beneath their ankle-length cotton night shirts.

"What is wrong?" Susannah asked, although she was much reassured by Patsy's complacent manner.

"You need not have disturbed yourself, Mrs. Susannah. Little Davey just had a nightmare," the young maid said, hugging her upper body against the wee hours' cold.

"Oh, well, back into bed with you, then, before you take a chill. I will see to the children," Susannah said, placing the candlestick onto a table. While Patsy returned to her cot in the next room, Susannah walked to the fireplace, added two large cedar logs to the dying embers, and poked up the fire.

Moving to Davey's side, she bent over to tuck him back under the covers. The child scooted on his rear from Susannah's reach and cowered in the corner of the bed next to the white wall. He turned a panicked face toward her and began to whimper like a lost puppy.

"Are you going to whip Davey?" Ethan's belligerence echoed through the small room.

Stunned, Susannah spun around, her robe billowing around her ankles. "Of course not. Why would you assume I would do something so cruel?"

Ethan knelt in the middle of his bed, his hands clenched into pugnacious little fists.

"Whenever Davey had a nightmare, Miss Ginnie whipped him with a strap for waking her up."

Susannah covered her mouth in horror. "Oh, no! That is appalling." She did not have to ask who Miss Ginnie was. She could only have been one of Benedict's mistresses. But she felt as if she had dropped into a nightmare herself when Ethan glared at her, his stony blue eyes condemning. "Her hair was like yours, lady. All curly and short and flamy red. You and Miss Ginnie look exactly the same."

Susannah stared at him. In his young mind Ethan was equating her with Benedict's brutal mistress based solely on her appearance. She was dismayed, but she forced calm and reason into her voice, and said, "In London society many ladies wear their hair short. It's the fashion."

Ethan maintained his combative stance. "I never saw red hair on no one but you and Miss Ginnie."

"I know most people have dark hair the color of your papa's or Mr. Josh's or blond hair like yours and Davey's, but, Ethan, although you have never seen them, there are many ladies and men, too, with red hair. It does not mean they are bad people who would hurt a little boy."

"Mrs. Tremont said all Papa's ladies were sinners who hid

their Godless ways behind pretty faces, but Miss Ginnie was horrible."

"Mrs. Tremont took care of you?"

Ethan nodded.

Susannah, at a loss for words, turned back to Davey. Joshua's theory was apparently right, but even he would be shocked to find that Davey had suffered real abuse, not mere unkindnesses, at the hands of at least one of Benedict's mistresses. How could her brother have allowed such excesses to go on under his roof?

Susannah stood beside Davey's bed. "Davey, I am not going to whip you. I would never do that."

The child sniffed and drew the long sleeve of his nightshirt across his nose and mouth.

Susannah held out her hands to him. "Come here, Davey, please," she coaxed. Surprising her, the child immediately crawled on his knees across the mattress. She wrapped him in a bed cover and carried him to the rocking chair beside the fire. Once in her lap, he settled himself comfortably against her bosom.

Susannah rocked him back and forth in the maple rocker.

"You hollered at Ethan when Nellie ran away," he said wistfully.

"Yes, I did," she admitted. "And I cannot say that I will not scold either you or Ethan again when you do something wrong, but I will never lay violent hands on you."

Davey yawned. "And you won't tell Mr. Josh, will you, that I woke you up with my screaming? He calls me his big boy. If he knows I cry in the night, he will think I am still a baby and be 'shamed of me."

"Even grown-ups have nightmares, darling," Susannah said, holding him closer. "Mr. Josh will understand."

Davey struggled to sit up, and his lips began to tremble. "Please don't tell him, lady! I don't want him to know I wake people up in the night!"

Since the child was on the brink of tears, Susannah quickly promised, "I won't say anything to Mr. Josh," to placate him.

She calmed Davey for a time with soothing, crooning sounds before laying him back in his bed where he coiled into a ball and closed his eyes.

Susannah knew from Joshua that the children had been raised in near isolation. Evidently, Mrs. Tremont had denounced Benedict's women to the impressionable boys. But both Ethan and Davey were too young to make moral judgments. The housekeeper's damnation of Benedict's mistresses had been misconstrued by them. Mrs. Tremont had been speaking of fallen virtue while to Ethan Miss Ginnie's evil had to do with Davey's batterings. Joshua had been right. Susannah's age and sex and her close physical resemblance to the most notorious of Benedict's ladybirds had incriminated her in the children's eyes. Her brother's other women must have had a different look about them. A ridiculous delusion. But, there was no logic in delusion.

Susannah kissed Davey on the forehead and turned toward Ethan, determined to get to the bottom of Benedict's neglect. The boy's head was propped up on one elbow as he watched her warily.

He seemed so small and vulnerable that Susannah wanted to clutch him in her arms. But the leeriness in his stony eyes deterred her good intentions. Ethan would spurn a show of affection. She sat down on the edge of his bed.

"Why did no one stop Miss Ginnie from whipping Davey?" she said, keeping her tone matter-of-fact, although she was furious not only with the faceless Miss Ginnie, but with Benedict and, even, Mrs. Tremont. Had both of them been blind?

"I tried, but she knocked me down."

Susannah bit her lip and put out her hand to offer comfort, but Ethan eluded her, pulling back beyond her reach. Susannah roundly cursed Benedict.

"What of your papa or Mrs. Tremont? Couldn't they help?"

"When Papa drank too much wine, no one could wake him up. Miss Ginnie came in the night when Papa was in his cups."

"And Mrs. Tremont?"

"Miss Ginnie said if we snitched to Mrs. Tremont or Papa, we would be very sorry. I was afraid," he said sadly.

Susannah shuddered. "Ethan, listen to me. I am not Miss Ginnie or anything like her. You are not too young to understand that it is nonsense to believe that a person's red hair or curls or anything else about her appearance has any bearing on her character."

His mouth remained unyieldingly grim. "But Papa's other two pretty ladies did not hurt us. Mistress Lane even bought us sweets sometimes. And Miss Flora didn't pay much attention to us one way or the other. But Miss Ginnie pinched me when she was out-of-sorts. I think she wanted Papa to get rid of us, but he would not."

"This is bad, Ethan," Susannah said. "I think you should talk this over with Mr. Josh. You trust him."

"No!" he shouted. "You promised Davey. You tricked him!"

"Sh, you will wake your brother. I did not trick Davey. I mean to keep my promise, but I thought you might want to speak with Mr. Josh on your own."

"No, Davey would be ashamed, and Mr. Josh doesn't have to know about Papa or Miss Ginnie. He won't like us as much."

"Of course he would. He would know that none of the bad things she did was your fault."

"You better not tell him!"

Resigned to Ethan's misguided fears, Susannah said, "I won't." She got up and walked to the door. She wouldn't tell Joshua. There was nothing he could do now. But if she showed Ethan that she could be trusted, he might come to see on his own that she was not another Miss Ginnie. She made a last bid at persuasion. "Ethan, think over what I said about judging a person by their looks. You are seven years old, not too young to reason out a problem."

Ethan hunched down under the covers with his back to her. When Susannah picked up the candlestick from the table where she had left it, she said, "Good night, Ethan." But there was no response. She stepped into the hall and closed the door behind her.

Davey sat up in bed, bracing himself on both elbows. "Ethan?"

"What?"

"We don't have to be afraid of lady, do we? She said she is never going to hit us."

"No," Ethan said, "she isn't going to hit us."

"Mr. Josh said I was brave because I didn't cry a lot when Nellie ran away. But I get real scared at night. He'll be 'shamed of me if lady tells him."

"Go to sleep. I don't think she will tell Mr. Josh, but I will watch her tomorrow and catch her if she does."

"Ethan?"

"What now?"

"Is it all right to like lady?" Davey waited for his brother's response. When none came, he sighed and crawled back under the warm covers.

"Call her Auntie, Davey. Mr. Josh says to say lady by itself is rude."

"Why?"

"I don't know. It's all right to say *my* lady, but not just lady. It has to do with manners. But she wants us to call her Auntie or Aunt Susannah."

"Oh, but, then, can we like her?"

"Maybe," Ethan hedged.

"Our auntie doesn't act mean to us, and Mr. Josh likes her a lot," Davey said. "Can't we like her, too?"

"Go to sleep. I'll decide. You are only five. At seven, I'm old enough to reason it out," Ethan said importantly.

SEVEN

Ethan leaned against a sundial close to where Susannah sat on a stone bench in the garden talking with Joshua. It was evident to Susannah that the child had his ear cocked to pick up her conversation with the solicitor. While she felt safe from the boy's misguided sleuthing, for she had no intention of breaking her word to him and Davey, she longed to set Ethan upon her lap and talk away his unfounded suspicions and remove the painful wariness from his young blue eyes. But apparently it would take more than words to convince him that she was not a monster.

Davey had squeezed onto the seat beside her, his small hand lying on her lap. Joshua was positioned facing Susannah with one brown-booted foot resting on the bench, his arms on his knees. His dark eyes were fraught with unspoken questions.

Earlier Susannah had sent him frantic pleas with her eyes. She had coupled those silent signals with barely perceptible shakes of her head to implore him not to quiz her about Davey's newly displayed warmth while they were in the child's presence.

Susannah had no illusions that Joshua could be fobbed off for long. Only yesterday, she had been lamenting her inability to win over the children. He would demand an explanation for Davey's sudden transformation. She prayed she could invent a fib that would satisfy him. It was important that she not let down the children.

Playing with Davey's fingers, she looked up to see a footman rushing from the house. He stopped before her and delivered a message that Mrs. Susannah was needed at the sheep barn. Susannah excused herself and walked off to see to the emergency.

Although consumed with curiosity, Joshua put aside his first impulse to join her and get an immediate answer to the peculiar development.

He considered asking a few lawyer-type questions of Ethan and Davey, but he sensed that Susannah would be vexed if he queried the children, however gently. To distract himself from inadvertently reaping her disfavor, he collected the boys and took them to the paddock for a long overdue riding lesson.

An hour later, Joshua and Davey returned to the house where they found Susannah in the dining room, overseeing a kitchen maid who was setting out a cold collation for the midday meal. Ethan had gone to speak with Ezra Stark and made a tardy appearance for luncheon. All politeness, he apologized and said, "Auntie, may I ride with Mr. Stark to the village to pick up farm supplies? I will have to put off lunch, since he has to leave immediately. He wants to be back in time to give the sick sheep their medicine."

Joshua had to admire Susannah's poise, for her heart had to be soaring to hear Ethan's civil tone directed at her. "Well, then," she said, "let me fix you a picnic." She lifted the cheese dome and removed a wedge of cheddar from the china plate beneath, added a thick slice of bread, and wrapped the sustenance in a white linen napkin. "You can eat this in the wagon," she said, handing him the small bundle.

Ethan's sunny smile brought a look of unmistakable joy to Susannah's face. To know that the glow on her cheeks was because the boy's stony eyes had softened and that Ethan had changed his mind about her, for he must have, made Joshua smile, too. He wondered how it had happened.

At the table, he listened with pure delight to something he had never heard before. Davey was talking to his aunt. The jokes and repartee which passed between them were like the sweetest melodies to Joshua's ears. Spearing slices of a second helping of cold beef from a large platter, he transferred the meat to his plate. For now, he was content to leave the hows and the whys of the radical conversion until he could speak with Susannah in private.

When he finished eating, Joshua laid his knife and fork across his empty plate and said to Susannah, "The fishing paraphernalia for which I sent arrived yesterday. Ezra has bragged that the river on your southern boundary has excellent fishing. Would you care to join the lads and me for a picnic there tomorrow?"

Susannah agreed at once. "My father was a serious angler. I know his favorite fishing spots where the river is little more than a brook and deep pools abound with trout."

Without a great deal of conscious thought, Joshua decided to put off asking Susannah how the children had come to have a change of heart. Since she did not volunteer the reason, he intuitively suspected that his pressing her might bring a pallor to her face and remove all that wonderful mirth from her beautiful green eyes. In truth, he was reluctant to step on her happiness merely to satisfy his curiosity.

Then, too, he admitted to himself, he wanted her in a pliable mood. His mind already had leapt past the moment to his promise to Susannah that first night. He had said that he would stay until the children were settled, which appeared to have been quite suddenly accomplished without his intervention. It was time for him to end his visit and put to the test the results of his, heretofore, passive courtship by raising the stakes.

Susannah sat beside Joshua on the box of the one-horse wagon as he drove down a dirt track which had been worn by frequent use into a crude road. The boys were in the wagon bed with the picnic hamper and the fishing gear. The river was visible through the breaks in the willows and the blackberry bushes which grew thickly along the banks.

Susannah could hardly believe that Joshua had let several opportunities pass when he could have probed with impunity to discover the reason for the children's drastic change in behavior. Not that she would have given them away. She was prepared to say that she had gone to tuck them in one night, and the next day all seemed to have changed in their attitude. It was not the full truth, but neither was it exactly a lie, except by some important omissions. Of course, she thought wryly, his normal baritone would probably rise into that stunned tenor that he affected whenever he was skeptical. Joshua would not be easy to fool.

"Here is the place I had in mind for our encampment," Susannah said as she recognized the scythed field and the huge oak tree under which she had often picnicked with her father.

Joshua brought the horse to a halt, took stock of the low grass and the neighboring river that ran clear and free over the black rocks. "Looks perfect to me," he said. He fixed the vehicle's brake, jumped from the box, and lifted Ethan and Davey down to the ground.

He reached up for Susannah. "I am quite capable of disembarking on my own," she said, standing up. Joshua ignored her with a rakish gleam in his eyes. He spanned her waist and swept her into his arms, drawing her hard against him.

"It seems I have wanted to hold you like this forever," he said. He lowered his mouth toward her lips, but Susannah put her palms on his chest and backed away, opening some distance between them. Peering from under the wide brim of her gypsy hat with gaily colored silk flowers around the straw crown, she said, "The children," although the wagon shielded them from the boys, who had run to see the river. Joshua took on the arctic look of a man whose patience was running thin, but he released her without comment and busied himself unhitching the horse.

Susannah found herself in a muddled state. She wanted Joshua to kiss her, and yet something held her back. Her eyes were on him when Joshua turned the horse into the meadow to graze, returned to the wagon, and lifted the picnic basket from the wagon bed. Then, with a sudden, more immediate concern, Susannah began to worry that he might continue to show his displeasure for her evasive tactics and ruin the day.

But to Susannah's intense relief, his smile was back in place when he came to where she had spread the carriage blanket and asked her, "Where shall I put this?"

She took the hamper from his hands and looked for a shady spot to store the food. Having rid herself of the basket, she turned back toward Joshua and stifled a gasp.

Susannah took one long look at him before she pulled off her stylish hat and sank to the ground beneath the oak tree. Her mouth dried to cotton. His neatly folded brown coat and snowy cravat were on the grass. Joshua had unfastened three buttons on his cambric shirt placket and rolled up his sleeves past his elbows.

Susannah fanned her flushed cheeks with her hand as she took in his respectable set of muscles and strong chest. He had eschewed the constricting coats and breeches that cinched a man's body like a second skin and required the services of a valet to get into. His less confining clothes had masked his fine athletic form. She now understood why he had been able to stop a runaway horse.

Sporting a lazy grin, Joshua stood over her. "You have a queer expression on your face, ma'am," he said. "Have I given offense by taking the liberty of making myself a little too casual for your taste?"

"No, not at all," she fudged, smoothing the skirt of her spring green muslin frock in a nervous gesture. "In rural areas, the rules of proper dress which would be strictly enforced in the city may be bent." She suspected that she was stretching a point, for unless a gentleman was working in the fields beside his farmhands, he would probably not show all that male skin in the presence of a lady.

Susannah could only be thankful that comments on his state of undress were brought to an abrupt close when Ethan came over to them and asked, "When can we fish, Mr. Josh?"

Joshua removed a gold watch from the pocket of his breeches and snapped open the scrolled case.

"It lacks better than forty minutes to midday," he said. "We will have our picnic then, and do our fishing afterward. Help me carry the rods and creel and tackle box from the wagon."

Once the paraphernalia was brought from the vehicle and dumped onto the blanket, Joshua sat cross-legged in the midst of the jumble of fishing equipment like another happy boy while Ethan and Davey knelt beside him to better examine the unfamiliar gear.

Joshua lifted the tackle box's lid and rummaged among the corks, hooks, and lines. "It has been an age since I have looked in here." His face lit up. "Lord bless me," he said and removed a strange little collage of faded materials tied together into a bunch. "I made this when I was not much older than you lads."

"What is it?" Ethan asked. "This part looks like a bird's feather."

"Yes, from a jay, and the yellow is a piece of wool, and this is a bit of red silk, who knows from where, all tied together with a long hair from a horse's tail. The whole is called a fisherman's fly and is used to lure fish to one's hook. I made many similar lures to this one during my boyhood, but it seems this is the only one that has survived."

"Why must one use a fake fly to attract fish, Mr. Josh? Don't fish like real ones?" Ethan asked, his small mouth musingly pursed.

"A thoughtful question, Ethan. Yes, trout are known to jump right out of the water to snag an insect from the air."

Ethan took the lure from Joshua's hand and stared at the crude device with focused concentration. "Then, why don't you use a real fly when fishing? Flies are easy to come by." He pointed to the cart horse in the field. "See, even now, Matilda is swishing them with her tail."

"Once one swats a fly," Joshua explained, "its body and wings are battered and the insect loses its proper color and its appeal. But a clever fisherman can trick a fish with a colorful fake fly. Old Man Trout thinks he is in for a rare treat."

Joshua dug down in the tackle box and pulled out three professionally tied lures. "We can use these to fish," he said.

"I want to make my own fly," Ethan declared, "like you did." He scanned the landscape eagerly, an idea forming. "There must be lots of birds' feathers around here, and we can pull a long strand of hair from Matilda's tail."

"Whoa, lad," Joshua said on a crack of laughter. "You try that trick, and Matilda is liable to give you a swift kick. It would be much safer to ask Mrs. Bixby for a piece of thread from her sewing box when we return to Berryhill."

Ethan shook his head. "That won't do, Mr. Josh, for I would not be able to test the fly if I must wait to assemble the whole when I return to Auntie's house."

"Point well taken, Ethan," Joshua said, remembering what it was like to be an impatient little boy. "I daresay, we can comb through Matilda's mane with our fingers and come up with what we need."

Ethan broke into a sunny smile. "Come on, Davey," he said. "Let us look for feathers to make a fly to catch Old Man Trout." Susannah watched the children walk off with their eyes pinned to the ground, searching for feathers.

Last night at bedtime, Ethan and Davey had spoken a little of their father and some happy times with him. She did not quiz the older boy about his altered opinion of her. Ethan would not want to be reminded of his folly.

"I suppose, despite his poor choice of companions, Benedict had a softer side, or he would not have raised such good children," she said without thinking.

Joshua stopped stacking the gear he had begun to form into a neat pile on the edge of the blanket and looked at her with a slow-breaking expression of dawning.

"My theory was on the mark, wasn't it? The boys' resentment of you *was* related to their father's mistresses. Did they tell you that the harlots were cruel to them?"

Susannah recoiled when she realized what she had carelessly given away. She could have pretended that he was off the mark, but instead she merely parried any further conjecture on his part by saying, "Josh, I beg of you. Don't say anything of that sort in front of the children."

"Do not break into a pelter, Susannah. I am not completely shatter-brained. I won't say a word to them. I just cannot understand why you refuse to be more forthcoming with me." Hurt flared in his eyes.

Susannah sighed. "Is it so important that you know every detail? For myself, I thank God for giving the children such resilience. Can't you just leave it?"

Joshua raised both hands in a sign of surrender. "Peace, then. Just do not poker up again." He got to his feet and approached her.

Before Susannah could guess what he was about, Joshua had stretched out on the grass with his head in her lap.

"You are aware, sir, I am sure, that you are taking an improper liberty."

"Take pity, my dear," he murmured in shammed inertia. "The ground is so very hard and your, uh, thighs are so very soft."

Susannah groaned. Any proper lady would swoon, or at least pretend to swoon, at the mention of that part of her body by a man.

"Thighs?" she echoed. "Joshua, you are incorrigible. No gentleman mentions that word to a lady. My reputation would be in shreds without the least hope of redemption if what has passed between us this day were to be made known in Society."

Joshua turned his eyes from the blue sky where only the merest puff of white clouds showed here and there to Susannah's lips. How he wanted to kiss that luscious mouth. Throwing caution to the winds, he hooked a strong hand behind her head and pulled her face down to his and molded his lips over hers in a sweet, unexacting kiss.

"In for a penny; in for a pound, sweeting," he whispered

against her lips. His mouth became more demanding, but before he could part her lips, Susannah lifted her head, breaking contact.

Joshua got to his feet and looked down at her. The river burbled in the background. Susannah did not have to look at him to tell he was annoyed. "I have to bring my holiday to a close. I want you to return to Chelsea with me."

Caught unaware by his peremptory petition, Susannah was hard put to say anything for a few seconds. Finally, she asked, "Are you inviting me to visit you?"

"Yes, you and the children. I want you to see my house on the river. I keep a small yacht docked on the Thames. While you are there, we could go sailing. You have mentioned that Ethan and Davey need new clothes. There are some good shops on Cheyne Walk where you can make the necessary purchases."

"We are very busy on the estate this time of the year."

"You will not be missed for a few days. Ezra Stark is extremely competent and well able to run things in your absence."

Ethan and Davey, returning from their hunt for birds' feathers, cut off further fencing between them.

His mouth down-turned, Ethan opened his fist and showed Joshua the dull plumes he had crushed in his hand. "We could only find gray feathers," he said. "You said Old Man Trout is attracted by bright things."

Impulsively, Susannah moved onto her knees and reached for the straw hat with the bright-hued silk flowers around the crown.

"Josh, cut off some posies with your pocket knife," she said. "The tiny ones from underneath barely show. You can snip bits of different colors to spark up the drab feathers the boys found."

"Are you sure you want to lop off those flowers?" Joshua said, his brow raised in disbelief. The hat was obviously a creation of an illustrious London milliner and looked new and costly.

"Sacrificing a few blooms from among such a plethora of

blossoms will not ruin the hat," she said. She smiled at Ethan. "What would a fishing fly be without a spot of vividness?"

"Aunt Susannah, you are a great gun," Ethan cried and flung his thin arms around her neck in a swift hug.

Still rejoicing in Ethan's spontaneous, first-ever show of affection, Susannah unpacked their picnic lunch with one eye on Joshua as he removed the buds from her hat and helped the boys fashion a lure. Her mood became serious as she considered his invitation to visit him in Chelsea.

She could invent an excuse for not being able to leave the estate for a few days, but none would hold water under closer examination. Joshua was right. Ezra could manage laudably by himself.

When Joshua sat down to their picnic and picked up a fried chicken leg, Susannah said, "I will go to Chelsea with you."

"Day after tomorrow too soon?" he asked with a shadow of a smile on his face.

"No, not too soon. That will be fine."

Ethan began describing the riverside house in glowing terms when Joshua revealed the planned journey to the boys.

Susannah stayed out of the ensuing discussion, for she found that her feelings had quite sharply taken an ambivalent turn. She hardly knew what to make of them. If she had refused Joshua's invitation to accompany him to Chelsea, she sensed that she would have lost him forever. She was so much in love with him that his soft kiss beneath the oak tree had made her blood race through her veins with a desire that had frightened her. She had drawn back, but Joshua had forced her hand. It came to her that a gentleman invited a woman to his home only if he planned to ask her to marry him. Lord, marriage meant living with one's husband wherever he set up his establishment. How could she give up Berryhill and move to Chelsea? Absentee ownership inevitably eroded an estate's assets.

She felt a weakness invade her. She wanted Joshua, but she could not give up Berryhill. Her anguish was effectively silenced by the children's raillery which drew her from her un-wittingly wretched thoughts.

While Joshua helped her clean up the remnants of the picnic and pack up the leftovers and the dishes and the wineglasses, she hid all her uncertainties behind smart banter. She was not going to let him see how mixed up she was.

She had intended to read a book in the shade of the oak tree while Joshua took the boys fishing up the river. However, he insisted that she come with them.

"Here," he said, picking up her flowered hat and arranging it prettily over her red curls with the skill worthy of a lady's maid. He tied the striped ribbons into a becoming bow under her chin.

"You are going to show me those deep pools where you claim your father caught all those trout."

"Claim, nothing. He did catch them," she said. His light-hearted mood infected her, and her worries receded with her own determination not to spoil the day. He gave her the tackle box to carry while he bore a large fishing pole and two smaller ones in his right hand. Susannah's free hand ended up tightly laced in his. They both laughed over nothing and hurried after Ethan and Davey, who walked ahead, one carrying the wicker creel, the other a short-handled scooping net.

EIGHT

Susannah left for Chelsea the day after Joshua, who did not like to linger when traveling. He rode his horse Wizard back home with his meager effects packed in his saddlebags.

During her more leisurely journey, Susannah made frequent stops by the wayside. She and Patsy stretched their legs while the boys played tag and jumped and ran which kept them from becoming restless during the longer intervals of confinement in the closed carriage.

When Susannah's luxury coach rolled up to the curb in front of the two-story, gleaming white stucco house in Chelsea, Joshua, who had been waiting on pins and needles for her arrival, all but dashed through the colorful anterior garden with his loose-limbed stride. Staving off the uniformed footman who was assigned to open the carriage door, Joshua sprang the polished brass latch himself. Susannah stepped to the sidewalk and into his open arms. He held her close against him and whispered for her ears only, "I am so glad you are here, my sweet. I feared you would change your mind."

Her face asmile, Susannah relished the brief moment in his arms, a glow in her heart from just being near to him again.

Joshua released her and reached for the children. Ethan jumped down nimbly, unassisted, while Davey tumbled deliberately into the lawyer's strong arms.

After he helped Patsy down, the solicitor directed Susannah's coachman to the mews to park the carriage and stable the horses, and his own footman to drive along to help unload the luggage.

With a light hand on the elbow of her dark green traveling suit, Joshua guided Susannah to the gate which was ajar in the wrought-iron fence that defined the front yard. Sending Patsy and the boys up the brick path to the front door, he and Susannah walked behind them at a slower pace. Flowering shrubs and beds of tulips and daffodils afforded a charming buffer between the elegant house and the busy street.

Joshua pressed Susannah's fingers and asked, "What do you think of the house?"

While Joshua had been acquitting his duties at the carriage, Susannah had been admiring the classical decorations on the upper facade and the arched windows. The pleasure of being by his side eclipsed all her lesser emotions, but she said truthfully, "It is a beautiful house. I particularly love the front garden. What a fine initial impression it makes on your visitors."

Quite contented with her enthusiastically favorable response, Joshua clasped her about her slim waist. "I want very much for you to like it all," he said with feeling. "I think the interior will not disappoint you."

Inside, where the vestibule was made bright by a large fan-light over the door, Susannah was introduced to Mrs. Kiley, Joshua's austere, middle-aged housekeeper, and Arlene, a pretty, dark-haired, much younger woman, who would serve as Susannah's abigail during her stay.

Susannah drew Patsy forward and made her known to the two servants. "She looks after the boys," she said.

Mrs. Kiley, staid in her black bombazine, took charge of Patsy and the children with a conspicuous show of competence. She indicated that they should follow her up the stairs to their rooms on the second floor.

Joshua turned to the abigail, dressed in a neat gray serge dress and starched white apron, who was standing by for her instructions. "Arlene, show Lady Taylor to her bedchamber and see that she has everything she needs to freshen up. When she is ready, bring her down to the drawing room."

Joshua and Susannah traded warm smiles. Arlene curtsied to her employer and led Susannah up the impressive winding staircase to the best guest bedroom.

Sometime later, Susannah had renewed herself and changed into a raspberry muslin frock with tiny puffed sleeves. The well-trained abigail escorted her downstairs, opened the drawing room door, stood aside for Susannah to enter, and withdrew, closing the door behind her.

Joshua rose from a large brocade parlor chair and waited for Susannah to come down the room to him. The excellent furniture and tasteful decorations were functional rather than ornately spectacular, making the room very livable.

As she walked forward, Susannah looked past Joshua to the tall, curtainless windows that gave an unobstructed view of the beautifully cared for backyard. The long lawn ran down to the river where a tall-masted sailing vessel was moored at the wooden dock.

Susannah stopped in front of the wall of glass and said, "How perfectly lovely."

Joshua came to her side, conjuring in his mind more provocative visions than the landscaping. "Ethan and Davey are upstairs with Patsy, looking through the telescope I have pointed up the river," he said. "Their preoccupation with the sights should afford us some privacy."

He brought Susannah's hand to his lips and pressed a kiss onto her wrist. "I've missed you desperately." His voice was a combination of tenderness and deep desire.

Susannah teased, "It has been but a day, sir." But she knew what he meant when he said, "It seems more like a month," for she felt exactly the same.

She casually freed the hand Joshua held, looked up at him, and asked a question that was very much on her mind. "Whose room is next to mine?" The connecting door was locked with the key on her side; nevertheless, the arrangement had made her wonder.

"The room is mine," Joshua said. The honest eyes that Mrs. Bixby, from the first, had found so compelling stared directly at her. "But before you jump to conclusions, my dear, your chamber is the best bedroom, other than the master suite, for seeing the gardens and the river from above. I chose it for you for that reason. No other."

Susannah merely nodded. She took him at his word and felt that no verbal comment was warranted. Moving closer to the windows, she took in the groomed beds of abundant flowers blooming in every direction she looked. Here and there, fancy iron benches under tall shade trees offered sheltered places to watch the traffic on the river.

"You must have a talented gardener," Susannah said unimaginatively.

"Several," Joshua replied. It was on the tip of his tongue to make some bland observations about the scene outside the window. But he found that it was becoming increasingly difficult to cap his emotions. He did not want to talk about gardens when the desire to make love to her consumed him. He moved behind Susannah and slipped his strong fingers over her slender shoulders and down her bare arms.

Susannah leaned into him and shivered under his seductive touch. "No more games," he said huskily, his breath warm on her neck. "I love you, sweeting, with all my heart. What of you?"

"I love you, too, Josh," she admitted as his warm lips brushed her nape and sent a frisson of ecstasy into the pit of her stomach.

Joshua turned her to face him. His hungry mouth covered hers. Kiss followed kiss until the growing fire that was generated soon flamed into uncontrollable, exploding passion.

Susannah never knew afterward how the sound of light footsteps and childish chatter on the stairs had ever cut through the dizzying, heavenly rapture.

"Patsy and the children are coming downstairs," she murmured languidly against Joshua's hot mouth.

He moaned. His wandering hands stilled slowly, and his lips parted from hers unwillingly.

"We will have to continue this later," he said, breathing hard. He sank into the brocade chair as the drawing room door was flung open. When the boys burst into the room, he gave the impression that he was totally absorbed in watching a small ship passing by on the water.

Susannah took a deep breath to calm her wild heartbeat and stepped forward to intercept the children.

"We saw men fishing for eels through the telescope," Ethan proclaimed, looking from her to Joshua.

"Really," she said, managing somehow to maintain her outward composure. "Tell me about it." She drew Ethan's attention from Joshua, who still breathed oddly.

Susannah sent Patsy to take refreshments in the kitchen and pointed out the tea service and the plates of fancy sandwiches and luscious pastries on a low table to the boys. Four chairs had been placed around the appetizing spread.

"Look at the delicious cakes Mrs. Kiley has set out for us," she said. Ethan and Davey took their places and turned greedy eyes on the repast while Susannah poured the tea into delicate, rose-patterned china cups.

Joshua came over and sat down beside her. "That was well done, my dear," he said, with the intimate smile of a conspirator.

After the evening meal, Susannah played a board game with the children at a large library table in Joshua's study until Patsy came to collect them at their bedtime.

"I will come upstairs in a few minutes to tuck in the boys," Susannah said to the young maid. Joshua drained the last of his after-dinner wine which he had sipped intermittently from the crystal glass that had remained at his elbow while he sat in his favorite chair reading a periodical.

He bid Ethan and Davey good night, rose from his comfortable seat, and moved to the table where Susannah was picking up the game pieces and placing them in a wooden box.

"Leave that," he said and pulled her up into his arms. Susannah made no effort to resist him, but Joshua sensed a tension in her. He backed off and stroked her upper arms. "Do you think you could be happy living here as my wife?" he asked.

She hesitated much too long for his peace of mind.

"Do you love me?" His voice was curt.

"Yes." To Joshua's relief her answer came promptly this time.

"But, there is an impediment?"

She nodded. "An estate the size of Berryhill needs a hands-on owner living on the land."

Joshua bit back an oath. He dropped his hands from her shoulders and stared at her incredulously. "You love me, but not enough to give up Berryhill to marry me?"

Susannah knew it needed saying, but she could not talk about it now. "It has been a long day for me," she said, looking at the tall clock in the corner. "I must give the boys their good-night kisses."

She moved to the door and turned back to face him. "Joshua, I will retire now, too," she said, her voice a bit hollow. "I will see you in the morning."

Stunned, Joshua stared at the empty doorway.

For the first time in his thirty-odd years, he had met a woman with whom he wanted to share his life, and she had turned out to have queer notions. Did Susannah expect him to move to Berryhill and give up lawyering and become a farmer? When a man proposed marriage to a woman, it was her duty to become the mistress of his household. In the marriage vows, the groom endowed the bride with all of his worldly goods, not the other way around. *She* promised to love, honor, and *obey* him.

He paced and vented his anger with a few earthy expressions

directed at Susannah, but which he was too much of a gentleman to express in her presence.

He stood at the window and called himself all kinds of a fool for loving such a woman. He sat down at the library table and leaned on his elbows, sinking his fingers into his hair. But self-pity was not in Joshua's makeup. He was a man of action who never let a problem defeat him.

Resting his chin on his palm, he asked himself one question. *How badly do you really want her?* With the answer, he swallowed his pride and went to work to come up with a foolproof solution that would get her to agree to be his wife.

Unable to sleep, Susannah had been curled up in a wing chair before the fire in her bedroom for over an hour, completely lost in deep thoughts of her marriage to Aaron. A dutiful daughter, she had made a match with her parents' choice, a kind and considerate man. She had been very fond of Aaron and truly believed herself in love with him. But what she felt for Joshua was an ardor a thousand times more potent. How could she love him with such unadulterated passion and be unwilling to give up Berryhill to marry him? She hated the way it made her feel: indecisive, petty, heart-hurt.

She jumped, startled by a commanding knock on the door connecting her room with Joshua's. Susannah got up from the chair and pulled her cherry silk wrapper more tightly around her and walked to the door.

Putting her ear to the wooden panel, she asked, "What is it, Josh?" her heart still pounding a little from the unexpected summons.

"Open the door, Susannah," he said, his impatience evident when he rattled the doorknob.

"What? No," she said indignantly. "Joshua, are you foxed?"

"No, certainly not! What do you take me for?"

"A sober gentleman does not attempt to break into a decent woman's chamber."

"Oh, Lord. I was merely testing the lock."

"This is highly improper, Joshua. I can't allow it."

"Deuce take it, woman. Your virtue is safe. I have no intention of ravishing you. I simply want to talk."

"Can't it wait until morning?"

"If I don't settle things now, I will be awake all night."

Susannah chewed her lower lip in vacillation.

"Come on, Susannah," he snapped. "Open up. Dash it all. You have my word. I shan't touch you."

Still ill at ease with the idea of admitting Joshua into her bedroom, Susannah, nevertheless, turned the key in the lock and let him in.

When he pushed past her and walked across the flowered rug to the wing chair beside hers, she became even more uncomfortable, for he was not in street clothes, but wore a black night robe, braided in gold, and had black slippers on his bare feet.

He sat down and patted the seat of the companion chair.

"Don't look daggers at me, sweetheart," he said. "Come sit down and hear me out. I am about to make you the happiest of women."

Susannah complied, and her discomfiture eased, for his voice was gently mocking.

"This is what I have decided," he said without further prelude. "I have my legal practice here in Chelsea. Understand me, my dear. I cannot give up the law. But, on the other hand, I can understand your reluctance to surrender your hold on Berryhill Manor, given the history of your hard work to bring the estate up to snuff."

Susannah leaned forward in her chair and listened with curiosity and interest, although her head was muzzy from the late hour.

"Among our class, husbands and wives rarely remain in each other's pockets. We could go on in our separate occupations even though we were married."

"How?" Susannah asked, rubbing her temples.

"Compromise. Chelsea is less than a day's drive from Berryhill. There will be slow times in the office when I can come to you, even for a day taken here or there. You are not needed on the estate during fallow periods and can stay with me for even longer spells," he said. He gave her a thin smile. "I daresay, we will end up being together more than most of our married peers. Now, what do you say to that?"

Somehow Joshua had expected Susannah to fall into his arms in a spasm of thanksgiving. He was puzzled by her hesitation. The plan was perfect. She should be eagerly accepting this olive branch which said far more of the depth of his love and how much he wanted her than any routine proposal.

"Well?" he said, rather brusquely.

"I don't know," Susannah said. The hour was late. She was exhausted from her journey. It was all so unexpected, and, while it sounded good, her head was spinning. "Let me think about it."

"What is there to think about now that your main objection has been removed? Either you want to marry me or you don't. Didn't you hear me? You can keep on running Berryhill." His voice had roughened. He was on his feet, facing her.

"Josh, please."

Joshua's back was to the fireplace, his hands linked behind him. Her lack of gratitude irritated him. When Susannah had kissed him this afternoon with such unexpected fervor, he had thought he would rather die right there than never have her. No other Englishman of his class would have humbled himself as he had just done. Suddenly, he was hurt by her foot dragging.

"Just what does it mean? 'Josh, please,' " he mimicked.

"I suppose it means that it is late at night and that I am tired," she said, resenting his badgering.

Joshua bent forward and leaned his hands on the arms of her chair, his peppery face inches from hers.

"For a woman who professes to love me, you are exceedingly slow, madam, in saying yes to what should be the answer to your prayers." His inner pain and anger were all out of proportion to the situation. He knew that he was behaving badly. Without conscious thought, he gave in to a boorish itch to get back at her.

Joshua's eyes hardened into chill black agates. "You have run me a merry chase, my love, but this is the end. Think what this cost me. And to have it thrown back in my face . . ."

He made for his room without a backward glance. When Susannah heard the click of the lock, she could only be indebted to him for not slamming the door. His injured pride had made him very angry. And with some cause. *Think what this cost me.* Joshua had turned his marriage expectations upside down in order to win her. Instead of hemming and hawing, she should have accepted his amazing offer at once. What a henwitted idiot she was. With one word, she could have had both Joshua and Berryhill. As he had said, his unprecedented proposal was an answer to her prayers.

Susannah half rose in her chair to go to him, but on second thought sank back onto the cushions. If she called Joshua back, the afternoon's heated love scene would be reenacted with different results. Her gaze fell on the four-poster with its blue silk canopy. She had no doubt that she would go to bed with him, something she had promised herself she would never do with any man outside of marriage. Susannah ran a contemplative finger over her lower lip. But she was a widow, not an innocent. And she would not be the first woman to anticipate her wedding night. In the end, however, Susannah's weariness, as much as her principles, won out over wanting immediately to pacify Joshua. Tomorrow, she decided, when she felt more the thing, she would accept his proposal.

NINE

Susannah awakened to the bells warning of fog on the river. She paid scant attention to the shouts of workers on the barges and the rumble of cargo being moved. With a sense of urgency, she rang for Arlene, her whole being keyed to the earliest possible reconciliation with Joshua.

The abigail arrived promptly with hot water in a large Staffordshire jug which she poured into the matching ceramic basin. Susannah washed with the rose-scented soap of French milling and dried her face and hands on a soft towel.

Someone was moving about next door. The mantel clock's hands were nearing ten, so the rustle from Joshua's room must be caused by his valet, Susannah thought, for she had been apprised by Arlene that the solicitor had breakfasted at eight o'clock.

She did not fuss overly long with her toilette, but put on a simple blue muslin day frock and promptly went down to partake of the morning meal.

The breakfast room was made cheerful even on this gray morning by the jonquil-striped wallpaper, patterned with blue cornflowers, and the sunny yellow chintz curtains at the windows. Patsy and the boys sat at the table eating their porridge and chatting. Susannah surmised that Joshua must be in his study reading the morning paper, still cross with her.

The tantalizing aromas of bacon and coffee came from the kitchen. Being hungry made Susannah a bit grumpy, and she was more than a little nervous with the prospect of facing

Joshua, for he had been very upset last night. She decided to eat before confronting him.

Susannah said good morning to Patsy and dropped a kiss on the top of each boy's blond head. After making selections from the various dishes on the sideboard, she took her heaping plate and sat down beside Ethan.

Ethan put down his porridge spoon on the service plate beneath his cereal bowl. "Auntie, can we go for a walk along the river when we finish our meal?" he asked, bright-eyed.

"We must see what Mr. Josh has planned for us," she answered.

"He has gone from home," Ethan informed her. "Mrs. Kiley said he had to attend to some business at his law office this morning."

"Oh?" Susannah's spirits sank. Her stomach felt hollow and not from hunger. Joshua had taken such an aversion to her that he had fled rather than face her.

But Ethan and, now, Davey, too, blissfully unaware of Susannah's crestfallen mood, begged her to take them to the river park.

The appearance of Mrs. Kiley with a pot of fresh coffee interrupted the boys' entreaties and forced a shiny smile, which was required by propriety but was at odds with her emotions, onto Susannah's lips. She thanked the housekeeper for the rich brew that she poured into Susannah's cup. While Susannah added sugar and cream to the steaming coffee from the containers on the table, she debated the advisability of questioning Mrs. Kiley further about Joshua's whereabouts, but the housekeeper took the matter from her hands.

The tall, sedate woman set the silver coffeepot on a trivet and said in her practiced, efficient tone, "The master asked me to give you a message, my lady. He was needed at his place of business, but will return in good time to take you sailing this afternoon."

Susannah buttered a slice of toasted bread. This cold, sterile message from Joshua further deflated her, but there was nothing to be done, but to endure Joshua's absence and proceed with her prior agenda. Susannah asked Mrs. Kiley for directions to the stores and said, "I would like to do some shopping."

"I know where the best shops are, Aunt Susannah," Ethan interjected.

"So you do, Master Ethan, from when you stayed with us after your papa passed on," the housekeeper said. She turned to Susannah. "You can safely give your custom to any one of those merchants, my lady. Our Chelsea tradesmen, you will find, are less avaricious than those in London. The prices are fairer and deliveries are prompt."

With this assurance, Mrs. Kiley went back to the kitchen.

Susannah picked at her eggs and nibbled at her toast with a diminished appetite. Until she faced Joshua again, she would not know if his love had withered. She could not imagine such a possibility. It would just take a bit of humble pie on her part to bring a smile back onto his mopish face.

She pushed her plate of half-eaten food aside and glanced through a window into a side yard which was fenced in from the neighboring house by a high brick wall.

"The early morning fog appears to have lifted," she said, and when she added with a smile, "Shall we put on our wraps and be off to buy some clothes for you and combine our shopping with a visit to the river walk?" the boys cheered.

Fifteen minutes later Susannah strolled down Cheyne Walk, a street of splendid houses, including Joshua's, and superior shops. Holding Davey's hand, she walked behind Patsy and Ethan, searching for a store that sold children's clothes. She was pleased to find one that had a wide selection of attire for young boys.

Soon Ethan and Davey were trying on shirts, breeches, coats, and boots. Choices were made, and the purchases were boxed and wrapped, making a sizable pile on the counter. Opening her reticule, Susannah removed some bills and paid the clerk for the items.

"I am Lady Taylor. Please deliver the boxes addressed in my

care to Mr. Joshua Cameron's residence," she said and gave him the house number.

When she stepped back onto the sidewalk, Susannah would have liked to browse in the other shops, but the boys were already running ahead toward the elm tree-lined path which bordered the Thames and where fashionably dressed ladies and gentlemen took the air.

Following the children to the river at a more moderate gait with Patsy at her side, Susannah pointed out a lovely yacht on the river to the young maid. "What a magnificent boat," she said.

Patsy took in the sight without visible reaction and said, "Mrs. Susannah, must I go sailing with you and Mr. Cameron this afternoon?"

"Not if you do not want to. But I do think that you would enjoy the outing."

"No, ma'am," Patsy said, shaking her head. "I am very, very sure that I would rather keep me feet on dry land."

"Well, then, I can look after the children. You may have the afternoon free. Chelsea is a lovely village, and you might want to explore on your own."

Susannah's suggestion brought a horrified look to Patsy's face. "Oh, I couldn't. The roads are filled with a constant stream of carriages and carts that make a terrible clatter on the cobbled streets. And never have I seen so many people in one place, not even at the village fair. I'll just sit with Cook in the kitchen. She is not as starched-up as most of Mr. Cameron's servants."

Susannah kept her peace, but thought that Patsy seemed to be gaining precious little cheer from this visit to Chelsea and hoped that after she, herself, spoke with Joshua, she was not destined to remember her stay here as equally cheerless.

"Let's catch up with the children," she said, increasing her pace. "I don't want them to get too far ahead and become lost in the press of people."

* * *

Some time later, Joshua sought out Susannah in his study where she had gone to read the newspaper while she awaited his return from his law office. He crossed the room in what seemed a single stride and dropped down into his favorite chair with an assumption of ease. Susannah folded the London *Times* and lowered the paper into her lap.

If Susannah expected to see a pining lover, one look at Joshua's harmonious countenance disabused her. None of the previous night's bitterness was in evidence. He leaned back in his chair and stacked his hands behind his head.

"I regret having had to leave you on your own, but I had to consult with my clerks on some upcoming enterprises. What did you do to occupy yourself this morning?" he asked, quite amiably.

Susannah related her shopping trip and her stroll with the children on the riverside promenade. The conversation was congenial and free of the least rancor, but soon came to a close when Joshua took out his watch, snapped open the case, and said, "Mr. Bronson, a former seaman who captains my yacht, is down at the wharf with his crew readying the boat. I need to put on more suitable attire." He was dressed in the black lawyer's clothes he had worn the day he had brought the children to Berryhill.

Susannah could not keep still a moment longer about the fears that had been nipping at the edge of her mind since he had joined her in the study. "Josh, about last night," she began.

"Not now, my dear," he said, holding up an admonitory hand. "I don't want to miss the tide."

"But, Joshua . . ."

"Susannah, last night never should have happened. I must go now. Meet me in the vestibule in half an hour."

With those lowering words, Joshua took himself off.

Susannah's heart plummeted. Joshua had found her wanting. In his mind, he had already withdrawn his proposal. *Last night never should have happened.* Nothing could be plainer. The boat ride had lost all of its appeal, yet, for the children's sake, she must go through with it. But she would start packing tonight to return to Berryhill tomorrow.

Although the visit had become flat, once on board the small yacht, Susannah's spirits revived some. Mr. Bronson with the assistance of two young helpers hoisted the sails. The erstwhile seaman asked Joshua, "You, sir, or me?" and pointed to the wheel.

"You sail her downriver, Mr. Bronson," Joshua replied. "I might take over later." He took Susannah's hand and led her to a deck chair that faced the riverbank on the port side of the boat and sat her down. Ethan and Davey came dashing around the corner of the cabin into Joshua's entrapping arms.

"We are exploring the boat," Ethan said, squirming in a vain attempt to break the solicitor's iron hold, for he was eager to continue with his inspection of the vessel.

"Fine," Joshua said, "but there is to be no climbing on the rails or leaning over the side. I don't want to have to fish you out of the drink."

"No, sir," Ethan said. "Mr. Bronson says he is the captain, and he will tie us to the mast if we misbehave."

Joshua did not let his smile show. The old salt was more bluster than action, but as long as the youngsters believed him, they were not likely to break the rules.

Joining Susannah, he stood with his back against the rail. The boat sliced smoothly through the water while seagulls swooped around the mast. "Josh, this is wonderful," Susannah said, staring up toward the white sails flapping against the cloudless blue sky. "Where are we going?"

"Downriver toward Greenwich," he said. "I thought you would enjoy a river view of London."

"How splendid," Susannah replied. Joshua looked wonderful in a navy seaman's jacket and long trousers. Still conscious of an ache around her heart, Susannah kept her eyes averted from him so that he would not catch her openly admiring him. He might be able to snuff out his love like a guttered candle, but she could not. She lifted her chin, for she was mulishly determined that he would never read her internal misery from gazing at her face.

Davey crawled up onto the unoccupied deck chair next to Susannah's. And before long Ethan became bored with delving into the same nooks and crannies and joined his brother, taking a seat on the edge of the chaiselike extension of the same chair.

As Mr. Bronson sailed the boat closer to the city, Joshua turned toward the embankment and propped his arms on the rail. "The buildings you see there," he said, "are the Inns of Court. Lawyers have had their offices in some of those buildings since the fifteenth century."

"Isn't that St. Paul's in the distance, Josh?" Susannah said, spying the soaring dome and golden cross. "I have been there."

"Yes, the church is visible from almost anywhere in the city and has been since early in 1700. The old St. Paul's was destroyed in the fire."

"What fire?" Ethan asked, his interest piqued. He came forward to join Joshua at the rail.

"About one hundred and fifty years ago a fire started in an overheated baking oven a short distance from here. Thousands and thousands of buildings were destroyed." He pointed toward a nearby bridge. "Buildings burned there on London Bridge, but the bridge itself did not. The monument you see there was designed by a famous man named Christoper Wren to commemorate what is called the Great Fire of 1666."

"What is that building with the fish on top?" a curious Davey asked a little later.

"A rather large fish market," Joshua said.

"Billingsgate?" Susannah asked.

"Yes," he answered. "The market sells a prodigious number of fish daily."

"The fishermen in London must be much better anglers than you are, Mr. Josh," Ethan said, looking up at the lawyer. "You couldn't even catch one little trout in Aunt Susannah's river."

"You are a cheeky little lad, halfling," Joshua said, tousling the giggling boy's blond hair. "I explained to you before that it was the wrong time of day for trout."

Susannah found herself smiling at the nonsense between Joshua and the smirking child. The stony look had not been in Ethan's eyes for days now. Neither she nor the seven-year-old had brought up the subject of the redheaded Miss Ginnie again, but Susannah knew that Ethan no longer identified her with Benedict's mistress.

"What's that?" Ethan cried, breaking into Susannah's musings. She looked up to see the gray stone building that she recognized as the Tower of London.

"Susannah," Joshua said, his dark hair mussed by the wind, "I know you have been to the Tower, but it is only from the river that you can see the infamous Traitor's Gate."

Susannah listened as Joshua related a tale familiar to her of the entrance to the Tower that was gained only by boat. Once this had been a fearful place. Most of the prisoners who had come by way of the river were on their way to die and had been tortured and suffered cruel and violent deaths.

Mr. Bronson had sailed a little farther downriver from the Tower when he called out to Joshua. The children trailed after the solicitor as he went to answer the summons out of Susannah's sight. She watched the two young crewmen do things with the sails that she did not understand, but which caused the yacht to turn around deftly.

Susannah had thought that Joshua might have taken over the captaining of the boat from Mr. Bronson, but the solicitor soon came into view with the children walking beside him. The lawyer stopped out of earshot and put his arms around Ethan's and Davey's shoulders. Bending down, he spoke at length in a low tone to them, stood up, and put a finger to his lips in a sign of secrecy. His palm on the small of Davey's back, he propelled the child straight to Susannah's chair. Davey climbed into her lap without further prodding and nestled against her bosom as her arms came around his small form to secure him on her knees.

He said, "Are you enjoying the boat ride, Mama?" stressing the last word significantly, before clapping his hands over his mouth to smother a mischievous titter.

Susannah's heart did a somersault when Joshua's lively eyes sparkled with humor and real affection for her. "It seems you have been doing some coaching," she said to him. Soft laughter tumbled between them.

Ethan leaned on the arm of his aunt's deck chair. "But we do want you to be our mama, Auntie," he said, his blue eyes big and serious. "We never had a mother; leastwise, not one that I remember."

Moved, Susannah covered his small hand with hers. "I would be honored to be your mama," she said through a cramped throat which she cleared with difficulty.

Joshua hissed, "Ethan, the other part."

"Oh, yes," the boy said, responding to Joshua's prompt. "I forgot. If you are to be our mama, you will need to marry a papa to help raise us."

"A papa?" she said, genuinely taken aback.

The merry expression on Joshua's face took her by surprise. He would not be instigating this comic melodrama unless he still wanted to wed her. Somehow, she had gotten something wrong. Playing along, Susannah said, "Now, who would suit? Collins, perhaps. Too old, I suppose. How about Mr. Stark? A man who can make a swing would certainly be a handy father to have."

"No, Aunt Susannah," Ethan protested with fiercely beetled brows. "Mr. Josh has to be the papa."

"Mr. Josh," Davey insisted with a firm bob of his head.

"Really?" Susannah simulated dumbfounded amazement. Joshua's hands crossed his chest in an indolent pose, but his eyes held so much love that her heart bounced around in her throat. She swallowed and said softly, "If Mr. Josh is the one you both want for your papa, who am I to stand in your way?"

"Oh, but that is smashing," Ethan cried.

Joshua lifted Davey from Susannah's lap and set him on his feet beside his brother. "Lads, now that an auspicious future appears to have been assured for all three of us, why don't you see what Cook packed in the picnic basket for our refreshment. The food is in the cabin."

When the cabin door banged shut behind the children, Joshua pulled Susannah up into his arms.

"I love you so much," she said first.

"And I you," Joshua said, cupping Susannah's face in his hands and stroking her cheeks with his thumbs and whispering love words to her.

Susannah spread her hands on the front of his navy coat. "But, you said that last night never should have happened."

"Nor should it have. It was bad of me to behave like a dictatorial boor, swaggering and posturing about the sacrifice I was making. Of course you needed time to think. After all, you enjoy going into Society. You might not care for the idea of eyebrows being raised by such a radical marriage."

"Oh, no, Josh. It was never a question of that. In any case, as long as we appear at balls and routs together, Society will not care a fig. And we could easily accomplish that through the compromise you mentioned. If you had given me just another minute, I would have accepted you."

He pulled her fully back into his arms. "Do you forgive me for being all pumped up with my own self-importance?"

Susannah slipped her arms around his waist and snuggled closer. "There is nothing to forgive. But I don't want you to think that I am unmindful of the generosity of your marriage terms."

Joshua grimaced. "No more talk of gratitude. We love each other. That is all that matters." He brushed back a few copper wisps that were escaping from underneath her broad-brimmed bonnet. "Do you still doubt that you have a mother's heart?"

"No. How can I gainsay the sweetness that poured through

me when the children said that they wanted me to be their mama?"

He traced the outline of her lips with his finger before he met her upturned mouth with his in a slow kiss that threatened to last forever.

The cabin door opened on well-oiled hinges, and Ethan peered onto the deck. Davey wormed past his brother. "They're kissing," he hissed, scrunching up his face. Ethan tumbled onto the deck and pulled his brother down beside him. The two rolled around on the varnished floorboards at their new parents' feet, raising a ruckus meant to gain attention. But it was a long, long time before Susannah and Joshua, locked in an endless kiss, took any notice.

THE
PERFECT
MATCH

by
Juliette Leigh

Joe, Michaelle, Susan, Joelle, Mackenzie, Alexis, Madison, and Guess Who—not very original, but oh, so true: You light up my life. . . .

ONE

"There has to be a way," he whispered hoarsely.

Mr. Timothy Beresford sat stiffly on the bench as close as he dared to Miss Sally Rivers. He cast an anxious glance at her chaperone, Miss Timmons, and edged an inch closer. "There has to be a way, Sally," he whispered, his voice full of distress. "I can't bear not seeing you for a whole year."

"I know," Miss Rivers whispered back, glancing at Miss Timmons. That lady was busy with her tatting and hadn't looked at the pair for some twenty or thirty minutes. Miss Timmons was an excellent chaperone, in Miss Rivers' opinion, since she never stopped Miss Rivers from doing what she wished, and, better, she was known to be somewhat deaf, although she took pains to appear to hear everything. Miss Timmons chose that moment to look up and smile vaguely at the pair. "Lovely weather," she said with a bright smile. "Just lovely weather. I do hope we'll have good weather when we leave for Gibraltar in a fortnight." She peered once again at her tatting.

"Gibraltar!" Miss Rivers whispered in anguish and put her hand over her mouth to keep from crying. "I can't go to Gibraltar! Timothy, we must think of something! We must!"

Mr. Beresford nodded in agreement and frowned as he began to think.

* * *

Mincey Cottage stood a little back from the road that went through Crickford and wound on past the very imposing mansion belonging to the very imposing third son of Lord Fallstone. That very imposing son, Edward Walker Percy Evan, was in his carriage on the way to his holdings at Crickford to tend to a small matter involving his ward, Mr. Timothy Beresford. Edward Walker Percy Evan was not in the best of moods. He was, in fact, nursing a rather bad headache that he had acquired when he fell over some books that Mr. Beresford had left piled on the floor of the library in the London house. This, coupled with the disturbing report from Mr. Beresford's tutor, had put him in a black mood indeed. He was now on his way to Hannaford House to do the same thing to Mr. Beresford that his father had done to him at the same age—send him to the plantation in Jamaica until he learned how to behave. At the time, Mr. Evan had thought it a terrible injustice, but from his vantage point of forty years, he now saw it was much the best thing. Had he been left to his preferred devices, heaven only knew what scrapes he might have been in. As it was, he had been in enough brambles before his father intervened. He wasn't going to see that happen to young Timothy. He had promised William that he would look out for the boy, and, by God, he was going to do it if it killed him.

"I have it!" Mr. Beresford snapped his fingers as the idea hit him.

"What?" Miss Rivers stopped and looked at him, partly in adoration, partly in question. Miss Timmons stopped also. "Yes, they are lovely birds," she said absently. "What are they?"

"Uh, robins," Mr. Beresford said, not having a single notion about what distinguished one bird from another. "A special kind, I'm sure."

Miss Timmons nodded. "Lovely." She rose and gathered up her tatting. "I do believe we should be getting back now," she said with a smile. She waited until the two of them rose as well, and then she began ambling down the road toward Mincey Cottage.

"What, what?" Miss Rivers urged, falling back a discreet distance behind Miss Timmons.

Mr. Beresford frowned. "What do you mean *what?* I certainly don't know, Sally. I have no idea about birds. All I know is that they tweet, usually in the morning when one is trying to sleep."

"Not birds, Timothy. Why did you snap your fingers and say that you had something?"

"Oh, that." He looked pleased with himself and, with one eye on Miss Timmons marching ahead of them, hazarded enfolding Miss Rivers' hand in his. "Your mother is going to Gibraltar to marry Captain Price."

Miss Rivers looked at him crossly. "I know that, Timothy. That happens to be the cause of the entire problem. If she weren't going to Gibraltar, we could stay here with Grandfather and Grandmother Chapman."

"Do you realize," Mr. Beresford said in a dramatic whisper, "that if your mother married someone in the neighborhood, she would stay here? You wouldn't have to return to Gibraltar!"

Miss Rivers' expression fell. "Yes, Timothy, but there's no one around for her to marry. Besides, she's already promised to Captain Price." She frowned as she thought. "Still, she might be persuaded to break her engagement to him." Sally paused and worried her lower lip with her teeth. "If, of course, she fell madly in love with someone else."

"Then, it's up to us to find someone here for her," Mr. Beresford said confidently. "Didn't you tell me that she certainly has no particular feelings for Captain Price? Surely she can find someone here whom she has no particular feelings for." He hesitated. "Did I say what I hoped to say?"

"I'm not sure, but I do know what you mean." Miss Rivers sighed. "Mama told me she was marrying for security for the two of us. She said that Grandfather's illness has shown her that she needs to marry. I think that was why she accepted Captain Price's offer of marriage." Miss Rivers was thoughtful. "I don't think she really wants to get married. Not to Captain Price, at any rate."

Mr. Beresford looked puzzled. "I thought all women wanted to get married. My mother is off honeymooning with her fourth husband right now. Of course, she always marries really old men. Except for my father, of course."

"Mama wouldn't marry just to be marrying. I think she's marrying Captain Price just because . . ." She stopped and groped for words. "Well, because of what I said. He's certainly not as handsome and dashing as Papa was. We would need someone like Papa, I think. As for someone handsome and dashing in the neighborhood, there's no one around here like that."

Mr. Beresford frowned again. "Handsome and dashing—by heavens, I know just the person." He paused for dramatic effect, but Miss Rivers interrupted him.

"And we're leaving in a fortnight now that Grandfather is well. We can't possibly have someone introduced to Mama now and have him come up to scratch in a fortnight." She sighed. "No, Timothy, I'm afraid it's Gibraltar for me."

He shook his head and patted her hand, keeping his eye out for Miss Timmons. "No, no. This would be someone she knew years ago. My guardian."

Miss Rivers gaped at him. "Evan? Evan the Ogre! Oh, my, no! Timothy, how could you think of such a thing? That would never do!"

"Why not? He isn't really an ogre, you know. That's merely reputation. In fact, he would be perfect. Didn't you tell me that he and your mother knew each other from the cradle? That they had played together as children? He isn't married, and neither is she." He turned to her and seized her other hand. "Don't you see, Sally? It would be perfect. It would solve all our problems. They would be married, and we'd be able to see each other all the time."

Miss Rivers shook her head. "He'd never do it. We need to find someone else."

They walked in silence for a moment; then Mr. Beresford snapped his fingers again. "Cousin Alphonse," he said triumphantly. "That's the perfect one."

"Cousin Alphonse?" Miss Rivers frowned as she thought.

"You remember him," Mr. Beresford said, grinning with victory. "He's my guardian's cousin, and much his opposite. His mother was French, and he spent many summers at Hannaford House; so he knew your mother as a child, too."

"Alphonse Dewitt? I've heard Mama talk of him. She usually laughs when she relates some escapade they had as children. Do you think he would do it?" Miss Rivers asked cautiously.

"Alphonse would do anything for money and a little free lodging. I have my quarter's allowance saved up, and that should do it. I'll write to him this afternoon. No, by Jove, I'll go see him. He's cadging a week's stay over at Kemble's. That's only an hour's ride away."

"Timothy, I don't believe that I want Mama to marry someone who spends his time cadging free lodging from everyone. Her husband should at least be able to support her."

Mr. Beresford took Miss Rivers' hands in his. "Drat, Sally, she don't really have to actually marry Alphonse. He could just pretend to be in love with her long enough to delay her return to Gibraltar. That would give us enough time to find someone for her." He smiled triumphantly. "As I said, Alphonse is part French, and I'm sure he's as romantic as all get-out. Haven't you heard that about the French? I'm telling you, Sally, it's the perfect solution."

"Timothy, as usual, you're right. You have the best ideas!" Miss Rivers looked up at Mr. Beresford in adoration.

Miss Timmons turned around and looked in shock. "Children, children!" she said, walking back and placing herself between them. "This simply won't do. Come along." She moved the bag containing her tatting to her other arm and firmly marched them toward the cottage. As they walked the path,

Miss Timmons moved ahead again until they entered the small front garden. Miss Timmons walked on toward the front door, but Mr. Beresford and Miss Rivers stopped as they heard the noise of a carriage on the road. Timothy stood on tiptoe and looked through the bushes at the road. "It's Evan," he said breathlessly, looking at Miss Rivers. "He wasn't supposed to come here until next week, but here he is. I'll have to go straight to Kemble's and invite Alphonse to stay at Hannaford House. If I ask Evan about it, he'll say no. If I just do it, he'll be too polite to toss Alphonse out on his ear."

"Doesn't he like Mr. Dewitt?"

"Can't abide him, but that's a small matter." He paused a moment. "That's a little strong. Just say that Cousin Alphonse annoys Evan."

"Then, he may scotch our plan."

Timothy shook his head. "No, because I doubt that Evan will be here over a day at most. He's always off here and there overseeing Fallstone's holdings. Evan keeps the family finances together, you know." He chortled and rubbed his hands together. "Cousin Alphonse. It's perfect. This is quite a brilliant idea, if I do say so myself."

"I don't know." Sally's voice was doubtful. "Are you sure it will work? After all, with Evan coming here now . . ." Miss Rivers' voice trailed off. "He may stay longer. Maybe our plan won't work after all."

"It will. Don't look on Evan's arrival as a bad sign. As I said, he never stays here over a day or two at most. Even if he does decide to stay longer, that's to our advantage as well. That means that Alphonse won't stay in the house much, and what better place for him to go than to visit the lovely lady at Mincey Cottage. It's an omen, I tell you. A sign."

Miss Rivers thought about this for a moment, looked at Mr. Beresford, and nodded. "You're right as always, Timothy," she said. "It's an omen."

* * *

Mrs. Barbara Rivers was in the small back garden at Mincey, one of her favorite places to be on a lovely day. She was busy trimming dead flower heads and pruning wayward leaves from her roses. She was taller than most women of her acquaintance, with blond hair and startling blue eyes. Her eyes had been compared to everything from sapphires to limpid pools over the years, but she had resisted all flattery. It simply did not work with her. She preferred intellectual stimulation to flattery and officious speeches. She had but recently returned to Mincey Cottage from Gibraltar, where she had lived since her daughter, Sally, was less than a year old.

She paused in her flower cutting, remembering those days. She had met and married James Rivers in the space of just six weeks. They had met at a local assembly, just after she had decided that there would never be anyone for her. The major had been more than attentive, and she had married him almost immediately. Within another six weeks, she realized just what a terrible mistake she had made, but it was too late. She was already increasing. To her relief, Major Rivers was posted to Gibraltar. She stayed behind at Mincey with her parents, planning to go to Gibraltar right after the baby came. While she was home, she received disturbing posts that Major Rivers was acting much as an unmarried man.

Sally's birth had been difficult, so Barbara had stayed some months at Mincey to recover. Finally, for Sally's sake, she had felt she had to join her husband. She had just moved to Gibraltar with Sally when Major Rivers had been killed. He had always hoped to die bravely in battle, but had unfortunately been run down by a drunken sailor who had commandeered a carriage. The sailor had had no idea how to drive, and had promptly taken the carriage up on the sidewalk, right over an equally drunken Major Rivers. The demirep with the major had suffered no ill effects.

The newly widowed Mrs. Rivers had worn her widow's weeds for several years, deterring all suitors. Even after she removed them, she had discouraged any close friendships with the men who thronged into Gibraltar.

She had returned to Crickford some months ago to care for her parents, who still resided there. Her brother, Charles, an army captain, had not been able to return to Crickford, and that was all for the best, Barbara had decided. Charles was quite a hothead, and the army was far and away the best place for him. He didn't have the temperament to care for aging parents. Actually, she thought as she snipped a wilting flower head, Charles didn't have the temperament to care for anything except warfare and the excitement of brawling and drinking with his friends. The two of them were complete opposites.

Once, things had been different. She had been as daring as Charles, but that was long ago. Long before she became a mother. Now her life was settled, and she had Sally to fill it. Soon Sally would be married; then there would be grandchildren. Barbara paused and looked into space, visualizing Sally and a faceless husband, happy among a brood of lovely children. She smiled, seeing herself among them, taking the children for walks, introducing them to books and flowers. It was a happy thought. With a jolt, she realized that she had not visualized her intended, Captain Price, in the picture. She bit her lower lip, worrying. She had accepted his offer when her father was gravely ill. Now. . . .

She thought about the letter propped on her desk, the one crying off from the engagement. Every day she looked at it and wondered if she should mail it.

She sighed and put the thoughts of Captain Price from her mind. Right now, she had other concerns. If all those happy grandchildren were to be, she was going to have to find a suitable husband for Sally. There was little possibility that she would be able to afford a London season for her daughter. She had saved what she could over the years, but the small amount that Major Rivers had left to her just hadn't gone far. She could have come home during those years in Gibraltar, but . . .

She stood and looked at the riot of late buds that were left in the garden. For a fleeting moment she wondered what Evan would think, seeing her thoroughly domesticated. She smiled briefly, a wry smile. She had heard that he was returning to Hannaford House within a fortnight. With any luck at all, she and Sally would be on their way back to Gibraltar by the time he discovered her presence in the neighborhood. If he discovered it at all.

She was interrupted by her mother coming into the garden. "Here you are in the sun without your bonnet," her mother scolded with a smile. "How you managed to live in the tropical sun without ruining your skin is beyond me." Mrs. Chapman looked fondly at her daughter. "You can't know how wonderful it is to have you at home at last, Barbara. Your father and I do wish you'd reconsider and stay here with us. We have more than enough room for you and Sally, and you know we both want you to stay. You and Captain Price could move in here while your father and I could settle in the small cottage. It's large enough for us and Miss Timmons as well. I know she doesn't want to leave us."

"I know, Mother." Barbara sighed and avoided her mother's eyes. "But I need to return to Gibraltar. All my friends are there, as well as my music pupils. I don't feel I can stay away from them much longer. I told Miss Timmons she could stay here if she wished."

"You know she'd never leave you and Sally. She told me that you took her in when she hadn't a friend in the world, and she'll never leave you alone. She regards you and Sally as her family."

Barbara smiled. "Miss Timmons tends to exaggerate. Still, she's been with us so long that she seems like family. To be truthful, Mother, I'm rather glad she's returning with me."

"Barbara," her mother began, putting her hand on Barbara's arm. "As your mother, I wanted to talk to you about your marriage. Do you . . ." She stopped and turned away. "I just can't discuss it now. I need to see about your father. He was talking about coming outside, and I thought the fresh air might be good for him."

"It would be," Barbara said with a smile, glad that her mother hadn't pressed the topic of her marriage to Captain Price. "Why don't I go with you and help him outside? This day will be better for him than any medicine Dr. Small could prescribe."

She went inside with her mother and missed the sight of the black carriage going by the front gate. She also missed seeing Sally and Mr. Beresford looking at each other, nodding in complete agreement.

TWO

"I'm delighted you're in residence at Hannaford House," Mr. Alphonse Dewitt said to Timothy Beresford as they rode across the country toward Crickford. "I would have stopped by for a few days if I had known." His voice dropped a notch. "Evan doesn't happen to be there, does he?"

Mr. Beresford gulped. He was not by nature a dissembler; but desperate times called for desperate measures, and he had been careful not to mention his guardian's name. "He hasn't been there. Actually, the last time I talked to him, he was planning on staying in London for a few weeks." This was all, Mr. Beresford thought, perfectly true.

"Good. Evan and I, though cousins, don't exactly rub along too well." Mr. Dewitt grimaced slightly. "Actually, we don't rub along at all. Evan tries to ring a peal over me every time I see him. What a shame he has all this and we have nothing, eh, Timothy?" He pulled up his horse and looked out over the valley, letting his eyes take in all of the gleaming white of Hannaford House. "I'm glad we came this way so I could take a good look at Hannaford House. I have to hand it to Evan," Mr. Dewitt said, a touch of admiration in his voice. "He does see that the place is kept up. Those gardens are something to look at from here." He frowned. "There must be someone there. Look at all the activity around the stables."

"There was no one there when I left," Mr. Beresford said truthfully. "Perhaps someone else has come to visit."

Cousin Alphonse looked at Timothy and smiled. "No doubt.

I'll race you to the stables." He grinned his devil-may-care smile that always preceded one of his escapades, and had captivated many a London lass. Then he took off hell-for-leather down the grassy slope. Mr. Beresford didn't even try to catch up, as he wasn't the horseman either Evan or Alphonse was, and he knew it. Instead, he paused and looked at the picture Alphonse made riding down the slope and across the lea, the horse and man seeming almost as one. Alphonse was dressed, as always, impeccably, and his blond hair framed his face perfectly under his brown beaver hat. His Hessians glistened like mirrors, showing well the loving care his man, Cormak, gave his clothing. Alphonse was the envy of every young buck in London because of Cormak's devotion to him, and both men had been offered huge sums of money for Cormak's secret boot polish recipe—sums which had been politely declined, no matter how much under the hatches Alphonse was. No one could really understand why Cormak stayed with Alphonse, who, more often than not, was in arrears with the man's salary. Timothy, however, knew that Cormak stayed because Alphonse had a likable personality. That personality, Timothy fervently hoped, would exercise the same hold on Mrs. Barbara Rivers. He chuckled to himself and urged his horse down the slope so he could at least keep Alphonse in sight.

Alphonse was walking out of the stables when Timothy rode up. "You're going to have to do better than that, my boy, if you expect to be known as a horseman," Alphonse said with a laugh.

"I doubt that day ever comes." Timothy dismounted and turned to walk into Hannaford House when he saw his guardian coming along the path. As usual, Walker Evan was frowning, and his mouth was set in a straight, angry line.

"I believe," Alphonse said softly to him, "that Evan is here and in a mood. We'd make ourselves scarce, but he's already seen us."

Timothy gulped nervously and forced a smile to his face. "How do you do, sir," he said to Evan, his voice cracking. "Your presence here is unexpected."

"Obviously," was the chilling reply. Evan turned to Alphonse. "And how long have you been here, Alphonse? Are you leading my ward astray without my knowledge?"

Timothy interrupted. "Oh, no, sir. I had no idea you were coming here and, since I was here all alone, and Cousin Alphonse was visiting nearby, I just thought . . ." He groped for words. "Cousin Alphonse has just arrived."

"Then, I got here in the nick of time, I see," Evan said. "How long will you be with us, Alphonse?"

"Oh, for a while," Alphonse said easily. "Young Timothy asked me here for a month while he was in residence, and I made my plans accordingly." He smiled broadly at Evan. "How long will you be down?"

"I was planning on leaving tomorrow, but I may have to postpone my departure." He turned to Timothy and gave him the ghost of a frozen smile. "Have you made any other social plans in my absence?"

Timothy gulped again and saw his opportunity. "I had planned . . . that is, I asked. . . . Mrs. Rivers and her daughter are at Mincey Cottage, and I thought they should come for supper."

Evan's reaction surprised both Alphonse and Timothy. He stepped back a full step and paled slightly. If possible, his frown became deeper, and his voice was tight when he answered. "Mrs. Rivers? I suppose you mean Mr. and Mrs. Chapman's daughter. And granddaughter?"

"That's right."

"Fine." Evan's voice seemed to shake a little, and he turned on his heel. "Settle yourself wherever you wish, Alphonse. As you'll recall, we keep country hours here for dining." He walked back up the path toward Hannaford House, his shoes crunching on the gravel. He walked, as usual, proudly, his back straight and his dark head held high.

Timothy and Alphonse looked at each other, astonishment written on their faces.

* * *

Walker Evan didn't go into Hannaford House immediately; rather, he decided to take a turn around the gardens. Barbara Chapman home again. This was a surprise. He paused in front of a shrub, but didn't see it. Instead, he ran his fingers through his dark hair and tried to keep the thoughts from flooding into his head. He was not successful. Finally, he gave up and began pacing, not seeing the manicured loveliness of the garden, but looking inward to a time past.

Barbara Chapman. He had heard little of her since they had parted bitterly nineteen years previously. At that time, he had come home to Hannaford House, engaged to the current beauty of the season, Abigail Deane, an engagement arranged by his father.

Evan himself had not been consulted on the engagement—he had merely been informed that it had been done and he was to marry Abigail before Christmas. He had come to Hannaford House to enjoy one last summer before he married, and to apply to the Hannaford estates the knowledge he had won with so much difficulty during his four years in Jamaica.

That summer burned in his memory as the most wonderful, the most heartbreaking, time of his life.

He remembered the first time he saw Barbara that summer. He was expecting the coltish tomboy she had been when he left, but instead. . . . Evan closed his eyes at the memory. It was as raw now as it had been all those years ago. Instead, he thought, Barbara was eighteen and had grown into a beautiful woman while he had been away in Jamaica. He could see her now as she had been that summer: Lovely blond hair caught up with tendrils cascading around her face. A complexion that could put any other to shame, and those eyes—eyes of such a beautiful blue that there were no words for him to describe them. He remembered how he had gone to visit her when he first arrived. She was in the garden at Mincey Cottage, bent over a rose bush, trimming it. He had thought he was just going to greet a childhood friend, but when she turned to look at him and smiled, his heart was lost forever.

He had not told her about his engagement to Abigail Deane. He kept telling himself that he would do it, should do it, but he kept putting it off. In later years, he realized that he had been trying to discover ways to rid himself of Abigail so he could have Barbara, to no avail.

Finally, the truth came out in the fall when Abigail came to Hannaford House for a visit. He hadn't expected her, hadn't known she was coming. Lord Fallstone had come with her, along with her mother. They had wanted to complete the wedding plans. That day—Evan smiled bitterly to himself—that had been the day that he had told Barbara that he loved her.

That night, she had come to see him at Hannaford. It was just like Barbara to throw caution to the winds and come to declare her love for him. She had come and knocked on the door that dark, rainy night, her hair windswept and damp, her dress clinging to her in places that revealed just how beautiful she had become. He had come into the front hall when he heard her call his name. She had run to him and thrown her arms around his neck. "Oh, Evan," she had said, her eyes filled with love and happiness. "I do love you."

Then, looking over his shoulder, she had seen Abigail, and the joy had gone out of her eyes. The joy had gone out of his world as well. Even now, he flinched at the memory. It had been a terrible, embarrassing scene.

With a sigh, he went into the cool, dark house, pausing in his study to glance up at the picture of his late wife, Abigail. Theirs had been the unhappiest of marriages, and he still recalled with terrible guilt the feeling of relief he had felt when Abigail died. Worse, he still recalled Barbara that night. In his sleep, he could feel her smooth skin and drink in the wonderful scent of lavender and rainwater. He hated himself for the times he had slept with Abigail and remembered Barbara, wishing . . . wishing.

Evan turned and rang for the butler. "Mason, please tell the housekeeper to replace the painting over the mantel."

Mason's jaw fell. "Mrs. Evan's portrait?"

"Yes." Evan bristled. "And tell Mr. Timothy that I wish to see him privately as soon as possible."

"I believe he has gone," Mason said, looking out of the corner of his eye as several trunks belonging to Alphonse were brought inside. "He said he was going over to Mincey Cottage for a short visit."

Timothy Beresford and Sally Rivers sat in the small blue parlor at Mincey Cottage, looking at each other under the watchful gaze of Miss Timmons. As soon as Miss Timmons became absorbed in her tatting, Miss Rivers began whispering. "So tomorrow I am to have Mama walking along the lane where the bridge is, and you will have your cousin Alphonse there."

"Yes," Mr. Beresford whispered back, all the while smiling at Miss Timmons. "I think she should be attracted to him immediately—most women are. Cousin Alphonse has a way with women. As I said, it's the French thing."

"Anyone would be better than Captain Price." Miss Rivers punctuated her whisper with a sigh. "Mama just promised to marry him because he was so persistent. And," she added, "she got this feather-headed notion that I needed a father. I've been fine without one my whole life, but now she thinks I need one."

"Perhaps you could use that," Timothy said in a low tone while staring straight ahead. "Tell her that you would like Alphonse for a father." He paused. "That wouldn't be so bad, you know. Alphonse wouldn't bother you at all with any silly rules, and he's a great deal of fun and entertainment."

Sally nodded and looked at him with a smile. "What an excellent idea! I'll begin dropping hints just as soon as Mama meets him." She pulled a scrap of paper from the book on the small table beside her. "I've written down some ways we can throw Mama and your cousin Alphonse together." She passed the paper to Timothy. "There's church, of course, but we can also arrange a chance meeting or two in the village and perhaps suggest a touch of refreshment."

"Once they've firmly renewed their acquaintance, there's always a picnic and visits." Timothy paused. "Speaking of which, I told Evan that I was going to invite you and your mother over for supper. After we meet at the bridge, why don't you invite Alphonse and me here?"

"Why don't we forget the meeting at the bridge, and you can simply bring Mr. Dewitt here. After all, he is a guest at Hannaford House, so it would be perfectly proper for you to bring him along."

Timothy nodded. "Good thinking. That way we won't have to persuade your mother to go out. If we have to, we can have the chance meeting at the bridge the next day. Supper at Hannaford House could be the day after that. They should have renewed old times quite well by then."

"Excellent idea, Timothy." Sally slid her hand down between them and squeezed his hand. "We mustn't forget Miss Timmons, however. She'll have to be with us."

"Of course." Timothy squeezed her hand back and smiled innocently at Miss Timmons, who had glanced up from her tatting. "It's been a lovely day, hasn't it?" she asked, putting up her work. "Would you join us for supper, Mr. Beresford? Mrs. Rivers told me to ask you, so it's quite all right."

"I'd be delighted," Timothy said, giving Sally's hand another surreptitious squeeze.

The next day, Sally mentioned in an offhand way that Mr. Beresford was bringing his cousin to visit them since the cousin was staying at Hannaford House and had nothing to do.

Barbara Rivers stood suddenly and dropped her mending on the floor. "Cousin?" she asked with a catch in her voice. "His guardian?"

"No," Sally said, bending to retrieve the mending. "His cousin, Alphonse Dewitt. I believe that Mr. Evan and Mr.

Dewitt are cousins. That's why Mr. Dewitt is staying at Hannaford House." Sally missed the sigh that eased the tension in her
mother's body.

"Alphonse? I haven't seen him in years. Not since we were
children," her mother said. "However, I promised Father that I
would go out with him on his rounds this afternoon. He feels
well enough to get out, and I thought the fresh air would be
good for him."

"Would you like me to go with you?" Sally asked innocently.
"I'm sure Mr. Beresford and Mr. Dewitt will be gone before
then. I'll be glad to help you with Grandfather."

Barbara smiled fondly at her. She never understood just how
Major Rivers could have sired a child as good as Sally. "I'd be
delighted to have you along," she said, "and I'm sure Father
would as well." She came over and put her arm around Sally's
shoulders. "You make me so proud of you."

To Barbara's surprise, Sally burst into tears. "Oh, Mama. No
matter what, know that I only want the best for you. You de-
serve to be happy."

"I am happy, sweeting." She dried Sally's eyes with the corner of her apron. "Perhaps we should go up and change. I
would hate for the gentlemen to find us in our everyday clothes
and aprons."

Back at Hannaford House, all was not going well with Mr.
Beresford. He was standing on the carpet in front of Mr. Evan's
desk. "I understand, Timothy," Mr. Evan was saying, "that you
were asked to leave school for a term with the understanding
that you were to catch up on some studies while you were out.
I also understand that you have neglected your studies while
here." He paused. "By God, sir, I won't have it! I promised your
father that I'd see you had a good start in life, and you're going
to do it. Do you understand?"

"I understand," Mr. Beresford mumbled.

"Good." Mr. Evan leaned back in his chair. "Since education

doesn't seem to be working for you, I think it would be a good idea for you to go to my Jamaican plantations and see exactly what running an estate is all about. That will be information you will need in the future."

Mr. Beresford choked. "Jamaica! I promise to study! I promise to go back to school and do my best. You can count on me."

Mr. Evan shook his head slightly. "No, Timothy, I think Jamaica is by far the best plan. You're not going into government or planning to write poetry. You are planning on running your father's estates. I've taken good care of them for you, and I want you to be ready when the time comes. You inherit when you're five and twenty; so that gives you six years to learn, and I can't think of a better place than Jamaica."

"I'll begin writing poetry if you let me go back to school," Timothy said in desperation. "I can't leave! I simply can't!"

"Miss Rivers?" Evan lifted an eyebrow. "I've heard that you've been spending a great deal of time there. I'm surprised that her mother would allow it."

Timothy was spared having to answer as Alphonse walked into the room. "There you are, Timothy," Alphonse said. He was elegantly attired for the country, as always. Every item of clothing was carefully chosen; every single blond hair was in place. "I believe you wanted to make a call this morning?"

"Yes. No. That is . . ." Mr. Beresford sputtered and gave his guardian a chagrined look.

"If you have plans, by all means go on," Evan said, pulling a pile of papers toward him. "I plan to make the arrangements we discussed. You should be ready to leave for Jamaica within two months."

Timothy started to protest, then thought the better of it. "Yes, sir," he said dully. He went out the door without looking at either Evan or Alphonse.

"So you're doing to the boy what your father did to you," Alphonse remarked, watching Timothy's stiff back disappear into the hallway.

"It's none of your affair," Evan said shortly.

"None at all." Alphonse's voice was as cheerful as always. "You came back from Jamaica a different person, though. I would hate to see the same thing happen to Timothy. You went over there a friendly, outgoing lad who loved to play pranks and listen to music. You returned a dour old man."

"I was one and twenty when I returned."

"It doesn't matter. You were already middle-aged." He gave Evan a quick look. "You were mentally the same age you are now." He took a step toward the desk. "Do you realize, Evan, that I haven't seen you laugh since we were children? What happened? Was it all Jamaica?"

Evan looked at him coolly. "There's no time for laughter in my life, Alphonse. Unlike you, I have work to do. If I didn't keep the estates going, you certainly couldn't enjoy the life you do."

Alphonse grinned at him. "Touché," he said. He went toward the door chuckling, then paused a moment before he went out. "By the by, Evan. Timothy is taking me to visit Barbara Chapman-Rivers now—and her daughter over at Mincey. Weren't you two good friends at one time? You should come along."

Evan tried to make his voice light, but couldn't manage it. "That was a long time ago, when we were children. And as for going with you—I have work to do, Alphonse. Someone has to keep a watch on the money."

"As long as you keep my allowance coming on a regular basis," Alphonse said with a laugh. "Just by way of repayment, I'll give you a report on Mrs. Rivers."

"I'm not interested." Evan realized that he had whispered, and that he was talking to an empty room. He had to restrain himself from knocking the tidy stack of papers to the floor. He realized after a few minutes that he wasn't really seeing the words on the papers, so he pushed them aside and got up, walking restlessly around the room. The painting of Abigail hadn't been replaced yet, and he paused for a moment in front of it. Abigail was painted beautifully, and he had to admit that she had been beautiful in life. The artist had caught her perfectly—the lush body, the slight pout, and the icy blue eyes. She had been the toast of London, and everyone thought Fallstone had done so well to nab such a beauty for his third son. Little did they know that all Abigail had wanted was enough money to spend and no husband to bother her. Evan had caught her in a dozen liaisons during their few years of marriage. Oh, she had been discreet, causing him no embarrassment, but. . . .

She had often accused him of being cold, and perhaps he had become that way. He had never really been in love with her, and often thought that as bad as the pain of their marriage was for him, he could not have endured it if he had loved her. As it was, indifference had saved him.

In death, Abigail had been just as discreet as she had been in life. She had not told him that she was with child. Perhaps, he thought bitterly, that was because she wasn't sure of the identity of the father. At any rate, Abigail had taken measures to rid herself of the child. Instead, bleeding and fever had killed her. He had tried to feel grief, but found himself unable to conjure that emotion. She had used him, and both of them had paid.

He turned on his heel and rang for a footman.

"John," he said shortly to the footman, "please remove the portrait of Mrs. Evan and box it up. I want it shipped to her family. Immediately." He turned and went outside to pace again through the garden, unable to rid himself of his memories.

THREE

Timothy Beresford sat in the rustic, wooden chair in the garden and looked at Sally Rivers in a knowing way. He was quite pleased with the visit. The day was perfect—warm and sunny—so the conditions were excellent for the meeting between Sally's mother and Alphonse. He couldn't have arranged it any better. The four of them were seated around the small table that was placed under a large shade tree in the garden, and the warm breeze wafted the scent of roses over them. Mrs. Rivers had changed into a lovely dark blue gown that made her eyes, if possible, even bluer and more beautiful. Her blond hair glinted in the dappled sunlight and shade. Alphonse hadn't been able to take his eyes from her since they arrived.

Sally glanced over at Timothy and nodded imperceptibly. The plan was working beautifully—her mother seemed quite interested in Mr. Dewitt. The two of them had chattered on and on about mutual childhood acquaintances and what had happened to them since that time.

Mr. Beresford had news of his own to impart to Miss Rivers and, furthermore, thought a little time alone would not be amiss; so he suggested a turn around the garden to Sally, and they set off. As soon as they were at the far corner of the garden, Timothy looked back at the pair at the garden table and grinned.

"What did I tell you, Sally? Give Cousin Alphonse a week, and your mother will forget Captain Price. Give him a fortnight, and she'll be ready to stay here for the rest of her life." His voice bubbled with glee.

"As usual, Timothy, you were right." Sally smiled as she looked at her mother. "I can't recall when I've seen Mama like this. She's like a different person. She's laughed more today than she has in the past year."

Timothy nodded. "What did I tell you—Alphonse has a way with women."

"Well, I don't want Mama tangled with a skirt-chaser." Sally frowned. "Is he a fortune hunter? Because if he is, Timothy, I don't want him around Mama. Her portion is enough for us, but it's certainly no fortune."

"Alphonse would never think of that." Timothy became serious as he knew he had to tell Sally his news. He took a deep breath and turned Sally to look at a large rose bush. "I have bad news, however." He paused to find a gentle way to break the news, but could think of none, so he said it baldly. "Evan wants to send me to Jamaica. He says it will be the making of me."

Sally put her hand over her mouth to keep from crying out. "Jamaica! Timothy, that's worse than Gibraltar! How can we get him to change his mind?"

He shook his head slightly. "I don't know. I've thought about it all the way here. I even thought about trying to marry him off to your mother—"

"I won't have it!" Sally said, interrupting him. "The man is horrid. I hate him with all my heart!"

"He's not a bad sort," Timothy said, turning to walk along the edge of the garden. "He was sent to Jamaica, and so he thinks it's the thing to do. What we have to do is figure out a way to convince him that it's not the best thing for me."

"You could enlist in the army."

Timothy grimaced. "I can't say that I care to do that. I like the uniforms, but there's always the chance of getting killed. Besides, they would send me to the Peninsula, so we'd be apart anyway." He paused. "No, we have to think of some way to keep us together."

Sally licked her lips. "We could get married." Her voice was just a whisper.

Timothy stopped in his tracks.

"Come, you two," Barbara Rivers called. "We have lemonade and macaroons on the way. Do join us."

"We'll do that," Timothy said. He couldn't keep the tiny quiver out of his voice.

Timothy and Sally had barely seated themselves when there was a commotion in the front of the house. In just a moment, Mrs. Chapman came into the garden. All four of the people at the table caught a breath at the same time. Looming behind the tiny figure of the white-haired Mrs. Chapman was the imposing, dark-clad Edward Walker Percy Evan.

Barbara felt the blood drain from her face. She had thought about this moment for almost twenty years. She had always dreamed that she would meet Walker Evan face-to-face at some ball or the other. She would be elegantly gowned, her hair perfectly dressed, and she would be the envy of every other woman there.

She would meet Evan and give him the cut direct in front of everyone.

That was her dream. In reality, she stared at him across the small garden and willed herself to smile at him. "How do you do, Mr. Evan?" she asked through stiff lips, wondering if she would even been able to make a sound, until she heard her voice. She sounded strange and faraway.

"Quite well. How do you do, Mrs. Rivers?" he asked in return, giving her a slight bow. He made himself release his grip on his hat brim. His knuckles and fingertips were white from the strain. He tried not to look at her, but it was impossible. Lord, she was beautiful! If anything, the years had made her more lovely, lusher, riper. He tried not to look at the mature swell of her figure, but his eyes betrayed him.

"I thought I heard my ward say that he was coming here. That is, Alphonse mentioned that they might . . ." He took a deep breath.

"Won't you sit down?" Mrs. Chapman asked, smiling at him.

"We have lemonade and macaroons. If I recall correctly, when you were a boy, my macaroons were a favorite of yours."

"Thank you." He sat in the chair beside Barbara.

Timothy stared at him a moment. "You liked macaroons as a child?"

Barbara laughed, and the sound took Evan back. Coming here had been a mistake. He felt as if he would explode if he didn't get away. He couldn't even look at her. "I do believe, Evan," she said, "that your ward can't ever imagine you as a child."

"I can't," Timothy said earnestly.

Evan forced himself to smile even though his face felt brittle. He experienced a surge of rage as Barbara looked at Alphonse and laughed. Couldn't she see Alphonse for what he was? He had half a mind to. . . . He stopped as Miss Timmons joined them. Barbara introduced Miss Timmons, and she began chattering. Evan tried to listen, but could think of nothing except Barbara. His fingers itched to touch her hair.

"Do you, Mr. Evan?" Miss Timmons asked. She looked at him expectantly.

"I beg your pardon," Evan said. "I was woolgathering." He forced a laugh. "The thoughts of Mrs. Chapman's macaroons took me back to my childhood."

"Oh, wonderful," Miss Timmons said. "Personally, not much brings back my childhood unless it might be pork fat." She frowned. "Yes, pork fat. Definitely." She smiled and looked at Barbara. "Does anything remind you of your childhood, dear?"

"That's a period I'd rather forget." Barbara turned to Alphonse. "And you, Mr. Dewitt? What reminds you of those carefree days?"

"New-mown hay," he said promptly. "Evan and I always ran down to the fields as the hay was curing and played in it. We made mounds and castles and forts. It was great fun."

"I shudder to think how much hay we ruined," Evan said. He stood. "I really must be getting back to Hannaford House."

"Without your macaroons?" Barbara's voice held the hint of laughter he always remembered.

"I'm sorry. Do tell your mother that I couldn't stay." He looked at Barbara's smile and felt himself getting dizzy. Grasping for control, he looked over Barbara's head at a point toward the back of the garden and concentrated on that. "Timothy told me that he wished to ask you to supper one evening, and I thought I would stop and extend a personal invitation. We'd be delighted to have you any evening."

"Tomorrow?" Timothy asked promptly, a smile across his face. He moved over as Mrs. Chapman came in with a tray of macaroons, followed by the maid bearing a pitcher of lemonade and some glasses.

"I heard you say you're leaving. Do let me pack a few macaroons for you." Mrs. Chapman picked up several and wrapped them in a towel.

"Did you hear the invitation, Mother?" Barbara asked. "Mr. Beresford and Mr. Evan have asked us for tomorrow evening."

Evan nodded. "If that's convenient."

"We'd be delighted," Mrs. Chapman said. "I know the outing will do Mr. Chapman a world of good. He's been ill and is just now able to be up and about. We've been encouraging him to go out." She turned toward Barbara. "Barbara and Sally are planning to take him to the village this afternoon. I know he'll feel so much better for it."

Alphonse leaned in slightly toward Barbara. "Do allow me to escort you, Mrs. Rivers. I had planned to visit the village this afternoon, and this will provide a delightful diversion. I'll be glad to assist with your father."

"What a wonderful idea!" Mrs. Chapman said. "Thank you so much."

Evan bit down on his lower lip. "I'm sure you'll have a wonderful outing," he said, wondering all the while why Barbara didn't slap Alphonse for his impertinence. Evan's anger seemed to come right up his body into his head, and he wanted to slap Alphonse himself. He grasped the brim of his hat and made his goodbyes. Outside, he dismissed his driver and began walking along the overgrown path that led from Hannaford House to Mincey Cottage. The path had once been well-worn. He realized that he hadn't been over that path since the day he had told Barbara that he loved her.

There had been a large rock about halfway along the path. He and Barbara had often sat there, beginning from their childhood when they had played knights and a damsel in distress. He paused and looked for the rock. It was there, overgrown with vines. He pulled a few of them away and removed the moss that had covered part of the rock. Then he sat down and looked around him, remembering how his tutor had sat and talked to Chassie, the Chapman's maid, while he and Barbara played and ran in the field below the rock. That, too, had become overgrown and unused.

With a sigh, he rose and walked the rest of the way to Hannaford.

Back at Mincey Cottage, the group was laughing as they readied to walk into Crickford. Mr. Chapman had joined them and was telling stories. Six of them started out for the village in pairs—Mr. Chapman and Miss Timmons, Timothy and Sally, and, last, Barbara Rivers and Alphonse Dewitt.

"They make a handsome couple, don't you think?" Mr. Dewitt remarked, looking at Sally and Timothy. "You did know that Evan plans to ship him off to Jamaica."

Barbara caught her breath. "No, I didn't know. He's been a wonderful friend for Sally. He's made this an exceptional summer for her." She smiled briefly. "I think she was dreading to return to Gibraltar and leave him here."

Dewitt looked at her. "Gibraltar? I had no idea that you were returning. Do I dare hope that your return is several months in the future?"

"No, I plan to return soon. I told Sally to be ready to depart in a fortnight, but I really haven't decided exactly when to return." She smiled at him. "I've procrastinated. I kept telling myself that I couldn't book passage until Papa was better, but since then, I've come to realize that I keep putting it off because I don't want to return just now."

Alphonse smiled easily at her, the sort of smile that radiated warmth. "I hope you procrastinate even more, Mrs. Rivers. I'm being selfish when I say that, but I want to renew our old acquaintance."

She laughed. "Have we grown so old and so apart that you must call me Mrs. Rivers? You called me Barbara for years when we were children. Mrs. Rivers does sound formal."

"It does," he agreed, "but I don't want to push propriety." He chuckled. "Now, Evan would insist on all of us calling you Mrs. Rivers. He's quite a stickler for doing everything in the proper way." He paused. "Do you think he's changed?"

Barbara looked ahead and measured her words carefully. "I really don't know. He was much different as a child, but then we all were. I've hardly been around him enough to know if he's changed. Today was the first time I've seen him since before his marriage."

Alphonse lifted an eyebrow but said nothing. Instead, he began talking about the village and, once there, made himself indispensable in assisting Mr. Chapman. He even insisted that everyone return to Mincey earlier than planned so Mr. Chapman wouldn't get tired.

"A fine boy, that," Mr. Chapman said, watching Timothy and Alphonse begin the walk back to Hannaford.

"Which one?" Barbara asked with a smile.

"Both, but particularly Mr. Dewitt—Alphonse. We were talking about his childhood and his visits to Mincey Cottage, and he requested that I call him Alphonse as I did then." He paused. "He seemed most attentive to you, Barbara. You've been a widow for a long time. Perhaps you could consider . . ." He let his words trail off.

"Papa, you know I have an understanding with Captain Price."

Mr. Chapman smiled at her with all the wisdom garnered in a lifetime of being a vicar in a small village. "Yes, dear, I know. I also know that you haven't spoken his name in weeks, and haven't written to him in almost as long. Perhaps you should reconsider."

Barbara shook her head. "I promised him."

"I believe you told me that you agreed to marry him when you returned to Gibraltar. There's a great deal of difference in a promise and an agreement, Barbara." He paused. "I want you to be happy, dear, you know that. I just don't think you could be happy with someone you cared nothing for." He hesitated. "Look how unhappy you were with Major Rivers. I know you didn't love him."

Barbara paled. "How did you know that, Papa? I've never said a word."

He smiled and squeezed her hand. "You didn't have to, child. I knew from your reluctance to join him, and from the unhappiness in your letters after you arrived in Gibraltar. My only sorrow was that you were so far away from us."

"Don't ever tell Sally," she said, averting her eyes.

"I won't." There was a silence. "Look at me, Barbara."

She turned to gaze into eyes that were much like her own.

"Child, I want to see you happily married before I die. Your mother and I could ask for no greater gift than that. I don't think you'll be happy with Captain Price."

Barbara bit back a sob. "I have a letter written to him breaking the engagement. I just haven't had the nerve to send it."

"Send the letter, dear. Send it tomorrow."

The next day, Barbara was in the small parlor, the letter to Captain Price in her hand. She had thought about taking it to the post when she went to the village to take Mrs. Bascomb some comfrey leaves, but couldn't bring herself to do it. It seemed cold and unfair to Captain Price.

Barbara knew that Sally was planning to take a letter to be

posted this afternoon, because she had heard Sally promise
Mrs. Chapman that she would post her grandmother's letter to
a friend. The family always put letters to be posted on the small
silver tray in the front hall, and Barbara noted that it was empty.
Her mother must not have written her letter yet, so Barbara still
had time to make a decision.

She had gone so far as to place her letter to Captain Price on
the silver tray, but then she picked it up again. This had happened three times. Each time she put it down, an image of
Captain Price came into her mind. He was kind, bluff and
hearty, and would always be good to her and Sally. He had
courted her for years, Barbara knew, but she had only cared for
him as a friend. It seemed to come down to a question of
breaking his heart by refusing him, or dooming herself to a
lifetime of living without love. She propped the letter up on the
mantel and looked at it, trying to decide what to do.

She was still trying to decide when the maid, Chassie, announced Mr. Evan. Barbara turned to see him standing in the
doorway, almost filling the room with the force of his personality.

"Do come in, Evan." She sat down on the small striped chair
next to the fireplace. "Chassie, will you please bring some tea."
She glanced at Evan and smiled. "Macaroons, too, I suppose?"

"As always." Evan walked toward her, turning his hat in his
fingers, absently smoothing the brim. He put the hat on the
small table and sat across from her in a chair. "It's been a long
time, Barbara," he said huskily as soon as they were alone.

"Yes." She tried to keep embarrassment from flooding her
face as she recalled their last meeting. She wondered if he
thought of that time—it had been the worst moment of her
entire life. She had gone to give herself completely to the man
she loved, and she had discovered him at home with his fiancée,
planning their wedding. She had felt she could never face anyone again, and that was the reason she had married Major Rivers. She knew he was going to Gibraltar, and she thought she
could get away.

"How have you been?" he asked formally.

"Fine. And you?"

He gave her no answer except a nod, and they sat in silence until Chassie came in with their tea. Barbara poured and handed him a dish of tea. He held it awkwardly for a moment, then set it down. "I didn't know you were back in England," he said. "I've tried to keep up with what was going on in your life, but Gibraltar is a long way from here."

"Yes." She kept her voice carefully neutral. "I've heard that your life has changed here and there. Mother wrote me that your wife had died. My condolences, Evan. That must have been very difficult for you."

He swallowed, wanting to shout to her that it had been a relief, that it had meant that he was free. Instead, he looked at her and said, "Yes." He turned his gaze to the floor, frowned, and took a deep breath, wondering why this was so difficult.

"Barbara, I . . . I . . . ," he began, but was interrupted by Chassie announcing another visitor.

"Mr. Dewitt is here, mum. I told him to come in and join you, seeing as how you were already here with tea and all."

"Fine, Chassie." Barbara smiled at her as she disappeared to fetch Dewitt. "As you can see, Chassie hasn't changed at all. She'll never be a proper maid, but she suits Mother and Father." She chuckled. "She's good for them because she still has the same wonderful, warm heart."

"That's the really important thing in this world, isn't it?"

Barbara looked at him in surprise, but said nothing as Alphonse came in. He had been out riding and looked wonderful this morning. His blond hair was windblown, his clothes were, as always, perfect for the occasion, and he radiated good cheer and health.

"Evan, what a surprise," he said with a smile. Chassie brought an extra tea dish, and Barbara poured him some. "Perfect tea," he remarked, sipping it slowly. "I was looking for Timothy as we were planning on doing some fishing this afternoon. I thought he must have gone with you somewhere."

"I haven't seen him this morning," Evan said. "He's somewhat overset at my suggestion to send him to Jamaica for two or three years. I thought I'd give him time to become accustomed to the idea."

Chassie came back into the parlor. "Begging pardon, mum, but have you seen Miss Rivers? Your mother was wanting her to read aloud to your father, but I can't seem to find her about."

"I haven't seen her since I returned from Crickford," Barbara answered. "Perhaps she's in her room."

Chassie shook her head vigorously. "Oh, no, mum. I've looked all over the house and garden. She's not here."

Alphonse chuckled. "Another wayward child. The two of you are going to have to attach bells to Timothy and Miss Rivers."

Evan sat up quickly. "You don't think that—" He stopped and began again. "Surely they couldn't—" He shook his head. "Pardon my thoughts. It's impossible that they could have gone off together."

Chassie shook her head as well. "Oh, no, that couldn't be. Although I didn't see Mr. Beresford leave this morning. He and Miss Rivers was a-walking around the garden. I didn't see them after that."

Evan stood up in alarm. "Come, Alphonse, I believe we'd better find Timothy immediately."

Alphonse frowned at him. "I hardly think they've headed for Gretna, Evan. I'm sure we'll find them. They're probably sitting on the other side of the house. If they're even together," he added.

"Gretna!" Barbara stood quickly and put her hand on Evan's arm. "Surely not! I'll go up and see if Sally's things are all here. I know she holds Timothy in esteem, but . . . Gretna! It isn't possible!"

FOUR

"Gretna Green! What's this?" Mrs. Chapman came into the room. "Who's off to Gretna?"

Chassie looked at her, her eyes wide, her mob cap askew. "Oh, mum, everyone thinks that Mr. Beresford and Miss Rivers has done run off to Gretna Green!"

Mrs. Chapman reeled back against the wall in shock. "What is this, Barbara?" she asked faintly. "Surely not!"

Evan helped her across the room to his chair while Barbara poured her a restorative cup of tea. "We seem to have misplaced both Timothy and Sally," she told her mother.

"I doubt they've gone to Gretna," Evan said with a smile. "Don't you recall, Barbara, that several of us were always getting out of pocket when we were younger. We could usually be found down by the old mill or over at the old ruins." He picked up his hat. "I believe I will go try to find them, just to ease our minds. Alphonse, would you like to come along?"

"But of course." Alphonse stood and gave Barbara and Mrs. Chapman his best smile. "Don't worry a whit about those two. I'd stake my life on Timothy's integrity. I'm sure they've just gone for a few minutes and forgotten to tell anyone." He risked a sidelong glance at Evan. "Although I do own the boy is distraught about being sent to Jamaica. I'm hoping Evan will reconsider."

"This is neither the time nor place for such a discussion." Evan headed for the door with long strides. "Why don't I walk down to the mill, Alphonse, while you check at the old ruins."

"But of course," Alphonse said. He turned at the door and gave Barbara a smile. "Evan is always so intense," he said in a stage whisper as he went out.

Evan and Alphonse had been gone a good half an hour when Barbara heard chattering in the garden. Dashing outside, she ran right into Timothy, Sally, and Miss Timmons. "Mama, you're home. We went into the village, and look at the beautiful ribbon I found. There was a street peddler coming through, and he had the loveliest ribbons and bits of lace. You should go to Crickford. I think the man is staying through evening."

Barbara sat down weakly and caught her breath. "How could you leave without saying anything to anyone! Do you know how worried I've been? How worried all of us have been?" Her voice sounded strident.

Sally looked at her in confusion. "But I told Grandmother I was going to go mail her letter. And I left a note for you and gave it to Chassie. Miss Timmons and I looked for you, but Grandfather said you were in the village with Mrs. Bascomb. I thought we would see you on the way." Sally's lower lip began to quiver. "I'm sorry, Mama."

Barbara closed her eyes a moment. "No, I'm sorry for yelling at you. I was merely overset because . . . I thought . . . that is, Mr. Evan and I thought that . . ." She stood. "Never mind. Do you want to come in, Timothy? We have tea and macaroons."

"Oh, yes. I never turn down macaroons." Timothy shepherded them inside and followed close behind. Chassie came in as Barbara rang for fresh tea.

"Oh, mum, I see you stopped them from going to Gretna!" She smiled broadly. "That's by far the best thing. Every girl needs a proper church wedding, don't she?" She marched out of the room.

"Gretna?" said Miss Timmons in confusion, catching only the one word. "Are you planning to go to Gretna, dear?" she asked Barbara. "Is Captain Price going to meet you there?"

"No, Miss Timmons. This is all a muddle. No one is going to Gretna."

"What a shame." Miss Timmons sat down across from the tea tray and eyed it hungrily. "I've always wanted to travel north. I've never been there, although my cousin did send me some drawings." She glanced around. "It was quite a fatiguing walk to the village. And dusty, as well. I, for one, could use a cup of tea to tide me over until we eat."

Barbara poured tea as Chassie bustled in. "Oh, mum," she said, bobbing slightly, "Miss Rivers left me this note to give you, and I just remembered it right here in my apron pocket." She fished a scrap of paper from her pocket and handed it to Barbara. "Will you want more macaroons, mum?"

"No," Barbara said, at the same time that Miss Timmons, Sally, and Timothy chorused, "Yes!" Chassie looked at them in puzzlement. "It's close to nuncheon," Barbara said. "We'll have the macaroons with some fruit for dessert."

She glanced down at the scrap of paper. It was written in Sally's almost illegible hand on the back of what appeared to be a note from someone else. "I saved paper, Mama," Sally said. "You always said that I should." Sally frowned. "Mama, did you think I had eloped to Gretna? Was that what all this was about?"

Barbara hesitated, then decided to make a clean breast of it. "Yes, Sally, it did cross my mind. Mr. Evan and Mr. Dewitt are out looking for the two of you. We didn't get your note, so we had no idea where you were."

Sally looked aghast. "Mama, you know I would never do that! Furthermore, I would never leave the house without Chassie or Miss Timmons with me."

Timothy gulped. "Did you say that Alphonse and my guardian are out looking?" he asked.

Barbara nodded and smiled at him. "Don't worry, Timothy. I'll see that they understand what happened."

"Perhaps, if you don't see them before, you might explain when you come to supper." The worried expression was still on his face. "Evan can get overset in no time. I might be on a ship for Jamaica tomorrow."

Sally burst into tears.

Evan and Alphonse returned in the middle of the afternoon. They were dusty and hungry. Barbara hastily explained what had happened and mentioned that Timothy had hurried on to Hannaford House.

"Wait until I get my hands on the young whelp," Evan said, mopping the dust from his face.

"Be easy on the boy," Alphonse said. "It was a natural misunderstanding. It could have happened to any of us. Miss a message, overlook a note, and everyone is at sixes and sevens. It's happened to me before."

Barbara laughed. "I daresay that it's happened to all of us at one time or the other. Could I offer you two rescuers some refreshment?"

Evan shook his head. "I need to get back to Hannaford, and no doubt Alphonse does, too. I believe we're expecting your company for supper tonight."

Alphonse hesitated a moment as Evan waited for him at the gate. He leaned over, clasped Barbara's hand, and bowed slightly over it. "I'll be counting the minutes," he said softly, giving her a smile.

From her upstairs window, Sally saw and heard the exchange. She moved back into her room, a smile of satisfaction on her face.

Much to Mrs. Chapman's and Sally's delight, Evan sent his glossy carriage around to take them to Hannaford House. "Such consideration," Mrs. Chapman said. "Even as a child, Walker Evan was always a considerate person. Such a sweet, innocent boy."

"I agree he's considerate, but I daresay he's changed in other ways since then, my dear," Mr. Chapman noted. "I believe that now his time is consumed by his estate, and I heard he's been quite successful in some of his investments. Fallstone made such a mess of his estate in Kent that he needed Evan to come get things running smoothly again." He shook his head slightly. "Pity Walker Evan wasn't the heir. He's the best of the lot, I'd say—even after all that about his wife."

Barbara couldn't resist. "What about his wife? Do you mean his devastation at her death?"

Mr. Chapman and Mrs. Chapman exchanged glances. "Indeed," Mr. Chapman said. "You're looking fetching tonight, Barbara. That rose color becomes you." He glanced out the carriage window to see Hannaford House glowing a mellow gold in the last of the setting sun. "Lovely place, isn't it?"

Barbara glanced out, and all the embarrassment she had felt years before came flooding back. She remembered the rain, the happiness she had felt, the faintly scratchy feel of Evan's coat as she had flung herself into his arms. Worse, she could almost hear Abigail's voice as she emerged from the drawing room door. "And who is this, Evan? I don't believe we've met." Barbara could hear in her mind the faint drawl, the touch of arrogance and possessiveness. And the very worst recollection was the look of pure horror on Evan's face. . . .

She closed her eyes to try to block out the memory, but it stayed there, as fresh and vivid as when it had happened.

They sat stiffly in the drawing room before they went in to dine. That was, everyone sat stiffly except Alphonse, who was perfectly at ease and regaling Barbara with witty stories. Timothy and Sally sat off to one side, looking straight ahead, trying to pretend they weren't talking to each other.

"I think it's working," Timothy whispered. "She seems taken with Alphonse."

"You're right." Sally smiled at Evan, who was scowling. He didn't smile back. "What's wrong with your guardian? He's looked like a thundercloud since we got here."

Timothy sighed. "I don't know. He's been acting strange since he arrived. At first, I thought it was because Alphonse was here and he doesn't like Alphonse at all, you know, but now I believe it must be something else. It's probably either a woman or money." He nodded sagely. "Those would be the only two things to annoy Evan."

"Perhaps he'll leave." She turned to Timothy, her eyes wide. "A woman? Perhaps he'll go back to London and forget all this business of sending you to Jamaica."

Timothy shook his head. "No, Evan never forgets anything." He sighed. "If we can persuade your mother to marry Alphonse, perhaps the two of them can convince Evan that I'd wither in Jamaica."

"If it can be done," Sally said, "we'll do it." She smiled with satisfaction as her mother relaxed and laughed aloud at something Alphonse said. They made a handsome couple, both of them blond, both of them so much alike.

During supper, Alphonse entertained the table with his droll stories. He knew everyone in the *ton,* it seemed, and his stories were always amusing, but never cutting. All in all, Sally mused, he would do very well. Her mother seemed quite taken with him. He was so much different from Evan, who sat at the head of the table glowering at everyone. Mrs. Chapman did her best to talk to him, but he was no more than polite.

"Poor Evan," Mrs. Chapman remarked as they were driven back to Mincey Cottage. "He seems so sad and angry. You were so right, my dear. He has changed—he isn't at all like the boy I knew."

"Circumstances change people," Mr. Chapman said, patting her hand. "I suspect that the old Evan is there somewhere underneath the shell he's built around himself."

"He should be more like Mr. Dewitt," Sally remarked, trying to see her mother's face in the pale light. "I truly like Mr. Dewitt."

"He's always been likable," Barbara remarked. "Frivolous and feather-headed, but immensely likable."

Sally went into her mother's room right before they went to

bed that night. She picked up a hairbrush and began to brush her mother's hair. Barbara looked in the mirror, surprised, her blue eyes questioning. "You haven't done this in a long time," she said. "Is there a reason?"

"Mama, how can you think such!" Sally put her arms around Barbara's shoulders. "I've neglected you of late, but you've been so busy with Grandfather and Grandmother. I haven't wanted to disturb you."

Barbara put her hand on Sally's. "No, I'm the one who has neglected you, dear. I have been busy with them, but that will change now. When we get back to Gibraltar, I promise that—"

Sally began brushing her hair again and interrupted her. "Must we go back, Mama? You know that I want to stay here. Grandfather and Grandmother want us to stay as well. At their ages, they need us to watch over them here."

Barbara sighed. "I know. Believe me, the closer we get to our departure date, the more I realize that I should stay. But . . ." She let her words trail off.

"Mama." Sally paused, wondering just how to frame her words. "Have you ever thought about marrying someone like Mr. Dewitt? He's the kind of man I would like for a father, and he seems to care for you." She glanced in the mirror at Barbara's surprised expression. "I don't mean to interfere, Mama, but I do so want you to be happy."

"And you don't think I would be happy with Captain Price?"

Sally shook her head. "No, Mama, I don't. And I don't think you'll be happy in Gibraltar. I know I won't be happy there, but that's of little consequence. I do think you and Captain Price will rub along all right, but I don't think you'll be happy." She bit her lower lip. "There, I've said it. I'm sorry, Mama, but that's the way I feel." She fell to her knees beside Barbara. "All I want is for you to be happy, Mama. I know that sometimes I seem selfish and want my own way, but the thing I want most in the world is for you to be happy. I wish I could give you the present of happiness." She put her head in Barbara's lap.

Barbara stroked her hair. "That's the most wonderful thing

you've ever said to me, Sally. Your happiness is mine, too, sweeting, and you've just given me that present."

Sally looked up, her face shining. "Then you'll think about staying here where your heart is?

"Yes, sweetheart, I'll think about it." Barbara smiled at her and kissed her lightly on the cheek. "Go to bed now and have pleasant dreams."

Sally got to her feet, smiling. "I will, Mama. I truly will." She paused at the door as though she wanted to say something else, but she merely blew her mother a kiss and went out.

Barbara waited a few moments, then got up and looked out her window. In the distance, she could see the high top of Hannaford House silhouetted against the starry sky. She took a deep breath and picked up her candle. She went downstairs, picked up the letter to Captain Price, and put it on the little silver tray in the hall.

Over at Hannaford House, Walker Evan was sitting in his chamber. His man, Ledger, had come in to ready him for bed, but he had sent him away. Instead, Evan removed his coat and cravat and poured himself a stiff brandy. He walked over to the window where he could see a faint glimmer of light from Mincey Cottage. He took a long swallow of brandy and, standing there in his shirtsleeves, berated himself for being five kinds of a fool.

Jealousy, he thought. That's what it had been. He had recognized it, and still had been able to do nothing about it. The whole evening Alphonse had been charming and witty, the very epitome of what an urbane gentleman should be. Evan knew Barbara had been enchanted. He had seen it in her eyes, heard it in her laughter. At the sweet curve of her lips as she smiled at Alphonse, he had wanted to strangle the man with his bare hands. Evan had heard the warmth in her voice as she answered some remark Alphonse had made, and he had had to clench his hands into fists to keep from pummeling the smile from Alphonse's face. Couldn't she see that Alphonse was all veneer? She knew Alphonse from childhood—why couldn't she see that he hadn't changed at all?

She hadn't changed. Oh, she was older, but that had just enhanced her beauty. It was odd, he thought. Those fine lines around some women's eyes made them look old and tired, but they seemed to make Barbara look even better. A man looking at her knew that here was a woman who would be a confidante as well as a lover.

A lover. He caught his breath at the thought and leaned his head against the cool glass of the window. He wanted her. He had wanted her before, when he had discovered what love really was, but this was different. This was wanting because he knew he needed her to be complete. All these years, there had been only half of him existing; he had been living half a life. Barbara was his complement, and he didn't have her.

Evan groaned and hit the side of the window casing with his fist. He looked back at the tiny glimmer of light from the bedroom window at Mincey. He didn't even know if the light came from Barbara's room, but he thought it probably did. He could imagine her there now, getting ready for bed. In his mind, he saw her taking her hair down, pulling the pins out of it, and shaking it loose until blond cascades slid down her back. Then mentally he saw her taking off garment after garment, until. . . .

He cried out and surprised himself. In a red rage, he wheeled and threw the brandy glass against the fireplace, where it shattered into a thousand shards.

FIVE

Sally stopped by the front parlor as her mother was placing a bonnet on her smooth blond hair. Sally's eyes widened as she looked at her mother. Barbara was dressed in a dark sapphire dress that she hadn't worn for the better part of a year. Sally had always thought that the dress flattered her mother beyond words, had insisted that her mother pack it, and had often urged her to wear it during their stay at Mincey Cottage. Barbara insisted that the dress was too much for a place like Crickford and should only, she had once noted with a smile, "be worn when one wishes to impress." Now she was wearing it and, to Sally's delight, was also wearing an outrageously becoming bonnet that tied with matching ribbons. There could be only one answer, Sally thought to herself: her mother was going to impress Mr. Dewitt today.

"Are you going to the village?" Sally asked casually, entering the room.

Barbara whirled and a touch of red stained her cheeks. "No, Mr. Dewitt is coming by to take me on a short carriage ride." She glanced in the mirror. "I couldn't decide if this was suitable or not. What do you think?"

"It's perfect," Sally said with admiration. "Here, let me fix your bonnet ribbon." She straightened the ribbon and puffed it slightly just as Chassie opened the door for Alphonse.

"A charming picture, I must say," he said with a smile. "You two are rapidly becoming the standard by which I measure all other females, and"—he made a face—"they are all coming up short." He gave Barbara a devilish grin. "See, madam, just how you have turned my existence topsy-turvy. What will I do when I'm out in Society again? Every woman will be only an insipid copy."

Sally noted that her mother's cheeks had a faint blush, and that she smiled back at Alphonse. *Our plan is really working!* she thought to herself, as she had to fight down the urge to break into a little dance. *Mama is falling in love with Mr. Dewitt.*

"I'm off to read to Grandfather," she announced, hoping that Alphonse would whisk her mother off. "Do have a wonderful ride."

"I have no doubt of it," Alphonse said, offering Barbara his arm as they went outside to the waiting carriage.

Upstairs, Sally dashed into the front bedroom so she could watch the two of them go down the road. She had to lean out as, to her surprise, they weren't going toward Crickford, but instead headed down the main road toward Beddenbury. It was going to be a long ride if they went that far. Sally pulled back inside and shut the window, a very satisfied smirk on her face. Then she went off to read to her grandfather.

She had just gone into the parlor to pick up a copy of *Lyrical Ballads* to read to her grandfather when Chassie announced another visitor.

"I've come to see Mrs. Rivers," Mr. Evan said, again turning his hat brim in his fingers.

"She isn't here," Sally said bluntly. "She and Mr. Dewitt have gone for a carriage ride." She couldn't resist a chuckle. "In your carriage, I believe."

Evan nodded. "He told me he wanted the carriage, but I didn't ask the purpose." He hesitated a fraction of a second. "Will they be back soon?"

"Oh, I don't think so. They went toward Beddenbury, and that's quite a drive, you know. I don't expect them back until early evening, although Mama didn't really give me a time."

She dropped her voice conspiratorially. "Mama seems to enjoy Mr. Dewitt's company. I'm sure they'll have a wonderful day."

"I'm sure." Evan turned abruptly. "Good day, Miss Rivers."

It was all Sally could do to keep up with him and see him to the door. He left, mounted his big white horse, and began riding at a good clip across the fields. Sally hoped he had put his hat on firmly as he was in real danger of losing it. "A strange man," she muttered to herself. "No wonder Timothy is in awe of him." She smiled as she closed the door and started down the hall. "Perhaps we can find a wife for him—just as soon as we get Mama married off." She paused a moment by the hall table as an envelope caught her eye. "Captain Price," she breathed, picking it up and noting the address. "Mama is writing to Captain Price. She must be breaking her engagement." She smiled in satisfaction. "I'll post this myself this afternoon." She put the envelope back onto the little silver tray and went off to read to Mr. Chapman.

Evan pushed his horse harder and harder, trying to ride off his feelings. How could Barbara be taken in by someone like Alphonse? Couldn't she see what kind of unsuitable man he was? Evan rode hard for the better part of half an hour before he realized that he had turned his horse toward Beddenbury. He would not spy on them—he would not allow himself to do it. He reined in his horse and let the animal drink from a small stream, then turned back toward Hannaford House, trying with every step to keep himself from thinking of Barbara.

He was not successful.

The day was fine and sunny, so Timothy slipped away from Hannaford House in the middle of the afternoon and went over to Mincey Cottage. He found Mr. and Mrs. Chapman, Miss Timmons, and Sally sitting in the back garden. Sally was reading aloud to them. He paused to listen to her voice, thinking it sounded as he imagined angels would sound.

"Do come join us, Mr. Beresford," Mr. Chapman said, motioning Timothy into the garden. "We're just about to stop for some refreshment. I know Sally is exhausted after reading to us." He chuckled. "She read for an hour or so this morning, but we were so enchanted that we asked her to continue now." He patted her hand. "We'll finish tomorrow, dear. Do have some lemonade and rest your voice."

Timothy sat and tried not to gaze continuously at Sally. "It's a lovely day," he finally said.

"Yes," Mr. Chapman agreed. "Sally and I had planned to walk into Crickford and post a letter this afternoon. It will be a fine day for a walk."

"Perhaps we could all go together," Timothy suggested.

"Oh, my, no," Mrs. Chapman said. "Miss Timmons and I have several things planned in the garden. The rest of you go ahead."

Without waiting for anyone to change plans, Sally dashed into the house to get her bonnet and the letter. She tucked it safely into her reticule and went off to mail it in Crickford.

They were at the coaching inn, mailing the letter, when Wicket, the footman from Hannaford House, came in with a letter to be posted. "Mr. Evan wants this to go to the skipper of the *Pretty Maid* at Plymouth Harbor," he said to the man who handled the coaching inn posts. "Without fail, he says. He wants the skipper to have it afore he sails for Jamaica."

Sally caught her breath and glanced at Timothy, who had paled considerably. "Do you suppose that could be about you?" she whispered in a stricken tone.

"It probably is," he whispered back. His voice was hoarse. Evan usually did what he said he would do, but Timothy had believed he had more time than this. "I'd like to see what's in that one." He turned to Sally. "There's nothing I can do now to persuade Evan to let me stay."

"We'll think of something," Sally said as Mr. Chapman motioned them over to his table to meet one of his friends. They were forced to sit for a while and listen to talk about the good old days. Finally, Sally excused herself for a moment. She was gone for several minutes, and when she returned, she was pale. "Would you like some air?" Timothy asked.

"Ye . . . yes, I would. Do you mind, Grandfather? Mr. Beresford and I could take a turn around the churchyard."

"By all means," he said, waving his hand at them. "When you feel like returning, just come by and collect me."

They had walked halfway around the church when Sally sat down on an old tombstone. "I've done a terrible thing, Timothy," she said, twisting the cords of her reticule. "I . . . I . . ." she paused. "I've stolen your letter. Not your letter, but Mr. Evan's letter." She reached into her reticule and drew out a crumpled envelope, then handed it to Timothy.

Timothy looked at it. "What did you do? Why?"

Sally looked miserable. "I don't know why. I needed to find the necessary, and the letter was just there on the counter, practically calling out to me to pick it up. I grabbed it, then realized that I couldn't do that, but then people came in and I couldn't put it back." She looked up at him with stricken eyes. "What shall we do? I can't steal Mr. Evan's letter, but I certainly can't let him send you to Jamaica!"

Timothy looked at the letter and sighed. "We'll have to take it back. I'll go inside and pretend that I found it on the floor." He weighed it on the palm of his hand. "I'd give a pony to know what's inside that, but I can't break the seal. Drat!" He pulled her up by her hand. "Don't worry, Sally. I'll protect you. I'll get the letter back, and no one will be the wiser." He looked sadly down at the letter addressed to Captain Dogherty of the *Pretty Maid*. "I suppose there's nothing left to do except to try to convince Evan not to send me away."

"We should try to find him a wife, Timothy! That's what he needs. If he had a wife, then he would pay absolutely no attention to you."

"Well, the only eligible female around is your mother, and

we've already fixed her up with Alphonse. I don't know anyone else."

Sally sat back down. "Well, I don't either. Besides, I don't want Evan for a father. He's simply horrid sometimes. He might even send me away to Jamaica."

Timothy laughed at her. "I promise he wouldn't do that. We'll give the matter some thought, and I'm sure we'll come up with something." He pulled her up. "Now smile for me and we'll collect your grandfather and get back to Mincey Cottage."

"After you return the letter."

"Of course."

Sally was in her room, sobbing, when she heard the carriage wheels outside. She made herself get up and look out so she could be sure it was her mother and Mr. Dewitt. She saw Alphonse lift her mother from the carriage, laughing all the while. Her mother laughed back, a joyous sound that Sally could hear inside her room. She turned away from the window, satisfied on that score. It was the first time in a long while that she had heard such mirth in her mother's voice. She glanced in the mirror to see her own swollen eyes.

Barbara stopped by Sally's room on her way to change clothes. "Sweeting, whatever is wrong? Are you ill?"

Sally turned her face away so her mother couldn't see. "Nothing. I have a headache, that's all."

Barbara sat down on the side of the bed and turned Sally's face toward her. "What is it? You've been crying, and for a good while, unless I miss my guess."

"It's Timothy." Sally stopped and burst into tears. "And Mr. Evan. I hate that man. He's going to send Timothy off to Jamaica."

"Hush, hush." Barbara smoothed her hair back. "I'm sure Evan would do no such thing. He's a fair man, and I'm sure he'll do what's best for Timothy."

"No, no, no," Sally blubbered. "It's true. He's going to send him away. He said his father had sent him to Jamaica, and he's going to do the same to Timothy." She looked at Barbara through tear-filled eyes. "Timothy is a different person. That may have been all right for Mr. Evan, but it isn't for Timothy. You know Mr. Evan, Mama. Do you think you could talk to him?"

"I . . . I . . ." Barbara hesitated. "It isn't my place to interfere between Evan and his ward."

"Please, Mama, please." This was said with a fresh torrent of tears. "He's the most horrid man I can imagine. He's had no children of his own, so he doesn't know the first thing about how to treat Timothy. He's selfish and uncaring."

"Sally, I don't want to hear such things about Mr. Evan. You don't know him at all." Barbara felt an unexpected surge of irritation. "He's a good man."

"Then, talk to him. Convince him not to send Timothy away."

"If I see Evan and have an opportunity to say something, Sally, I will. That's all I can promise. I doubt that I'll see him."

Sally sat up. "I'm sure you will. He came by this morning, right after you and Mr. Dewitt left. I'm sure he'll be back." She managed a shaky smile. "I know you can talk to him, Mama. After all, the two of you grew up together."

"I'm not promising that I will, Sally." Barbara sighed. "I once thought I knew Evan well, but I was proven wrong. I will speak to him if the opportunity arises, but that's all I can tell you."

Sally threw her arms around her mother. "You're the best mother in the world," she said. Then she drew back, smiling. "How selfish I am to talk about nothing except my troubles. How was your day? Did you have a wonderful time with Mr. Dewitt?"

"I did. We visited some mutual friends in Beddenbury. I hadn't seen Rosalind since before I was married. We spent our time remembering things past." She paused a second, remembering her agony when Rosalind had mentioned Evan. Rosalind had assumed that Barbara had refused Evan's offer of marriage and that was why he had settled on Abigail. Barbara had quickly changed the subject and begun talking about Gibraltar.

"Mr. Dewitt is very good at that sort of thing, isn't he?"

Barbara smiled. "Yes, he is. I've heard he's the perfect house guest, and now I believe it. He was very attentive all afternoon. We left Rosalind's, and then we went to—" She stopped as Chassie came to the door.

"Oh, mum, there you are. Mrs. Rivers, I mean." Chassie wiped her hands on her apron. "There's a caller to see you if you're in. Of course you're in, but I could say you weren't. That wouldn't be exactly true, and he knows you're in anyway, but those things are done. What do you want me to tell him, mum?"

"Who is it, Chassie?" Barbara stood and smoothed the deep sapphire cloth of her dress.

"Oh, did I forget that? I'm sorry, mum. I certainly didn't mean to do that." She glanced at Barbara's puzzled expression. "Oh, it's Mr. Evan, mum. Are you home or not?"

Barbara glanced back down at Sally and saw the pleading in her eyes. "Tell Mr. Evan that I'll be right down, Chassie."

Evan was in the front parlor when Barbara went downstairs. He was wearing black, and his presence filled the small room. He wheeled around when she came into the room, almost knocking over Mrs. Chapman's prized Chinese vase.

There was an awkward silence. "Barbara," he said finally. "It's good to see you again. You look . . . you look lovely."

"Thank you, Evan." She sat down in a chair flanking the fireplace and motioned for him to sit opposite her. "It's good to see you as well."

He sat down, knocking a filigreed silver statue off the small table at his elbow. He reached down and picked it up. Barbara could never remember him being awkward. In fact, she had always thought of him as very graceful and agile.

She racked her brain for something to say as they sat there and looked at each other. She had thought often of the time she would meet him alone. She would be witty and charming, and he would regret not marrying her. Now she merely sat. "Would you like some tea?" she asked.

"Yes. Yes, I'd like that very much."

Barbara rang for tea, and they sat quietly until Chassie brought a tray in, their only conversation a few remarks about the weather. Barbara thought she had never been so uncomfortable. "How was Gibraltar?" he asked as Chassie set the tray down.

"It was very nice. After my husband was killed, I decided to stay there for a short while." She smiled at him as she handed him a dish of tea. "That stretched into several years. Sally and I were very comfortable there."

"That's good. I was afraid you were lonely." He paused. "I kept up with you, you know. Every time I came to Crickford, I asked about you."

Barbara gazed at him, startled. "I didn't know that, Evan. Of course, Mother kept me informed of you through her letters. As I told you before, I'm truly sorry about the death of your wife. That must have been quite a blow to you."

He looked at her, sitting in the chair in her sapphire dress that made her eyes glow like jewels. He wanted to tell her that Abigail's death had been a blessing, a relief, but he couldn't. He wanted to seize her and hold her next to him, the same way that he had wanted to hold her all those years ago when she had come to Hannaford, rain-soaked and wild. A million times since then he had imagined how it would have been to taste those rain-drenched lips and whisper love words through her tangled hair.

Instead, he sipped his tea and nodded gravely. "It was a shock, of course. I'm sure the death of your husband was a shock as well."

"Yes," Barbara said, only her thoughts were on how mortified she had been to find Abigail there at Hannaford House. How she had listened to Evan leave her late that afternoon, telling her that he loved her. She had hugged the words to her like a blanket that warmed her heart. That night, even though it was raining, she had impulsively run to Hannaford House through the rain to give herself to him. The warm feeling was chilled by thoughts of how he had betrayed her. She made herself return to the present.

She put her tea dish down on the tray and concentrated on her half promise to Sally. "As you know, Sally seems to have developed a deep friendship with your ward."

He grinned slightly. "After the Gretna Green scare, I think it may be more than a friendship."

"Perhaps," she suggested, "we may be reading more into it than actually exists. At any rate, she's distressed at the thought that he may be sent to Jamaica."

Evan sighed. "I've been thinking on it. I thought it might make a man out of him. I know it made one of me."

Barbara looked at him, remembering again. "Did it, Evan?" she asked softly.

He put his tea down and stood up, as though the chair was too confining. "Of course it did. I was much different when I returned. You know that."

"Yes, you were different, but I've often asked myself if you had changed for the better or the worse. If you had stayed here, what would have been different in your life?"

He leaned against the mantel, his chin on his fist. He wanted to tell her how he had longed for her in Jamaica, how he had thought about coming home to see her. He wanted to let her know that his father had planned his life for him, and he had felt obligated to do what was necessary. He wanted to tell her about Abigail, and how she hadn't been his choice at all.

Most of all, he wanted to explain to Barbara that the words he had said to her were from the depths of his soul. He must have been insane to tell her he loved her. Oh, it was true, would always be true, but he should never have said the words. He was the one who had created the scene in the hall at Hannaford that had so embarrassed her. It had been his fault, and he had done nothing about it.

Instead, he turned around and looked at her slowly. "I would have had a different life, I think," he said. "I was headstrong in those days. Going to Jamaica showed me that I had to subordinate my own wishes to whatever was best for the family. Overall, it was probably the ideal thing for me."

"And subordinating your own wishes and desires is what you've done since?"

He looked at her sharply, then nodded. "Someone must take responsibility for the family and its lands. They all depend on me." Without thinking, he ran his long fingers through his dark hair. Barbara noticed a few strands of silver at his temples.

She gave him a long look. "I didn't realize that everything was on your head, Evan. Perhaps it's time to delegate some duties to the others. In my experience with the army in Gibraltar, I saw that often people will let you do as much as you will. When you stand firm and force them to be responsible, they will do it."

"I can't imagine my life without work."

"Perhaps Timothy doesn't need to have the sense of responsibility that you do."

Evan took a deep breath. "He will have his father's estate." He paused. "However, I suppose you're telling me that Jamaica may not be the best thing for Timothy. He won't have family responsibilities as I have."

Barbara smiled at him. "I'm just asking you to look at the problem from all sides."

He turned and looked out the window. "All right, I'll think on it." He paused. "Barbara, I . . . I . . . I wanted to . . ."

Miss Timmons came into the room. "There you are, dear. I do hope I'm not interrupting, but Mr. Dewitt is here. He says you left your reticule in the carriage and he's returning it. Shall I show him in?"

Evan turned back to look at Barbara as she heard this. Her face brightened, and she smiled softly. A smile, Evan thought, that could melt ice. "Of course, Miss Timmons," she said. "As close as it is to supper time, why don't you ask Chassie if there's

enough for more? I'm sure Mr. Dewitt would like to join us."
She turned to Evan. "And you as well, Evan, if you wish to stay
to supper."

Evan felt as if someone had just thrown cold water on him.
"Thank you for the invitation, but I must be leaving," he said
formally. "I do hope I'll be seeing you again."

"Do stop by at any time, Evan," Barbara said with a smile.
"You know our door is always open to you, just as it has always
been."

He nodded and went out, passing Dewitt in the hall. He made
himself smile and nod to Alphonse, and even comment on the
weather. Alphonse was charming and managed to answer him
as well as turn his charm on Barbara. Evan raged inwardly.
Alphonse's knack for doing just the right thing socially was
something that Evan would never have. Feeling defeated, he
perfunctorily muttered his farewell and left.

Outside, Evan started to ride home, then tugged on the reins
and began walking, berating himself for acting like a fool as he
went, thinking about Barbara and Alphonse looking at each
other and laughing as they ate together. He veered off the path
halfway to Hannaford House and sat down on the big rock—
their rock—to think. He could remember how he and Barbara
and Alphonse used to play kings and knights, using the rock as
a fort. This was where he had said those fateful words to Barbara, all those years ago.

He closed his eyes a moment, letting the past wash over him,
leaving a bitter taste in his mouth. Then he thought of his conversation with Barbara and the things he had revealed about
himself. He would have revealed so much more if they hadn't
been interrupted by Miss Timmons. He had been just about to
declare himself. Thank God he had seen how she reacted to
Alphonse before he made a total fool of himself.

He put his hands over his face and gripped the top of his head
with his fingers, wishing he could rip out the memories. He
couldn't. The more he tried to forget, the more he thought about
Barbara. Now he relived the scene at Mincey—his only

thoughts were of what Barbara had said and done. He went over every single word, thinking especially of Barbara's comments about his work. He couldn't give up his work—he simply couldn't. He couldn't possibly delegate anything, for if he didn't stay overwhelmed and busy, he would have to think, and he didn't dare do that. His work was his salvation. It had been since the day he saw the look in Barbara's eyes when she had first known he was to marry Abigail.

For the first time since he was a small boy, he had the terrible urge to put his fists over his eyes and cry. Instead, he remembered he had some accounts to check. He stood wearily, not even dusting off his clothes. He picked up the horse's reins and began walking back to Hannaford House.

SIX

Barbara stopped by Sally's room that night before bedtime. "I talked a moment to Evan today about his plan to send Timothy to Jamaica."

"Did he say he would change his mind?" Sally danced across the floor and hugged her mother. "Oh, Mama, I'm so happy! Thank you!"

Barbara gently untangled her arms. "Don't thank me yet. He said he would think about it and try to come up with the best solution. I have no idea what that might be."

Sally's expression crumpled, and she sat down in the small chair by the door. "Oh, Mama, how terrible. He's going to send Timothy away. I just know it. Just because the man has had a horrid life, he wants Timothy to have one, too. He's just a bitter old man, that's all."

"Old?" Barbara sat down across from her. "Dear me, Sally, Evan is only slightly older than I am. He's forty, to be exact. As for being bitter—I doubt that. He's perhaps overworked, but I doubt that you could term him bitter."

"Oh, he is. Timothy hinted that his marriage had not been happy, and when Grandfather and I were in the village one day, I asked Mary Rose Taylor about it. You know what a gossip her mother is, and Mary Rose is just like her mother. She knows everything."

"And tells everything," Barbara added dryly.

Sally missed her tone. "Yes, she does. That's why I knew she would be the perfect person to ask. She told me that Evan and his wife had a terrible marriage." Sally lowered her voice. "She had lovers."

Barbara leapt to her feet. "Sally!" Her tone was horrified. "How can you possibly say such a thing! How can you possibly know about such a thing?"

"Really, Mama, I am grown." Sally raised her eyebrows. "Many females my age are already married. I know all about such things. Not only did Mary Rose tell me that Mr. Evan's wife had lovers, but she also said Mr. Evan's wife died because she had sent for the local witch woman to help her get rid of an unwanted baby. Mary Rose said—"

"Stop!" Barbara heard her own voice rise into a screech. "Stop that right now! I don't want to hear it, and I don't want you to ever repeat such scurrilous gossip! That Mary Rose should be taken out and horsewhipped. And her mother should be, too! Imagine ruining a good man's name by telling such nonsense." She jerked the door open and went out, slamming it behind her. She leaned up against the door frame, taking air into her body in deep gulps until she felt she could move. Then she went to her room and shut the door behind her. She sat there in the dark for a long time, thinking about Evan and what might have happened in his marriage.

Thinking over all the hints she had heard in the village, and her own parents' comments, Barbara didn't doubt for a moment that Mrs. Taylor and Mary Rose were telling things that had some basis in fact. The story made everything fit—Evan's bitterness, the changes in his personality, his complete immersion in his work. How he must have suffered over the years!

She put her head down on the bedside table in the dark and sobbed. She didn't know if she was crying for Evan or for all the things the two of them had lost.

Timothy and Alphonse came over the next morning. "And a beautiful morning it is, too," Alphonse said with his infectious grin. "I thought you ladies might like to walk over to Hannaford House with us and see Evan's new project. He's put in a pool with a hydraulic fountain just like the ones at Versailles. It's the perfect spot for a picnic."

"Timothy told me about the fountain, but I'm not sure I want to go if Mr. Evan is going to be there," Sally said.

"He's not there. I have no idea where he went, but his man Ledger said Evan was up and out at daylight. Ledger doubted that Evan will return before supper."

Sally turned to Barbara. "In that case, Mama, could we go? I've wanted to see the new fountain for ever so long—since I first heard about it. And it is a perfect day, Mama. Just look how lovely the weather is!"

"I do believe you've convinced me," Barbara said with a laugh. "It will take a while for us to get ready, however."

"I've thought of that," Alphonse said, pulling a letter from his pocket. "I need to go into the village to send a post, and instead of sending a footman, I thought Timothy and I could attend to that while the two of you prepare. On our way back, we'll stop, and all of us can go to Hannaford together."

Barbara looked up at him and laughed. "You were quite sure we were going, weren't you, Alphonse? And what would you have done had we refused?"

He smiled and took her hand in his for a moment. "There was never a doubt in my mind that you would comply. Remember that I know you from childhood, Barbara Chapman, and I know you'd never let a day like this go to waste." He paused and grinned wickedly. "Am I correct?"

"You are correct," she answered with a laugh. "We'll be ready when you return."

"You might check to see if there are any letters for us," Sally said. "I'm expecting a note from a friend in Gibraltar." She glanced at her mother. "I forgot to tell you that Amanda Rickford wrote to me that she was getting married, Mama. She promised to write and tell me all the details."

"Married!" Barbara's eyebrows shot up in surprise. "Goodness, Sally, Amanda is the same age you are."

"I know, Mama. What did I tell you?" Sally smiled smugly.

Suddenly feeling older than she had a few minutes before, Barbara gave Alphonse a look. He must have been feeling the same thing, as he laughed and squeezed her hand. He and Timothy left, promising to be back within an hour.

It was almost an hour and a half before they returned to find Sally pacing the floor. "We've been ready for ages," she said, picking up her bonnet. "Let me call Mama."

"No need," Barbara said, coming into the small parlor. She had on her bonnet and was ready. Alphonse smiled at her and offered his arm. "You look charming today, my dear," he said. "Blue is definitely your color. By the by, Miss Rivers, I asked about your post, but there was nothing there for you. The mail had been delayed today, and they suggested you ask tomorrow."

"Knowing Sally's friends, it may be months," Barbara said laughing. Smiling, Alphonse offered his arm, and they went out into the balmy sunshine.

The fountain was beautiful, Barbara thought. Evan had planned it down to the last detail, Alphonse had told her. He had installed a hydraulic system so that the fountain worked in the same way as the ones at Versailles. The water sparkled in the sunshine like diamond drops. The picnic which Alphonse had arranged was just perfect—the food was excellent, and the weather was made for dining alfresco.

After they ate, Barbara and Alphonse sat on a bench under a spreading tree and watched Sally and Timothy stroll around the opposite edge of the pond in which the fountain was located. Evan had even thought to install paving stones to make a walking path. It was perfect.

"Evan always did have a head for this sort of thing," Alphonse said. "He seems to attend to all the details."

"Too much so," Barbara said.

"Oh, I heartily agree. For the past several years, Evan has tried to hide his disappointments in his work. He usually manages to do it, I'd say."

Barbara hesitated. "I haven't kept up with Evan while I've

been in Gibraltar. Has he had an unhappy life? He seems rather contented to me."

"He'd like everyone to think so." It was Alphonse's turn to hesitate. "I don't want to tell tales out of school; but I know you were once close to Evan, so I suppose there's no harm, especially since most of the story is common knowledge." He took a deep breath. "Evan had a disastrous marriage. Abigail wanted a marriage in name only, one that would leave her free to, shall we say, pursue other interests. Evan tried to make things work, but to no avail. Abigail blamed him and even went so far as to tell friends in London that Evan was in love with someone else. Of course, everyone knew that was ridiculous—there was no breath of scandal attached to Evan, and he's never shown the slightest interest in anyone else."

Barbara closed her eyes against the bright sun. The glistening of the droplets in the fountain reminded her of the raindrops that had dampened her skin the night she had declared her love to Evan. "I'm sorry to hear that," she whispered. "I always hoped the very best for Evan."

"He deserves it," Alphonse said with his infectious smile. "Come, let's walk around the grounds. Evan has planned a surprise garden around the corner. Why don't you give me the benefit of your expert advice, and I'll pass it on to him."

"My gardening skills hardly qualify me as an expert," she said, smiling and trying to shake off her dark mood.

"You know more than I, and Evan asked my advice on this project." He laughed and offered his arm to her. "Just be sure to keep the names of the plants simple so I can remember them."

On the other side of the pond, Timothy and Sally watched them go around the corner and disappear from view. "Do you think he's going to offer for her?" Sally asked, her eyes wide. "I do think they care a great deal for each other."

"It's early days," Timothy said, frowning, "no matter that they did know each other as children."

"Love can happen in an instant," Sally said, matter-of-factly, "or it can be reawakened in just a second. Perhaps that's what has happened. Mayhap they really loved each other before, but just didn't realize they were in love."

"But now they do?"

Sally nodded. "Exactly."

Timothy turned as he heard the crunch of gravel behind him. Evan was there. He paused and lifted an eyebrow in inquiry.

"May I ask what the two of you are doing out here alone?" he asked, approaching them. "I'm delighted to see you, Miss Rivers, but you really shouldn't be here unchaperoned."

"Oh, I am chaperoned," Sally answered. "Mama is here with me."

Evan felt his breath catch in his throat, and he looked around quickly. "Where . . . ?" He let his voice trail off.

"She and Alphonse have gone around the corner of the house for a moment. We thought they might . . . that is, we hoped that Alphonse might . . ." Timothy stopped awkwardly as Sally nudged him in the ribs with her elbow.

Evan caught his meaning immediately and looked quickly toward the corner of the house. Barbara and Alphonse were nowhere to be seen.

"They've gone to see your new garden. That is, Mr. Dewitt thought Mama might have some suggestions he could pass on to you," Sally said.

Evan glanced down at his clothes and boots. He had been on horseback, out checking drainage ditches, and he was muddy to his knees. He had worn old breeches for that reason, and the rest of his clothing was spattered with mud as well. He hesitated for a second, then decided he couldn't wait to change. He had to see if Alphonse was offering for Barbara. As the one in the family responsible for finances, he had to stop Alphonse from taking on another obligation. He had to put an end to such an unsuitable match.

Quickly he paced around the paving stones, almost going in a lope. He rounded the corner of the house to see Barbara and

Alphonse deep in conversation, their heads close together. Barbara was smiling up at Alphonse, and he was looking down at her with an expression that held familiarity. Evan felt his hands curl into fists, and for an outraged instant, he longed to shove Alphonse's handsome, smiling face right into the fresh mud.

Instead, he took a deep breath, unclenched his hands, and walked toward them. Barbara saw him first and smiled at him. He felt her smile all the way down to his toes. "Evan," she said with a laugh in her voice, "I'm glad you're here. Alphonse has been trying to convince me that this garden needs a box hedge and a rose bed here. I think the garden is much too informal for roses and just needs flower beds." She paused and looked around. "All white, I think, with perhaps a border of pink."

"I agree with you," Evan said, immediately discarding any idea of roses. "That was precisely what I had in mind to do."

Alphonse sighed. "I told you my taste in gardens wasn't up to the mark. Now, if you want to know about waistcoats and boots . . ." He gave Evan a significant glance that took in his shabby clothing and mud.

"I've been out checking drainage." Evan looked chagrined.

"And you're quite properly dressed for that, I'd say." Barbara laughed and put her hand on his arm. "Would you like to join us for another turn around your fountain, Evan? Sally and I are fascinated by it. I, for one, would like to know how it works."

Evan smiled at her, silently thanking her for avoiding him any embarrassment, and they all went to the front of the house. Evan excused himself long enough to go inside to change and wash up, then joined them.

Timothy and Sally walked again to the far side of the pond, marveling again at the hydraulic system Evan had installed. They sat on a bench and watched both the water and the others. "I believe your guardian is attempting to explain the intricacies of his hydraulic system." Sally made a face. "I simply prefer to know that the thing works." She turned to look at Timothy. "Do you think Mr. Dewitt offered for Mama?" Sally asked hopefully.

Timothy shook his head. "I don't think so. I suppose Evan interrupted them before Alphonse got around to it." He sighed. "The Fates are against us, Sally."

"Do you mean the letter to Jamaica?"

Timothy nodded. "Evan never changes his mind once it's made up. He thinks through every possibility, then makes a decision. Once he's reached that point, there's no going back." He bit his lower lip. "I suppose I'll have to go."

"Maybe he hasn't really made up his mind. Mama didn't seem to think so. He told her that he would do what was best."

"He's decided. I'm sure of it." Timothy's voice was bleak. "Will you wait for me, Sally?"

Her voice caught on a sob. "You know I will, Timothy." She paused. "If we ran away together, would you have to go?"

He stared at her. "Run away? We can't do that." He reached down to hold her hand between them where the adults wouldn't see. "I hope to marry you, Sally, but I want no breath of scandal attached. No," he said flatly. "Running away is out of the question."

"Then, what?"

He sighed. "I don't know, but I'll think of something."

"You'll have to think of it soon."

"I know." He stopped and moved his hand as the three adults began walking around the pond toward them.

Evan declined to walk with the group back to Mincey Cottage as he had to meet with his steward about the drainage ditches. The other four set out across the fields. "Evan always has work to do," Timothy remarked.

"If the estates are to be well-run, someone needs to see to them," Barbara answered. "Evan should make his brothers and father do more."

"He may be thinking the same thing," Alphonse said. "He told me that he plans to divest himself of some of the responsibilities for the other estates and concentrate instead on turning Hannaford House into a model farm."

"Good." Barbara nodded approvingly. "He seems to hold Hannaford near and dear to his heart."

Alphonse smiled. "Yes. He also said that his fondest memories were there, and that was where he hoped to spend the rest of his days."

"I just wish I could say the same," Timothy murmured in a bleak voice.

The Chapmans spent a quiet evening at home. Sally read aloud to them while Barbara and Mrs. Chapman did needlework. It was a cozy setting. Barbara glanced around and realized that she never wanted to leave her parents or this place. It was home, and after all these years, she had returned at last to stay. She was glad she had written Captain Price. She hated to cause him pain, but it was by far the best answer.

"Do have Chassie bring us some chocolate before we go to bed, dear," Mrs. Chapman said.

Barbara pulled the bell rope, then pulled it again. "Chassie has probably gone off in a doze again," she said with a laugh. "I'll tend to the chocolate." She put her needlework down and went off into the kitchen.

Chassie was in the kitchen laboriously trying to form letters on a piece of paper. "I was just writing to my cousin in Plymouth," she said, turning the single sheet over. "I'll get whatever you need, mum."

Barbara sat down across from her. "Would you like me to help you with your letter, Chassie? I'd be happy to do so."

Chassie looked up, smiling. "Oh, would you, mum? I learned my letters, but it's hard to put everything together. I'd be most obliged if you'd write down what I want to say."

Barbara pulled the sheet of paper toward her and began writing as Chassie dictated. The letter was finished in just a few minutes. Barbara showed her how to fold it and seal it with a bit of wax. "There, Chassie, you're all ready to post it tomorrow." She picked up the tray with macaroons and chocolate that

Chassie had ready. "Do take time tomorrow to post it, or, if you prefer, I'll take it for you. I promised Sally that I'd walk in and check to see if she had a post."

"Would you do it, mum? I've only posted a letter or two, and I'd hate to get anything wrong."

The next day, Barbara made a point of getting Chassie's letter before she left for the village. It was a perfect day for walking—not too hot, yet not too cool. She loved days like this one. Gibraltar never had weather like this.

Halfway to the village, she heard a horse behind her and stepped to the side of the road to allow the rider to pass. Evan rode up to her and looked down from his horse. "You're looking fetching today, Barbara," he said as he dismounted. "Do you mind if I walk with you?"

She smiled at him. "I'd love company, Evan. It's a glorious day for walking."

Evan smiled back, and began to walk with her into the village, leading his horse by the reins. He glanced down at the letter in her hand. "Are you doing anything after you post your letter? Perhaps we could have some tea at the inn."

He had been awake most of the night, wondering if there were feelings between Alphonse and Barbara. He had agonized endlessly and, just before daybreak, had finally decided that he had to tell her how he felt. If she wanted to spurn him, then so be it, but he had to let her know of his feelings. He hesitated a moment. "I've been wanting to speak with you when it's convenient." He took a deep breath. *Speak* was a weak word for what he wanted to say, but this was neither the time nor the place. The inn was no place to declare himself. "Perhaps we could go for a ride one afternoon."

"I'd like that, Evan," she replied.

Right now, he merely wanted to be in her presence for a little while, wanted to reassure himself that she wasn't in love with

Alphonse, wanted to. . . . He made himself listen to her chatter about the weather and the village. It was much safer.

At the inn, Barbara posted her letter and turned to follow the innkeeper's wife into a small parlor that Evan had bespoken. She was halfway across the floor when the innkeeper called out to her. "I'm sorry, but I forgot that you had a letter today." He handed her a letter with a flourish and waited as Barbara searched in her reticule for money.

Inside the parlor, Barbara glanced at Evan and hesitated. "Would you mind?" she asked, glancing at the letter.

"By all means."

She quickly broke the seal, an unfamiliar one, and opened the letter. Her heart skipped a beat, and her breath caught in her throat as she saw it was from Captain Price. She wondered how he could have gotten her letter so quickly; then she looked at the date. It had been written before Sally had posted the letter to him. Barbara calculated the dates quickly.

With a sick feeling, Barbara realized that her letter had crossed with his in the post. She stood up, shoving the missive into her reticule. "I'm sorry, Evan, but I must be getting back to Mincey. I do hope you'll forgive me. Perhaps we can have tea some other time." She hurried out of the room.

As she walked along the road back to Mincey Cottage, she tried to sort things out, tried to decide what she would do or say. She had thought that her letter to Captain Price in Gibraltar would end their relationship quietly and with dignity. Now there was this.

Captain Price had written her that he was newly arrived in London and he would be at Mincey Cottage either tomorrow or the next day. He had something very important to share with her. Something, he wrote, so important that they needed to meet face-to-face.

SEVEN

Puzzled as he thought about Barbara's expression when she saw the post, Evan rode home. The letter that had so disturbed her could not have come from Alphonse. Unless, he thought to himself, Alphonse had mailed her a message to meet him. Evan shook his head. No, Alphonse wouldn't mail something—he would either send a note by a footman or go to Mincey Cottage himself.

Evan sighed. He wondered if there was someone else, someone he had never heard of. He had gently questioned the innkeeper and the housekeeper at Hannaford House some days ago, and both had mentioned that Mrs. Rivers was a model of propriety, always keeping close to Mincey Cottage and taking care of her parents. Between the two of them, they knew every time someone moved in Crickford, so surely there couldn't be anyone else, or they would have heard of it. Unless, he thought with a chill, there was someone in Gibraltar. . . .

Evan frowned at the thought as he dismounted. Distractedly, he gave the reins over to a footman and went inside.

Alphonse was seated in his study, waiting for him. "Morning, coz." Alphonse's voice was as cheerful as ever, with only the barest touch of the French accent that he had picked up from his mother. "I thought I was going to have to send a search party out for you. Timothy said you were coming right back."

"I was delayed." Evan leaned against his large desk and regarded Alphonse warily. "I take it you were waiting with a purpose in mind."

Alphonse grinned. "The usual—money." He hesitated only a fraction of a second before he continued. "I appear to have used up all my quarterly funds. And I'm sure you know that I hate to borrow money. I wondered about an advance."

Evan took a deep breath. "Alphonse, don't you think it's time that you found something to do other than live from invitation to invitation? I'd be happy to find you a position somewhere."

Alphonse lifted an eyebrow. "So I'm to be a working gentleman?" He stood and began to pace. "I'm quite aware, Evan, that you don't consider me anything more than a frivolous man who makes a good dinner companion, but I assure you that I'm much more than that." He paused. "I've been thinking of reforming my life, but my plans aren't set yet."

Evan could almost see Alphonse marrying Barbara and settling in at Mincey Cottage. "I suppose those plans include Barbara Rivers?" he asked icily, moving closer to Alphonse. "I suppose you'd like to live comfortably there for the rest of your life?"

Alphonse looked at him, surprised by the intensity in his cousin's voice. "Well, as a matter of fact, it had crossed my mind. Among other things."

Evan turned on his heel so he wouldn't have to look at Alphonse. The man disgusted him, and Evan clenched his fists to keep from striking him. "Barbara Rivers deserves better than you, Alphonse."

"Oh, I suppose you mean that she should be giving you all her attention." Alphonse's tone held an edge.

Evan turned back to face him. "You know what I meant, Alphonse. All Barbara would have if she married you is someone who would squander what money she has."

"You're just saying that because you're in love with her." Alphonse flicked a bit of lint from his coat. "Besides, what's wrong with me marrying her and living off her money? I don't know how much her portion is, but I'm sure we could be comfortable."

"You don't love her." Evan's words were flat. "You're despicable, Alphonse." Before he could stop himself, and even before he knew he was doing it, Evan wheeled and hit Alphonse on the jaw. Alphonse went down, then picked himself up, rubbing his jaw. "I should return the blow, or call you out, or both, but I'm not going to. One thing I have always been careful of is the reputation of the family. Even though I don't hold the purse strings, I am proud of the family and wouldn't want a scandal." He moved toward the door. "So, Evan, I suppose I'll take my leave of you and Hannaford House." He turned at the door and looked at Evan.

"You're in love with her, you know. If you love her that much, why don't you tell her so? I doubt she knows it. After all, her greatest memory of you is the night you threw her over for Abigail."

Evan sat down heavily in the chair. "Don't go, Alphonse. I apologize." He put his face in his hands and ran his fingers through his hair. Alphonse went over to the cabinet on the far wall and poured each of them a stiff brandy. Evan took it with gratitude.

"I didn't throw her over, Alphonse. Father had arranged everything, and I felt I had to go through with it. I wanted Barbara; but she left, and there was no way I could work things out." He looked at Alphonse, his expression anguished. "I still want her."

Alphonse walked slowly around the room, rubbing his jaw as he sipped his brandy. "Good Lord, Evan, I didn't know the depth of your feelings, or I would never have considered offering for Barbara." He hesitated. "I thought you cared, but not that much. I thought that was why you treated her so shabbily years ago."

"I treated her more than shabbily." Evan looked miserable. "I wanted to apologize, but there was no way I could. Abigail and Father saw to that."

"And now?" Alphonse asked.

Evan hesitated and then said nothing.

"We go back to the cradle, Evan," Alphonse said. "I know we've had our differences, and you don't particularly care for the way I live my life; but we're still family." He paused a second, searching for the right words. "I know that confiding in someone else doesn't come as easy to you as it does to me."

"Confidences don't come to me at all, Alphonse. I've always had to keep my own counsel." He walked over to the cabinet and poured himself another brandy, then another for Alphonse. He leaned on the cabinet, his head down. "I don't know what to do, Alphonse."

Alphonse smiled as he took the snifter from Evan's fingers. "For the first time in your life, I imagine. It's not a good feeling, is it?"

Evan shook his head. "No. I'm at a loss. I want to talk to Barbara, to try to explain what happened then, and tell her about my life with Abigail." He finished off the brandy and looked at the empty snifter. "I just don't think I can."

"Is there anything I can do?"

"I'm not sure there's anything anyone can do. I'm afraid everything was done on that night years ago. I wish I could make amends, wish I could wipe away the years, but I can't. Today, I had hoped to go over to Mincey and talk to Barbara and tell her of my feelings. We met at the inn, but that was no place for such a conversation. Before I could make any other suggestion, she had to leave." He turned around, his upper teeth worrying his lower lip. "I had hoped there might be an opportunity to apologize and explain."

"You do know she's promised to a Captain Price in Gibraltar."

Evan closed his eyes in despair. "I wondered." His voice cracked. He opened his eyes and looked at Alphonse, his face bleak. "What can I do?"

"You're just going to have to create an opportunity to tell her how you feel, and see how things fall." Alphonse stood. "In the meantime, I believe I'll pack. The Dentons invited me up for a fortnight or so, and this would be a good time to go."

Evan glanced up as Timothy came to the door. "Again, I apologize, Alphonse, and if you want to reconsider, you're always welcome at Hannaford House." He hesitated a moment. "In fact, I wish you would stay awhile. Both Timothy and I would benefit from your company."

"Perhaps at some later date." Alphonse smiled at him. "As for the other, apology accepted, but I think I'll go on and visit the Dentons. They have only one daughter, and while she's no diamond of the first water, she stands to inherit a respectable fortune." He chuckled. "It must be your staid influence. I've come to believe that it's time I put a little respectability in my life, Evan."

"I understand." The ghost of a smile touched Evan's lips. "Do come see me before you leave and I'll give you the money you need." He glanced at Timothy standing in the door, then added, "And, Alphonse, I'd appreciate it if you told no one of the matter we've been discussing."

"No one?"

"No one." Evan's voice was firm. "Please promise me."

Alphonse sighed. "I promise." He smiled at Evan and then looked toward Timothy. "I do suggest you take care of matters soon, however."

Timothy looked from one to the other of them, an amazed expression on his face. "What matters? You're leaving, Alphonse? Why?"

"It's time, Timothy, my boy. Why don't the two of us go over to Mincey Cottage where I can make my farewells," Alphonse said, putting a hand on his shoulder. "I'm sure Evan won't mind."

"Not at all." Evan's lips felt rigid. "Give the family my regards."

Alphonse steered Timothy out of the room, although Timothy kept turning back to look at Evan. "What is it?" he whispered to Alphonse. "I've never seen him look that way."

Alphonse smiled at him. "I do believe, Timothy my boy, that Evan has discovered how difficult it is to be human."

"What do you mean?"

Alphonse moved him to the front door and outside. "I mean

that Evan needs some time to reconsider his life. Shall we leave and give him that time?"

Timothy remained puzzled, but said nothing. Alphonse began to walk briskly toward Mincey Cottage, and after a moment's hesitation, Timothy ran to catch up with him.

Evan sat in the beautifully decorated room, his head in his hands, wondering how his perfectly ordered, perfectly rigid life had been turned so topsy-turvy. The pain he felt was as fresh as it had been on that rainy night all those years ago.

"I tell you, Sally, Alphonse told me right and proper. He said he was leaving, and Evan offered him money. Worse, Alphonse has a red spot on his jaw. He didn't say, but unless I miss my guess, he and Evan had been in a fight." Timothy interlaced his fingers in and out as he thought.

"Leaving?" Sally saw half of her hopes crash into dust. "Perhaps he could offer for Mama before he leaves. Do you think he's to that point?"

"I don't know." Timothy's voice was bleak. He looked up as Miss Timmons came into the back garden to join them.

"We have to do something to get them together, Timothy," Sally said brokenly. "This just isn't for us anymore. You have no idea how lighthearted Mama has been the past few days. She's even been singing around the house."

"But what can we do? Just tell me what to do and I'll do it." Timothy let his voice drop to a whisper as Miss Timmons bore down on them.

"There you are, my dears," she said, sitting and pulling out her tatting. "I don't think we'll be able to sit out here long. I do believe it's going to rain. If my old bones are right, we're in for several days of rough weather."

"I believe you're right, Miss Timmons," Timothy said with feeling.

* * *

Alphonse had left Timothy talking to Sally in the back garden as he went in search of Barbara. She was in the small parlor, finishing some embroidery she was doing for Sally. She put her sewing aside as Chassie announced Alphonse. He came inside the small parlor, his smile lighting up the gloom. "You shouldn't be sewing in this lack of light," he said easily, picking up the sewing and putting it where Barbara couldn't reach it. "It's going to storm. I can tell by the strange, yellowish light outside." He hesitated. "I need to get back to Hannaford House before the rain breaks, but I wanted to stop by and tell you that I'm leaving."

"Leaving?" Barbara raised an eyebrow.

Alphonse nodded. "Tomorrow. I thought I'd go visit with some friends." He smiled at her. "I did want to tell you how much you've made me enjoy this visit. I haven't enjoyed Hannaford House this much since I was a child."

Barbara smiled back at him. "I doubt I had anything to do with that, Alphonse. Often we require some distance from people or a place before we can truly appreciate them. I discovered that in Gibraltar. I had no idea how much I loved England or how much I missed my parents."

"Then, you plan to stay?"

"Yes." Barbara hesitated slightly, thinking of the letter from Captain Price. She would cross that bridge when she came to it.

"I'm glad you're staying," Alphonse said. It was his turn to hesitate. "Have you considered paying Evan a few visits?" Remembering his promise, he chose his words carefully. "I believe he would benefit greatly from your company. Evan is a very lonely man."

"He does seem to have changed."

"Actually, I believe he still feels the same." He waited for Barbara to ask him more so he could hint at Evan's feelings, but, instead, she began talking about other things until Mr. and Mrs. Chapman came in. Alphonse told them he was leaving and wished them all goodbye.

He collected Timothy, and they set out for Hannaford House

just as the first drops of rain began to fall. Sally stood at the back window and watched them as long as they were in sight. "Don't worry, dear. I believe they'll get back to Hannaford House before the rain begins in earnest," Barbara said to her.

Sally turned and looked at her as she lit a candle on the table beside her chair and sat down, picking up her embroidery. They were alone in the small parlor. The pale light from outside and the candle inside bathed Barbara in a golden light. Sally thought that she had seldom seen her mother look more lovely—or more troubled. "You truly like Mr. Dewitt, don't you, Mama?" she asked.

Barbara looked up as though coming from another place. "Of course I do, Sally. Remember that we knew each other in the past. I've liked Alphonse since he was a child." She smiled briefly, the action smoothing out the frown that worried her forehead. "He always worried about being half French, but Evan and I told him that he should be proud of that rather than ashamed of it. Alphonse has agonized for years over the excesses of the French Revolution." She paused. "Several relatives of his were killed then. He was only a baby, of course, but growing up he seemed to take it personally. I always told Evan he would grow out of it."

"And did he?"

Barbara laughed. "I believe he has. It's taken him a while, but I believe Alphonse is ready to settle down."

"I think he would make a wonderful father," Sally blurted.

Barbara looked at her in surprise. "I think so, too, dear." She turned her head and smiled as the sound of a bell clanged through the house. "I believe Chassie is calling us to supper."

After supper, Sally complained of a headache and asked to be excused. Barbara felt her head for fever and decided there was none. "Just a case of a growing girl," Mrs. Chapman said as they watched Sally go up the stairs. "I remember when you were the same way."

Barbara smiled to herself, thinking of those days. She certainly hoped her mother knew nothing of some of her activities.

"Would the two of you like for me to read to you?" she asked her father and mother. "I know Sally has just reached an interesting part in the book, and I hate to make you wait another day."

"Oh, would you?" Mrs. Chapman's voice held relief. "I was afraid I'd have to read it myself, and I'm not nearly as good as you and Sally are at reading aloud." She settled into a chair next to Mr. Chapman as Barbara opened the book and began reading.

Sally waited until they were engrossed in the book, and then she slipped down the back stairs, wrapped in her cloak. She could hear the rain outside, but there was no help for that. As she and Timothy had once agreed, desperate situations called for desperate measures. She peered around the corner to make sure Chassie wasn't there; then she slipped outside and pulled the cloak around her to ward off as much of the rain as possible. She braced herself and started toward Hannaford House.

Evan was working in his study when the butler came in to inform him that there was a visitor. "It's Miss Rivers from Mincey Cottage come to visit," Mason said with stiff disapproval. "She's alone, and seems to have walked here."

Glancing over the man's shoulder, Evan saw Sally, and a flash of remembrance stabbed through him. She was in the hall, and she was wet, her hair and cloak clinging to her. Just for an instant, she looked very much as Barbara had looked all those years ago. Evan went into the hall and brought Sally into the study where he insisted she stand in front of the small fire that had been lit to chase away the chill of the rainy night.

"I'm afraid Timothy isn't here," Evan said, wondering just how to handle the situation. Obviously he had to return her to Mincey without anyone knowing she had been here unchaperoned.

"I didn't come to see Timothy," Sally said, dripping water all over his Aubusson. "I wanted to talk to Mr. Dewitt."

"He isn't here either. A friend of his sent word that he was passing through Crickford and was spending the night at the inn. Alphonse and Timothy went to the inn to spend a while in conversation. I don't expect either of them to return until late."

Sally sank into a blue silk chair, not noticing she was getting water all over it. "Then, all is lost," she said dramatically. "He'll never offer for Mama if I don't talk to him."

Evan sat down suddenly in the chair opposite her. "Offer for her? Whatever do you mean?"

Sally put her hands over her face. "I wanted him to offer to marry Mama. I asked Mama if she liked him, and she told me that she did." Sally looked at him, and he couldn't distinguish the raindrops from her tears. "At first, I wanted to find her a husband just so she wouldn't move back to Gibraltar, but now I want her to get married so she'll be happy."

"And you selected Alphonse?" Evan's voice had a strange tone.

Sally nodded. "He'd make a good father. I asked Mama if she thought so, and she said he would. She said he'd grown up."

Evan smiled a little crookedly. "He's in the process, at any rate." He paused and took a deep breath. "Do you think I have any particular qualifications as a father?"

It took a moment for his question to sink in. Sally looked at him and stopped crying. Her jaw dropped as she stared at him. "You?"

"Me."

"Qualifications as anyone's father? Timothy's? You already act as his father."

Evan bit his lip and took the plunge. "I was thinking of applying for the post of your father." He looked at her, and the astonishment on her face again reminded him of her mother. It was like a knife twisting in his heart. He wasn't going to make the same mistake twice. He couldn't.

"I . . . I care very much for your mother. I always have."

Sally stared at him for a long moment, and things suddenly fell into place. "You." She closed her eyes.

Evan rose, thinking she had rejected his suggestion. He looked out one of the windows into the rainy darkness, seeing nothing except the crash of his hopes. "I know you feel I've been overly harsh with Timothy, but I made mistakes in my youth that I didn't want to see repeated with Timothy."

"Was my mother one of those mistakes?"

He turned to face her. "Yes, although perhaps not in the way you think. I should have married your mother when I had the opportunity. It's something I've regretted bitterly since that day." He paused as the words came hard to him. "I've always cared for her. Always."

"Since you were my age? Since you were children?"

"Yes. Probably not as a child. As I recall, I found her rather annoying at one stage of my life." He smiled. "However, once we were of an age . . . yes, I cared very much for her. I imagined she would always be in my life, but it didn't work out that way." He stumbled over the last sentence.

Sally sat in silence as Evan turned back to look out the window, lost in his own thoughts and years past. Finally, she broke the silence. "I think we could rub along well enough," she said. "I own that Mr. Dewitt is more amusing, but I'm trying to think of what's best for Mama." She paused as Evan looked at her, hardly daring to believe what he was hearing. "You see, I wanted to give Mama the best present I could. I wanted to make her happy, and I thought that finding her a husband would be the very thing. I admit that my motive was selfish at first, but after I saw how happy Mama was when Mr. Dewitt was around . . ." She stopped, realizing she was saying the wrong thing. "I think, looking on things from this perspective, Mama thinks of Mr. Dewitt as a dear friend."

"And me? How do you think she looks on me?" Evan tried to keep his tone light, but failed. His urgency came through his words.

"I don't know," Sally said slowly. "You'll just have to talk to her yourself and see. You may tell her that we've talked and I think you'd make a very suitable father, indeed."

Evan released the breath he had been holding. "Everyone keeps giving me the same advice," he said with a small smile. "Just go talk to her. Alphonse told me much the same thing."

"Then, it must be the best advice," Sally said. She stood and reached for her cloak. "Since we seem to have come to some sort of an understanding, Mr. Evan, I need to get back to Mincey."

Evan took the cloak from her fingers. "Oh, no. Part of a father's duties is to make sure no breath of scandal touches his daughter." He squeezed some water from the steaming cloak. "Or to make sure she doesn't catch her death of cold." He chuckled. "I'll get you one of my old cloaks and take you home myself. I believe we can slip in the back way and no one will know you've been here."

Sally smiled at him. "It may be part of a father's duties, but I must say that you sound remarkably like Mama."

Evan left the coach several hundred yards from the cottage so they wouldn't be heard. He walked Sally to the back door and there took his cloak from her shoulders and handed her the sopping wet one. "Try the door first to make sure it's unlocked," he whispered.

Sally's eyes widened. "I hadn't thought of that." She turned and pushed against the door, but it didn't budge. "Now what shall we do?" she whispered in alarm. "I don't know how to get in."

"Wait right here," Evan whispered back. He ran to the tree at the side of the house and began climbing. He slithered out on a limb and pushed on a window on the upper story; then he wriggled inside. In just a few moments, he had unlocked the back door from the inside. "How did you know to do that?" Sally whispered in amazement.

"Some things never change, do they?" he asked, his voice

full of laughter. "That window has been unlocked for the past twenty-five years." His teeth showed white as he smiled in the darkness. "Hurry upstairs and get out of those wet clothes."

"And you'll be back tomorrow to talk to Mama?"

He nodded. "Lock the door behind me. I'll be back." He went outside and disappeared into the darkness.

All the way back to Hannaford House he rehearsed exactly how he would propose to Barbara.

EIGHT

The next day, Evan dressed with particular care. He had forced himself to wait as long as possible. Alphonse had decided not to leave until the next day since his friend was staying another day in Crickford. "I'm going to talk to Barbara today," Evan confided in him.

"It's the only way," Alphonse told him, smiling. "The two of you have been fated to be together since we were children."

"I don't know about fated." Evan worried his lower lip with his teeth and ran his long fingers through his dark hair. "If anything, it seems that we've been fated to be forever apart."

Alphonse laughed as he picked up his hat and prepared to go to Crickford. "Ever the optimist, Evan! Your mood is as gloomy as this rain."

Evan gave him a rueful smile. "I hate to sound pessimistic, but looking back over our relationship—or lack thereof—it does seem that fate has managed to keep us apart."

"Now it's time to change that." Alphonse put his hand on Evan's shoulder. "If sincerity and faithfulness have ever been rewarded, she'll accept you."

"I certainly hope so," Evan said fervently.

Barbara was standing at the window, looking out at the rain and lost in thought, when Chassie announced Evan. Sally looked at him, and they nodded imperceptibly at each other as he came into the room.

"Mama, I've forgotten my blue silk thread," Sally announced. "I've got to go upstairs to get it."

"Just use mine, dear," Barbara said, reaching into her sewing bag and offering her a skein.

Sally shook her head. "No, it must be the exact shade. I have it upstairs, but don't remember where I put it. I'll go find Miss Timmons and see if she can help me find it." She paused by the door. "It might take a while." She dashed up the stairs.

Barbara looked at Evan, puzzled. "I don't know what's gotten into Sally this morning," she said with a smile. "She's been like a worm in hot ashes, jumping from one place to another."

She sat down on the striped sofa, and Evan sat down beside her. Then he realized that what he had to say was best said facing her, so he got up and pulled over a matching striped chair. Barbara laughed. "You're as bad as Sally this morning. Could I get you some tea?"

"Yes. No. That is, I don't think I care for tea right now." He glanced longingly at his hat as though wishing he had it to crush between his finger and thumb. He had to settle for flexing his fingers together. "We've known each other a long time, Barbara," he began.

"Yes, we have." She got up and put the fire screen in front of the small blaze that kept the room from the dampness outside. Evan watched her every movement, amazed that she should still be so graceful, so perfect. He waited until she sat down across from him again.

"I've been meaning to speak frankly with you, Evan," she said before he could continue. "I know we discussed Timothy, and I made you aware of my feelings about sending him to Jamaica; but I've been thinking about it since. It's none of my business, but I feel very strongly about this. I must tell you that I don't think the boy would thrive in Jamaica." She softened her words with a smile at Evan, and he felt his breath catch in his chest. "I implore you to allow him to stay here. I believe he'll apply himself to his studies, given the right encouragement."

"All right, he can stay." Evan managed to start breathing again. "Barbara, I . . ."

She reached over and took his hand. "Oh, Evan, that's wonderful. I thank you, Sally thanks you, and I'm sure Timothy will thank you as well."

Her touch on his hand sent Evan's head spinning. It was a moment before he could answer her. He put his other hand over hers to capture it. "I didn't come here to discuss Timothy," he said hoarsely. "I wanted to talk to you." He paused, as there was a commotion outside. Barbara pulled her hand away and went to the window. Evan could see her body go rigid.

"It's Captain Price from Gibraltar," she said woodenly, turning to face him. She hesitated, her face pale. "We are engaged, you know."

"I was unaware that you were expecting him." Evan stood abruptly, feeling that he had left his life in shards around his feet. "I'll leave you," he managed to say. He picked up his hat in nerveless fingers, dropped it, and had to retrieve it from the floor. It gave him a moment to compose himself. "I know the two of you have much to discuss."

"Goodbye, Evan," she said. He could have sworn that there was a sob in her voice, but he didn't pause to look at her. He knew that he was perfectly capable at this moment of either throttling Price or else throwing Barbara over his shoulder and dashing out the back door with her. Years of training came into play as he formally said goodbye and went out, passing Captain Price and nodding at him as he went. Captain Price was assisting a woman from the carriage. His sister, no doubt, as they looked much alike, Evan thought as he climbed into his own carriage.

He had the driver stop when they could no longer be seen from Mincey, and he got out. "You'll catch your death," John Coachman warned as Evan told him to return to Hannaford without him.

"No matter," Evan muttered, sloshing off across the field. He wanted to walk, to move, to try to get his feelings under control.

The weather mirrored his emotions perfectly. He was a muddy mess when he reached Hannaford House, and he didn't care. He tossed his coat aside in the hall and went into his study, searching for a bottle of brandy. For only the second time in his life he intended to get gloriously, royally drunk.

It was not to be. His steward was waiting for him with another problem with the drainage ditches. Evan put everything out of his mind except that problem. It gave him some room to breathe. After all, work had always been his salvation.

Captain Price nodded at the dark-haired gentleman who went by him. He didn't have time to do more than nod as he was busy helping Emma out of the coach. He had dreaded this confrontation, but knew it had to happen sometime. He had no idea how he had fallen in love with Emma, but he had. He had no idea how things had progressed to the point of marriage, but they had. He had no idea how he, a man of integrity, had so forgotten his promises, but he had. Now it was time to pay the piper. He had confessed to Emma about Barbara, and she had insisted that the three of them meet face-to-face. "After all," Emma had said to Captain Price with that superb calm and logic she had, "Mrs. Rivers is a woman wronged, and we owe her an explanation. We owe her an apology as well." As usual, Emma had been right, although Captain Price would have given a year's pay to be somewhere else right now. The South Seas would be nice.

Barbara greeted them courteously, not even looking curiously at Emma. She rang for tea, and it was left up to Captain Price to explain matters. To his and Emma's surprise, Barbara exhibited none of the rage, none of the tears, for which they had prepared themselves. Instead, she began laughing hysterically. She couldn't seem to stop laughing, not even when Sally and Miss Timmons rushed to her side. She laughed when her parents came in to see what on earth was happening. She was still laughing when she kissed both Emma and Captain Price and wished them happy for the rest of their lives. She was chuckling and smiling when she bade them goodbye as they began the journey back to London.

"Poor dear," Emma Price said to her new husband. "The shock addled her. That's the only possible explanation. I do feel sorry for her."

Captain Price nodded in agreement. Secretly, he was surprised that Mrs. Rivers had felt so strongly about him. He had been under the impression during his long courtship that she regarded him more as a friend. There had never been any passion between them. In fact, he remembered as he rode along, there had been only two chaste kisses, one when she had agreed to marry him, and the other at her departure from Gibraltar.

He looked at his new wife and frowned. "I can't believe she would be so shocked." He looked puzzled. "I doubt I'll ever understand women."

Emma Price nodded sagely. "There's no need at all for you to do that, dear."

Back at Mincey Cottage, Sally was in high alt, dancing around the sofa where Barbara sat, still smiling. "Have you ever seen such a perfectly matched couple?" Barbara asked no one in particular. "They should be quite happy. He'll do everything she tells him to do, and she'll feel quite satisfied managing his life." She took a deep breath.

"Oh, I know, Mama. Now your problem is solved. Now you can marry Mr. Evan!"

Barbara blinked. "Marry Mr. Evan? Dear me, Sally, where did you ever get such an idea?"

Sally stopped dancing. "He didn't ask you to marry him? He was here, and I made sure you weren't interrupted. He was supposed to offer for you." She plopped down in the chair Evan had used opposite Barbara. "How could he have botched it?"

"Whatever do you mean?" Barbara got up and lit a candle in the gathering dusk. "I do have good news. Evan is planning to let Timothy stay in England. Timothy will have to promise to do well in school, however."

"No Jamaica?"

"No." Barbara shook her head as she sat back down.

"But he didn't offer for you?"

Barbara looked at her in exasperation. "Sally, will you please explain yourself." She pinned Sally with the look that always managed to make Sally's secrets an open book. In just a few moments, Sally had confessed all the details of her trip the night before to Hannaford House. "And he swore to me that he cared for you, Mama!" Sally said, twisting her hands in her lap. "All I wanted was to get a husband for you to make you happy."

"I'm happy with you, Sally," Barbara said gently. She touched Sally's hand in much the same way Evan had touched hers earlier. "Are you telling me the truth? Did he truly say that he cared for me?"

Sally nodded miserably. "Yes. Even more, he said he always had. Even from the time you were children." Sally twisted her fingers with Barbara's. "He loves you, Mama. I didn't realize it at all until last night, but he does. I know it."

"Perhaps he'll return," Barbara said gently. "At any rate, the next move is up to him. Now, why don't we read to Mother and Father until bedtime?"

"How can you do that? How can you just sit and read, knowing that he cares for you? Loves you?"

Barbara smiled at her as she picked up the book they had been reading aloud and handed it to Sally. "I've learned patience," she said.

The clock struck eleven as Barbara tossed back the covers. Patience was eluding her tonight. She had tried and tried to sleep, but couldn't. She went to the window and watched the rain stream down as she looked toward Hannaford House. She could see nothing there, but knew Evan was inside. She could almost feel him calling to her, just as she had fancied him doing all those years ago. Almost without thinking, she dressed and put on her heavy cloak, the whole time calling herself a fool. It didn't seem to matter. All she could think of was Sally telling her that Evan cared for her. He had not said the word *love,* but caring was enough. She loved him enough for both of them. She always had.

Barbara slipped out the back door and felt the rain pelt her, washing away the years. She began to walk rapidly toward Hannaford House. By the time she got there, she was drenched. There was only one light toward the back of the house—Evan's study. She hesitated, then clanged the knocker. Nothing happened.

She banged the knocker again, harder this time. The door began to open slowly. Instead of the butler, Evan was standing there. "Barbara." His voice was hoarse.

Barbara went in past him, water sluicing from her cloak. She unfastened it and let it fall into puddles on the marble. "I've come, Evan," she said simply.

He reached for her, touching her rain-drenched face with his fingertips, pushing her wet curls back from her face. Rain mixed with tears to glitter in her eyes and on her lashes. "Barbara," he said again, a world of meaning in the word. "Barbara, my love."

The wedding was a simple affair at the church in Crickford. Timothy and Sally stood outside the church as Evan lifted Barbara into the open landaulet that had been decorated with ribbons and flowers. Even the horses were beribboned. Evan sat down beside Barbara and took her hand in his. Happiness radiated from the two of them.

Alphonse came up behind Timothy and Sally as they stood, tossing flowers. "Have you ever seen a happier pair in your life?" he asked, looking as Barbara and Evan drove away in a pelter of flower petals.

Sally smiled. "No, I haven't, and they have us to thank." She turned to Alphonse. "Timothy and I wanted to get a husband for Mama so she would be happy, and we did just that."

"I can't wait to tell Evan that he was wrapped and tied as a present for your mother." Alphonse chuckled.

"Don't you agree that they're the perfect match?" Sally asked.

"I thought as much when we were all children," he said with a laugh as he herded them back toward the church and Mr. and Mrs. Chapman. "Even then, they were perfect for each other."

Sally paused as she and Timothy watched the landaulet go out of sight, carrying the newly married pair. Just as they reached the curve in the road, when Evan thought no one could see them, he leaned over to kiss his bride.

"Well, we did it." Timothy snapped his fingers, quite pleased with himself.

"I knew we would," Sally said smugly.

THE
LAST CHANCE
GOVERNESS

by
Bess Willingham

To the most tenderhearted person I know,
my sister, Mary Kim Harris

ONE

Having lost a considerable sum of money at a Faro table in an unlicensed St. James's gaming hell, Hugh Parmenas, the Duke of Deramore, salvaged that late summer evening by consuming two bottles of Bordeaux wine from a very highly regarded and ancient vintage, along with one willing female of a very recent one.

His head ached as he later lurched through the front door of his Curzon Street town house. "Well, perhaps I have it all wrong," he remarked to Bevis, his valet, who awaited him in the foyer with a hot toddy and a steaming towel. Tossing off a pitifully rumpled cravat, the duke draped the hot linen around his neck. "Perhaps it was *one* bottle of old wine, and *two* very young women, that I consumed. Can't rightly remember, old man. The past twelve hours are something of a blur. What time is it, anyway?"

From under his bushy gray brows, Bevis glanced at the long clock that stood in the corner. "It is quite early, Your Grace. You have made it home before nuncheon for a change."

Hugh took the proffered glass, threw back his head, and quaffed the brandy. With a gasp and a shudder, he said, "Ah, a bit of the hair of the dog that bit me, eh, Bevis?"

"Just so, Your Grace." The aging man, who had been the duke's father's valet many years before, followed Hugh up the winding staircase. In his bedchamber, Bevis helped Hugh shed his boots, clothes and unmentionables.

A pair of maidservants, one of them too young to ignore her employer's sculpted physique, scurried in with buckets of scalding water. "Would you like me to rub yer back?" she asked, emptying her bucket into the bath.

Hugh tested the water with his toe. Not even trying to conceal his nakedness, he grinned at the blushing servant. "So thoughtful of you, Minnie. I'll ring the bell cord if I need you."

"Quit gawking and get out of here, you two!" barked Bevis.

As the women scampered out, Hugh lowered himself into the tub. "So thoughtful of you, Bevis, to have my bath prepared ahead of time."

"It's a tricky task, keeping your bath warm, my lord, when I never know what hour of the day or night to expect you home. And I do wish you wouldn't flaunt your, um, manhood in front of the female staff. Minnie won't be good for anything the rest of the day!"

"Do I detect a note of censure in your voice, Bevis?" Hugh slid into the water, submerging his head. When he could hold his breath no longer, he sat up, blowing water from his nose, and shaking the drunken fog from his head.

Bevis stood beside the four-poster bed, arms folded across his chest. "Not a mere *note,* my lord. *A symphony."*

Were it not for the years of faithful service Bevis had rendered to his family, Hugh would have taken umbrage at such insubordination. As it was, he smiled through clenched teeth. "What's on your mind, old man?"

"We are in a bit of a spot, Your Grace."

"We? By that, Bevis, do you mean that *I* am in a bit of a spot?"

"Yes, my lord."

"Christ on a raft! Let me guess. Some fretful mama has her tail feathers ruffled because I won't marry her daughter. Is that it?"

Bevis sighed. "As I've told you before, Your Grace, it isn't your refusal to marry these young girls that upsets the mamas.

It is that you persist in dabbling in conjugal relations with the innocent things, *without* the benefit of matrimony."

"I have never forced myself upon a lady, Bevis. Or any female, for that matter." With the wet linen towel draped over his face, Hugh's voice was muffled. "I haven't been challenged to a duel again, have I?"

"Thank God, no. The last time you were called out by a jealous husband, you almost got your head shot off."

"Good thing for me that silly cuckold was such a lousy aim."

"Good thing for you I paid the man's second to adjust the sights on his pistol!"

Hugh peeled the towel off of one eye. "I have told you, Bevis, not to interfere with such matters. I ought to fire you on the spot! 'Tis dishonorable to tamper with an opponent's dueling pistols. Dishonorable, I say!"

"You didn't do it; I did. What was I supposed to do? Allow you to get yourself killed? Over what? A pouty bit of baggage who couldn't keep her skirts down even if she had lead ballast sewn into her hemline?"

"I won't have you disparaging Lady Spraddlepate's morals, Bevis. Enough of that." Hugh covered his face again. "If I haven't been called out, or accused of fathering a by-blow, then what in the devil is the matter? And don't tell me the roof needs repair, or the scullery wench has been caught stealing the silver again, because such matters as those fall within yours and Mrs. Diggory's bailiwick, and I don't want to hear about them!"

For a long moment, Bevis stood silently, pursing his lips and staring at the ceiling, as if composing his thoughts, or deciding which ones of them were fit to be aired in the presence of his employer. At length, he signaled his readiness to divulge the latest calamity that had befallen the duke's household by clearing his throat.

Hugh, arms stretched along the sides of the tub, waited.

"It is little Lord Badwell, Your Grace. Alexander. Your son, to be precise."

"Yes, I know who he is," the duke growled from beneath his hot towel. "What has Sandy done now?"

"The little lordling, I'm afraid, has, at the ripe old age of six and one half years, earned himself the distinction of being the first viscount in the history of Mayfair society to be permanently removed from the client list of the inestimable Mrs. Inchcape."

"You mean, we can no longer count on Mrs. Inchcape to furnish us with nannies, governesses, and sitters for Sandy?"

"That is correct, my lord."

"Why?" Hugh was alert now, despite the pounding in his head. "What has Sandy done now?"

"Little Lord Badwell has, er, disposed of another governess, I'm afraid, Your Grace."

"What do you mean, he's disposed of another one? You make it sound as if he's killed someone, instead of merely running off a nervous nanny. What kind of mischief did he inflict on the poor woman this time? Spiders in her boots? Pepper in her snuff box? A toad in her hat box?"

"Snakes, my lord."

"Snakes." Hugh couldn't resist a chuckle. "Harmless garden snakes, I take it."

"Yes, Your Grace."

"Well, a little garden snake never hurt anybody. But, I suppose you're going to tell me that Sandy hid them somewhere where the governess would come upon them rather unexpectedly. Hell, she probably scared the snakes more than they scared her! And just where did our latest poor unfortunate governess discover these snakes, Bevis?"

"The late governess in question found them in her bed, my lord."

Picturing the middle-aged woman, who had struck Hugh as rather grim and humorless to begin with, drawing back her covers only to find a nest of squirming snakes upon her mattress, gave the duke a moment of amusement. The moment was short-lived, however, as Bevis's words slowly sunk into the cottony fuzz of his sluggish mind. "Did you say, *the late govern-ess,* Bevis?"

"Yes, Your Grace."

"By that, I take it to mean that she is no longer Sandy's governess."

"By that, my lord, I mean that Mrs. Tavistock is no longer with us."

Hugh lifted one corner of his hot towel, and peered at his valet. "Do you mean to tell me that Mrs. Tavistock is dead?"

"As a doornail, Your Grace. The fright of finding a nest of serpents in her bed was quite too much for her."

"She's dead? Because of a silly little prank orchestrated by my six-year-old son?"

"And a half, to be precise. Mrs. Tavistock, as it turns out, has some family in Dorset. A sister, I believe, who by chance showed up in London the day before old Lettie died. According to her, the sister, that is, she has for the past six weeks been receiving almost daily accounts of Alexander's behavior. The late governess was apparently a very conscientious correspon-dent."

"The sister, I presume, is displeased."

"Most. As fate would have it, the sister arrived for an un-planned visit just moments after the governess expired. Carried the body away in a rented hackney, as a matter of fact—very strange if you ask me. At any rate, the sister has expressed quite a bit of outrage, not to mention anger, and even, perhaps, the intention to demand some financial compensation from Alex-ander's legal guardian. As his father, that would be you, my lord."

"She's blaming Sandy, is she?"

"It would appear so."

Hugh threw the wet towel into the water and sat up. "But Sandy didn't mean to hurt Mrs. Tavistock! That's absurd. He's just a child, a high-spirited one, I'll admit, but a *child,* nonethe-less. A typical, rambunctious little boy who played a quite in-nocent joke on a woman whose heart was most likely—it was her heart, wasn't it, Bevis? Her heart simply gave out on her, is that it?"

"That would appear to be our best argument."

"The woman's time had come, and the Good Lord took her, and it just so happened that at that same identical moment, she pulled back her bed covers and discovered a couple of harmless little garden snakes, no bigger than earthworms, wriggling around on her mattress!"

"That is certainly one way of looking at it."

Water sloshed on the Axminster carpet as Hugh climbed out of the tub. "That's the only way of looking at it. Why, I won't have my child labeled a—"

"No, my lord. You should know that at the sister's request, the Bow Street runners have already investigated Mrs. Tavistock's untimely demise."

"How dare they?" Slamming one hand into his open palm, Hugh exploded with anger. "What sort of scavengers are these people? Looking to make a quick buck off their sister's misfortune, are they? Bloody hell, I suppose the next thing you're going to tell me is that they've hired a solicitor, and that they plan to sue!"

Bevis, entirely accustomed to seeing his employer stalk about his bedchamber in the nude, tossed a thick towel to him. "Luckily for us, the runners concluded that Mrs. Tavistock had a preexisting infirmity. Seems she complained of chest pains while in her previous employment, as well. At least that is what Mrs. Diggory and I testified to. Young Lord Badwell was not found to be the cause of the woman's death, as a result, and therefore you need not fear any court of law holding you accountable."

"That's a relief." Hugh rubbed his body with the towel, then tossed it back to Bevis. "How much did you have to pay them?"

"Whom, Your Grace? The runners, or the Tavistock sister?"

Crossing the room, Hugh felt a bolt of pain shoot through his head. "Oh, I don't want to know about it!" As he jerked back his bed covers, a picture of Mrs. Tavistock flashed before his eyes. For an instant, he stood stock-still, staring at his mattress, half expecting to see it squirming with snakes.

Behind him, Bevis muttered, "Don't worry. I've already checked."

Lying on his back, eyes closed, Hugh sighed. He might have asked himself where he had gone wrong with Alexander, but the hell of it was, he knew. He had never been a good father, had never shown his son enough attention, had never given him the kind of paternal instruction a young boy required. From infancy, Alexander's upbringing had been relegated to nannies, governesses and servants. If Alexander was a bad boy, it was because Hugh was a bad father. It pained him—so deeply that he couldn't bear to think about it.

And most of the time he didn't. Most of the time he pushed it from his mind the same way he pushed away the thought of Hermoine's death. But on occasions such as this one, when the reality of Alexander's unruliness was unavoidable, Hugh had to think about it.

"What should I do, Bevis?" he said quietly.

When the servant finally spoke, his voice was so near that Hugh was startled. He hadn't heard the servant cross the room. He didn't know the man was standing at his bedside, staring down at him. But, when he opened his eyes, another streak of pain, this one laced with regret, pierced his aching skull.

Bevis stared at him with unalloyed dismay.

Even to his longtime retainer, Hugh was a disappointment. A man who had wasted six years of his life. A man in the process of killing himself with too much brandy and too many demireps. A man too absorbed by grief to give his son the attention he needed.

"Don't worry, my lord. I've already taken the liberty of re-taining a new governess."

"But, you said Mrs. Inchcape refused to send another one."

"Yes, but this one is not from Mrs. Inchcape. This one is not from any agency."

Almost afraid to ask, Hugh said, "Don't tell me. I'll guess. You've hired an animal trainer from Astley's. Or one of Pierce Egan's proteges, some wretched bruiser with a broken nose and cauliflower ears."

"No, my lord. I have retained Miss Fiona Plunkett."

"Who the devil is she?"

"In some circles, my lord, she is known as the Last Chance Governess."

With a moan, Hugh rolled over, showing Bevis his bare back. The Last Chance Governess, indeed. "God's teeth, Bevis, is it . . . safe?"

"Safe, my lord?"

"I take it she specializes in taming wild children."

"I have it on good authority that she can domesticate even the wildest one."

"You don't think she will be cruel to Alexander, do you? Because I won't have it, Bevis. The instant she lays a finger on the boy, I'll toss her on the street."

"I understand," murmured Bevis.

"He isn't really bad, after all." Hugh's words trailed as sleep tugged at him. "He's just . . ."

Bevis sighed as he tucked the counterpane around Hugh's naked body. Straightening, he said softly, "No, my lord, he isn't bad at all. Poor little bugger is just like the rest of us. Wants to know he's loved, that's all."

"I do love him, Bevis. More than you'll ever know."

"With all due respect, my lord, the lad needs a mother."

A mother. Hugh fell silent, pretending to be asleep. Of course the boy needed a mother. But to get a mother for Alexander meant acquiring a wife. Which Hugh had no intention of doing. Wouldn't be right. Wouldn't be fair to Hermoine.

"Did you hear me, Your Grace? I said, the child needs a mother. Not a governess."

But Hugh, unable to answer, pressed his face into the pillow and faked a snore.

TWO

"Now, Sandy, I want you to be nice to Miss Plunkett." Hugh stood before the fireplace, anxiously awaiting the arrival and introduction of the new governess. "And stand up straight when she enters the room. Shake her hand, tell her it's a pleasure to meet her, then sit on the sofa like a proper young man and be quiet."

On the other side of the room, Alexander was standing on his head, small, booted feet kicking at the Chinese wallpaper above the chair rail. "Yes, Father." He let his feet fall to the floor, stood upright and dusted his hands. "Shame about Mrs. Tavistock. I liked her. Honest, I did!"

"Well, you certainly didn't act like it. Putting those snakes in her bed! What were you thinking, Sandy? You scared the poor woman, well, to death!"

With his bottom lip poked out, eyes downcast, Sandy replied, "Didn't mean to. They were just garden snakes. Who would have thought she'd get so scared that she would go back to Dorset to live with her sister?"

"Girls don't like snakes, Sandy."

Shrugging, the child walked to the chintz-covered sofa, stubbing his toes into the carpet as he loped along. The picture of juvenile petulance, he sat on his tail bone, wagging his feet and avoiding his father's stare.

"This is your last chance," Hugh tried to say sternly. "Mrs. Inchcape has refused to send any more governesses, you know. You've run them all off."

"Spoil sports, all of them."

"Be that as it may, Miss Plunkett is your last chance. If you run her off, then . . ." Hugh frowned. If Alexander ran her off, then what? What would Hugh do? Send Sandy to some remote boarding school in the country, where religious fanatics would try to break his spirit, and older boys would taunt him, pick on him, beat him up, or worse?

And they would, Hugh thought, staring at his son with a mixture of wonderment and guilt. Alexander was small for his age. Frail-boned but sinewy, he had big green eyes, luscious lashes, and a finely sculpted nose, just like his mother. Just the sort of little boy the bigger ones would tease and torment. Just the sort of boy who would find every bit of trouble he could, provoking the wrath of every bully he came into contact with. Sending Alexander to boarding school would be condemning the boy to a childhood of misery.

"Run this one off," Hugh managed to threaten, "and I'll send you to live with your grandmother. You wouldn't like that, would you?"

Alexander picked at his fingers. Shaking his head, he murmured, "No, Father."

Had it not been for the sound of the front door opening and shutting, Hugh would have crossed to the sideboard and poured himself a splash of brandy. Dealing with his son always made him testy. Perhaps it was because the child was so stubborn. More likely, it was because he couldn't look at Alexander without thinking of the boy's mother.

Hermoine. Hardly a name that rolled off the tongue. But she had been a lovely woman, with small hips and doe eyes. Had he known how delicate her health was, he would have never allowed her to get pregnant. But he had. In fact, he had been quite conscientious in his efforts to get her with child. And when she had announced her pregnancy, he had been ecstatic.

Swallowing hard, Hugh glanced at the tray of bottles and glasses arranged atop the sideboard. Suddenly, recalling the agony Hermoine endured while giving birth to Alexander, his throat felt parched. As a mother, she'd made the ultimate sacrifice. As a father, Hugh had been nothing but selfish and negligent.

Aware that Alexander was staring at him, Hugh lifted his brows. "What is it, son?"

"Mrs. Diggory and Bevis. They think I need a mother."

Hugh's chest squeezed. The few discussions he had shared with Sandy about Hermoine had been rife with pain and tension. Still barely able to say her name without choking, Hugh left those sorts of conversations and explanations to his trusted retainers, and his own mother in Kent. This was the first time, ever, that Alexander had brought up such a sensitive subject.

"Well, that's all very nice for Diggory and Bevis to think. I can't tell you how sorry I am that your mother isn't here, Sandy."

The child blinked. "But that's just it, Father. She isn't here. But you are. Well, some of the time, anyway. Mrs. Diggory says you can't let go of the past."

"Blast Mrs. Diggory! I shall have a word with her, I assure you. 'Tis not her place to say such things, especially in your presence."

"Well, why can't we have a mother, Father?" The little boy's voice rose a full octave. "I mean, why can't you have a new wife, and me a new mother? Bevis says it wouldn't mean you didn't love my real mother—"

"That's enough, Alexander. I think I hear your new governess below stairs."

Footsteps on the stairs signaled the approach of Bevis and the new governess. In a moment, the double doors swung inward, Miss Fiona Plunkett entered the drawing room, and Bevis vanished, pulling the doors shut as he did so.

Without waiting for an introduction, the tall, dark-haired girl crossed the room, gloved hand extended. "You must be Lord Deramore. How do you do, Your Grace?"

He shook her proffered hand, startled by the firmness of her grip. And by her prettiness.

Thin, almost to the point of being lanky, she had small, precise features and a quick smile. Her hazel eyes darted about the room, taking everything in, committing the details to memory. There was an intelligent look about her face, but without the dullness of a bluestocking. Not quite tomboyish, she was far from being frilly or frivolous. She was, Hugh thought, the sort of girl one's sister should be, the sort of girl who could be your best friend if she were a man or a dog, the sort of girl you would trust your six-year-old son with in a heartbeat.

One thing was certain. A bed full of snakes would not scare *her* to death.

Despite her cool exterior, Fiona was somewhat taken aback herself. When Mr. Bevis had contacted her, he told her that the child in question was the only son of a widowed duke who hadn't the time, the inclination, or the skills to raise a spirited young boy. She had pictured an aging aristocrat, a rheumy-eyed, middle-aged man who was too befuddled, or perhaps too bloodless in his emotions, to bother with raising a child.

She hadn't pictured anyone half so handsome as Hugh Parmenas, the Duke of Deramore. Tall and broad-shouldered, he wore his breeches like a coat of paint. Gleaming Hessians encased his sinewy legs, accentuating a lean, muscular body. A dark blue coat hugged his trim body while a perfectly tied cravat, not too stiff and not too fancy, set off his olive complexion to perfection.

Trying not to appear too obvious, Fiona studied his face. His nose was a little too large, his front teeth slightly overlapping. Brown hair, thinning at the temples, was shot through with gray. A dark, inscrutable gaze peered back at her with frankly masculine appraisal.

Clearly, he liked what he saw. Well, she was accustomed to that. What she wasn't accustomed to was the wave of nervous warmth that fanned through her body as he squeezed her fingers.

Withdrawing her hand, Fiona purposefully tore her gaze from the duke. "And you are Alexander, Lord Badwell, I presume?"

The child hopped off the sofa and made a leg. "Good afternoon, Mrs. Plunkett," he replied, his pretty little face split in a grin that was far too angelic to be real.

She read him like a book. "It is Miss Plunkett, not Mrs."

His eyes rounded. "You're not married, then?"

"Alexander!" Lord Deramore pushed off from the mantelpiece and stood beside his son, one hand harnessing the lad's shoulder. "Don't be precocious, my boy. Mrs., I mean, *Miss* Plunkett's marital status is no concern of yours. Or mine, for that matter."

"But I think it is," the child persisted.

Fiona swallowed her laughter, not wishing to encourage the child in such impertinent behavior. "If you must know, Alexander, I am not married."

"Why not?"

"Sandy, what did I just tell you?"

But she had anticipated this question. "Because I am a governess, and my work means everything to me. Taking care of little boys like you gives me great pleasure. If I had a husband, I would be taking care of him, I suppose. Frankly, I would rather be here."

Silence hung in the air while Alexander pondered that answer. While the duke poured himself a drink at the sideboard, Fiona settled on one end of the sofa. Perched opposite her, Alexander stared at his new governess as if he had never seen such an interesting creature.

"How old are you?" the child asked, as if it were the most natural question in the world.

From across the room, Hugh choked on his brandy. Sputtering, he quickly crossed the carpet and said, "Good heavens, boy, you've better manners than that! Don't you know, you are never to ask a lady her age?"

"At her age, she shouldn't mind telling me," the boy responded. " 'Tis only old ladies that don't like to tell their age. That's what Mrs. Diggory said."

"Who is Mrs. Diggory?" Fiona asked.

"Cook." Hugh took a generous swallow of his drink. "Been with us for ages. Practically runs the house, with Mr. Bevis's help, of course. We're frightfully fond of her. Since Alexander's mother, er, passed on, you see, Mrs. Diggory has been a great help in taking care of my son."

"Mrs. Diggory says I need a—"

"Miss Plunkett, where were you before you came here?" Hugh's voice drowned Alexander's. "I mean, Bevis must have hired you away from someone else. Should I feel guilty? Apologize to any of my acquaintances?"

"On the contrary. My work was done when Mr. Bevis contacted me. Do you know the Smythsons of Blossman Square? I was governess for their little girl, Penelope, for a two-year period."

"Won't they miss you terribly?" Hugh asked.

Fiona tilted her head, considering her answer. She would certainly miss Penelope, but even though she fell in love with every child she worked with, she made it a practice not to get too attached to her charges. She had made it her mission to help reform unruly children, and when her work was done, she liked to move on.

"To tell the truth, I don't think they'll even notice that I'm gone," Fiona said. "You see, Penelope is quite different now than she was when I first met her. I think the Lord and Lady Smythson feel they are getting to know their little girl all over again."

Hugh looked skeptical. "Little Penelope was, I take it, a difficult child?"

"Her heart was sweet. It was her disposition that needed a transformation."

"And do you believe that all children are sweet at heart?" Eyeing Fiona over the rim of his brandy glass, Hugh's gaze held an unmistakable glint of amusement.

"I've yet to meet one who wasn't, my lord. But I strongly suggest we discuss my philosophy regarding child rearing some other time." She glanced pointedly at Alexander. "I am far more interested in hearing about Alexander. What sort of education has he had thus far, for example? Is he in good health? Can he throw a ball, or roll a hoop, or hold his breath under water?"

"I can stand on my head," Alexander said brightly.

"Oh, can you? Well, I should like to see that some day."

Leaping from the sofa, the child ran across the room, placed his forehead on a pillow and kicked his legs up in the air. Fiona watched with interest as Alexander's boots scuffed the wallpaper above the dodo rail, and the duke pinched the bridge of his nose.

Turning to Lord Deramore, Fiona said quietly, "Quite a spirited little boy, isn't he?"

"You have no idea, Miss Plunkett. Really, I think he shall put you to the test. I hope you are prepared for it."

"Oh, I am, my lord. After all, I love a challenge."

Alexander's feet hit the ground with a thud. Grinning, he crossed the floor and stood before Fiona. "I think we shall get along famously, Miss Plunkett. And, don't worry. I won't put snakes in your bed."

"I am relieved to hear that," she said dryly.

"You see, I intend for you to be my mother. And Father here needs a wife. You seem the perfect sort, not too pretty and not too plain—"

"Alexander!" A fine spray of brandy misted the duke's breeches. Red-faced, he slammed his empty glass on a table and stood. "Go to your room this instant. And I forbid you to ever make such a foolish remark to Miss Plunkett again. A wife and mother, indeed! I should fire Mrs. Diggory on the spot for putting such foolish notions in your head."

Rising, Fiona resisted the urge to reprimand the father in front of the son. The duke's outburst was far too excessive a reaction to the innocent remark the child had made. It was a romantic fantasy the boy had, after all, a dream that his father would one day marry a woman who could take the former duchess's place. For a six-year-old boy to wish he had a mother surely wasn't unnatural.

What was unnatural was the strange, tingly sensation Fiona derived from imagining herself as Lord Deramore's wife.

THREE

Fiona stood, staring after Alexander, flinching when the child slammed the door shut behind him.

"High-spirited, indeed," the duke said, refilling his glass at the sideboard. "Please sit down, Miss Plunkett. There are several matters I should like to discuss with you."

A long silence ensued during which Fiona watched the duke. He took a healthy swig of his brandy, then stood before the mantelpiece, long legs planted shoulder width apart, one hip jutting provocatively. She wondered if he ever smiled.

"What do you think of Alexander?" he asked, at length.

She told the truth. "He is a bright little boy, desperate for affection, particularly a mother's affection."

The duke scowled. "He is the center of attention around here, Miss Plunkett. Bevis, Mrs. Diggory, a succession of nurses and nannies. Good heavens, the child doesn't want for anything! He has only to snap his fingers and someone comes running."

"How much of *your* attention does he get?"

"My attention?" Deramore stared as if he hadn't understood the question. "Well, I can't be expected to baby-sit a six-year-old all day, Miss Plunkett. I have other matters to attend to."

"What sort of matters?" asked Fiona, fairly certain that the duke's responsibilities did not include work. Most likely, he spent his days playing cards at White's or judging the horseflesh at Tattersall's.

Swallowing a mouthful of brandy, he winced. "Miss Plunkett, let me be entirely clear about one thing. You have been retained as Alexander's governess, not mine. I'll not have you commenting on my lifestyle, monitoring my comings and goings. I have been an unmarried man for over six years now, and my personal life is no one's concern except my own."

Fiona crossed her arms over her chest. "If that is your attitude, it is no wonder that Alexander so desperately wants to find you a wife. He has undoubtedly concluded that if you had one, you would focus more of your attentions on your home life and less on your, well, as you say, your *personal* life."

Not surprisingly, the duke received this admonition with an air of agitation. Swirling his glass, he stared hard at Fiona. "I presume you are independently wealthy."

Her cheeks stung. "Of course not. Do you think I would hire myself out as a governess if I had independent means?"

"I think, Miss Plunkett, that a young lady who wished to remain employed would not be so brazen as to insult her employer."

Refusing to be cowed, Fiona met the duke's penetrating gaze. "I am sorry if you took offense at what I said, my lord. We were discussing the child, Alexander. I have been in this house less than half an hour, and he has already announced that you need a wife and he needs a mother. Moreover, his demeanor is precocious and his lack of discipline obvious. All of which leads me to believe that he is starving for the most basic of human comforts, the love of one's parents."

When the duke didn't answer, Fiona said, "Often times a stranger sees at first glimpse the very thing that intimacy obscures. In your case, I meant to point out that your son's discipline problems stem from a deep desire to win your attention."

"Your conclusion is illogical, Miss Plunkett." The duke's lips were tight, his jaw as hard as stone. Fiona thought if he held his brandy glass any tighter, it would shatter in his fingers. "Alexander is simply high—"

"If you say high-spirited once more, then I *shall* leave," Fiona blurted. Instantly, she regretted her blunder. "Oh, I am sorry, Your Grace. Truly! Please forgive me."

Deramore plunked his glass on the mantel. Threading his fingers through his hair, he sighed. "This stuff and nonsense about a mother for Alexander is a waste of time. The child's mother died during childbirth. Hermoine was . . . everything to me. Since she is gone, I answer to no one. Least of all you. And, in the event you are curious, please be assured that I am not in the market for a wife."

"I *am* sorry," Fiona murmured.

He looked at her. Eyes wide and watery, she did, indeed, appear saddened. Perhaps his rebuke stung her, or perhaps he had tweaked her heartstrings by confiding the details of Hermoine's death. But, whatever had subdued Miss Plunkett, Hugh found himself wishing that the brazenness she displayed earlier, which he had so callously disparaged, would return.

"Shall we call a truce?" he asked softly.

"Let's." She offered him a wobbly smile.

A warmth he couldn't have predicted spread through his body. How odd, he thought, returning Miss Plunkett's smile. She wasn't the prettiest girl he had ever seen, not by half. She was appallingly candid, both with her opinions and her emotions. Lacking the curves he ordinarily favored in a feminine figure, she was all legs and high cheekbones. Yet her countenance intrigued him. And her intensity disturbed that careful balance, the one between inconsolable pain and drunken numbness, that he had so diligently cultivated these past six years.

"You must be tired," he said. "Come, I will introduce you to Mrs. Diggory. She'll give you a tour of the house and help you get settled in your new quarters."

When she stood, she was nearly as tall as he. "Thank you, my lord. I am pleased that Mr. Bevis found me. Alexander appears to be a very bright, energetic child, and I am certain that he will benefit from my tutelage."

"I hope so, Miss Plunkett." Gently touching her elbow, Hugh guided her toward the door. "But, whatever you do, you must disabuse him of this notion that I need a wife. As much as it pains me to raise a motherless child, I refuse to remarry for the sake of convenience."

"You are right not to, Your Grace. A man and woman should marry for love, not because they feel an obligation to one another."

As he opened the door of the drawing room and she crossed the threshold, he caught a whiff of her perfume, clean and faintly floral. The urge to tangle his fingers in her glossy chestnut hair was strong. Hugh resisted. After all, he was a confirmed bachelor. And Alexander's earlier announcement, that the duke needed a wife, made him all too aware of the loneliness that accompanied his bachelor status. It wouldn't do to toy with Miss Plunkett's affections. Eventually, he would break her heart, *or his own,* in the process.

"I don't like brussel's sprouts!" Alexander's fork clattered on the plate. Arms folded across his chest, bottom lip puffed out, he pointedly stared at a spot on the wall straight in front of him.

The duke's expression betrayed his frustration and bewilderment. But his voice was soft and coddling. "Now, Sandy, don't be a bad boy. Miss Plunkett will think unkindly of us if we can't mind our manners at the dinner table."

"I don't care whether Miss Plunkett thinks kindly of us. She said she wasn't going to marry you, or be my mother, so why don't we hire another governess?"

Curious to see how the duke dealt with Alexander's misconduct, Fiona held her tongue. Like a doctor, she felt that treatment depended on the proper diagnosis. Sometimes a child misbehaved because he wasn't given enough attention; sometimes he misbehaved because too much attention was lavished on him. In Alexander's case, she was beginning to think it was the wrong *kind* of attention that was producing the problem. Still, she wanted to be certain before she prescribed any regimen of medicine.

"Alexander Fairhope Parmenas, Viscount Badwell." The

duke pronounced each syllable with emphasis. "Please. I beg of you. Be a good boy and eat your brussels sprouts."

"No."

"Well, then." With a heavy sigh, Hugh cast Fiona an apologetic look. "If you don't eat your vegetables, you may not eat dessert. And Cook has prepared floating islands, your favorite. I would hate to see you miss out on such a treat."

"I won't eat my vegetables, but I will eat dessert."

"You'll do as I say, young man." Hugh's tone was anything but firm, however. When the child glared at him, the duke looked at Fiona, silently entreating with her to intervene.

"I quite agree with your father," she said. "But, as for me, I don't intend to have my own meal ruined. Isn't the mutton lovely, my lord? 'Struth, I shall gain weight if Cook prepares a meal like this one every night."

"A few extra pounds will not detract from your shapely figure," the duke murmured, his face darkening.

Fiona blinked. Was the man flirting with her? No, it wasn't possible. Returning her attention to her food, she ate in silence. Lord Deramore made several attempts to engage Alexander in conversation, but the child had fallen silent also. Arms crossed over his chest, Alexander stared first at Fiona, then at his father. The duke took his cue from Fiona, continued eating, and said nothing more about the brussels sprouts.

When a big bowl filled with a frothy cream concoction was carried into the dining room, Alexander's eyes widened. A maid served the duke first, carefully dipping out a cloud of meringue and placing it in his bowl. Fiona was served next, and her mouth watered at the sight of the confection. Then the maid moved to the side of Alexander's chair.

"No, no. Alexander isn't having any dessert, I'm afraid," Fiona said.

The maid, her spoon in midair, looked up in surprise. "What, ma'am?"

"No dessert for Alexander, thank you."

"I want a floating island," the child said through his little teeth.

"I'm sorry, but you made your choice." Fiona smiled sweetly. "No brussels sprouts, no dessert. Your father was quite clear on that subject. I'm sure you understood."

"He didn't truly mean it."

"Yes, he did." Fiona stared at the duke. "Are you in the habit of saying things you don't mean?"

The duke hooked his finger beneath his cravat and gave it a tug. When he spoke, his voice was hoarse. "No." Grabbing his wineglass, he drank deeply.

Turning to Alexander and the horrified servant, Fiona said, "I didn't think so. Perhaps, next time your father tells you to eat your vegetables, you will obey him."

"I want my floating island!" Alexander's pleasant features were no longer pleasant. In fact, they were downright menacing as he glared at Fiona, challenging her, testing her.

To the servant, with as much authority as she could muster, Fiona said, "You may take the dessert back to the kitchen."

Straightening, the young woman said, "Yes, ma'am."

Before she could step away, Alexander reached for the bowl, grabbed a small fluff of meringue and stuffed it in his mouth. Egg white and cream dribbled down his chin and onto the front of his immaculate white lawn shirt and scalloped collar. Very deliberately, he placed his fingers, dripping with cream, into his mouth—and licked them slowly, one by one.

Hugh gasped.

Fiona forced herself to appear somber despite the comic effect Alexander's appearance had on her. While the maid scurried away, she stared expectantly at Hugh. "It must pain you to punish your son. I know it pains me when I must administer discipline. However, it is a necessary method of teaching children what they may and may not do. More importantly, it is a way of telling them you love them."

Hugh stared back at her as if she were speaking Greek. "Wha-what do you expect me to do? I can't force the child to eat his brussels sprouts! What good does it do to deny him dessert?"

"Probably none. But you are the one who said if he didn't eat his vegetables, he couldn't have dessert. You must follow through with your promises, my lord. You are doing your child a disservice if you fail to."

Sputtering, Hugh tossed his serviette onto the table. "That is the silliest thing I have ever heard!"

"Lord Deramore, I am an expert in this field, believe me. When you make a rule, you must enforce it. Alexander must be able to believe what you say in order to trust you."

"But he's had his dessert now! What would you have me do? Turn him over my knee? Paddle his behind? Confine him to his bedchamber for the next fortnight?"

"How do you usually punish him?"

A long silence drew out while Alexander stared at the adults, clearly amused.

"Just as I thought." Fiona stood. "Well, tonight Alexander is going to be punished for his defiance of your rules. Let me see, I think an extra hour in the classroom tomorrow will serve as an adequate punishment. When your language teacher has left tomorrow, Alexander, you and I will spend an hour practicing your letters. Don't worry, your father will be there with you."

"What! That's impossible," said the duke. "I have business to conduct."

"Tattersall's will wait, my lord. So will White's and Watier's"

"An hour? Practicing his letters?"

"I shan't do it!" Alexander wailed.

"Oh, yes, you shall." Fiona smiled again.

"And what if I say that *I* shan't do it?" Hugh asked, his voice surprisingly boyish to be so deep and throaty.

"You are the lord of this house," Fiona replied deferentially. "I cannot dictate your behavior, or tell you what to do. I believe we established that in the drawing room. You are the employer and I am the employee. However, let me advise you: If you wish to see a change in your son's behavior, start enforcing your rules *now.* Otherwise, there is nothing I can do for you, or for Alexander."

"Are you threatening me?" the duke asked quietly. "Are you warning me that if I do not do things your way, you will leave?"

"You have retained me for a specific purpose, my lord. If I am to carry out my work, I need your cooperation and participation. If you wish to raise a hellion, then you can do that by yourself. After all, you have done quite a nice job of it so far."

Alexander hopped off his chair and bolted for the door.

"If you will excuse me," Fiona said and followed the child. Crossing the threshold, however, she paused, looking over her shoulder at a stunned Lord Deramore. "I know you think you are being kind by letting him have his way, my lord."

"I can't stand to see the child unhappy," the duke replied thickly. "He's already suffered so much unhappiness in his life."

"Spoiling the child will only lead to more unhappiness, I assure you."

The duke's tone was that of a man not accustomed to being rebuked. "How is it, Miss Plunkett, that an unmarried woman knows so much about raising children?"

FOUR

If her heart were an anvil, the duke's words would be its unrelenting hammer.

Lifting her chin a notch, Fiona pivoted on the heels of her sturdy and very practical half boots. It wouldn't do to let Lord Deramore know that his question had wounded her. In fact, it wouldn't do to let him know that he affected her at all. Trudging up the steps to her fourth-floor apartment, she clenched her teeth and willed herself not to cry. She ought to go to Alexander's bedchamber and speak with the child about his behavior, but she barely made it to her own room before the flood of emotion she had been beating back unleashed itself. Alexander's discipline problems would have to wait until tomorrow.

How is it that an unmarried woman knows so much about raising children?

Well, that was the rub, wasn't it? That was the cruel joke that fate had played on her. Throwing herself on her bed, Fiona felt the old uncertainties, the old, familiar insecurities, wrap cold fingers around her heart. Perhaps she didn't know anything about raising children. Perhaps she was a fraud, after all, as the duke had not so subtly suggested. Perhaps a woman who could never bear children was inadequate and ill-qualified to be raising other people's.

The words of Captain Edward Plunkett, her late husband, echoed in her mind. "A woman's worth in life is measured by the children she produces." She had been young, far younger than her husband, when those words were first uttered. When, after years of trying to get her pregnant, Fiona remained childless, the captain gave up and moved out. Eventually, he went to Spain and never returned. Fiona was devastated, not by her abandonment, but by her failure. For a long time, she had believed the captain's words were true, that she was inadequate as a woman because she couldn't conceive a child.

She was older now. Older and wiser. And, after years of taking care of other people's children, she knew that there was more to being a mother than simply giving birth. The pain of her former husband's criticism was blunted by the knowledge that she had developed somewhat of an expertise in the area of problem children. Her work was fulfilling and rewarding. Recalling the lack of sadness she had felt when informed of Captain Plunkett's death in Badajoz, Fiona reminded herself that she was, indeed, a *worthy* governess.

Still, the duke's question, full of scorn and condescension, rattled her. Fiona, her tears spent, pushed off the bed, quickly shifted into her night rail, then climbed beneath the counterpane. It was only her first day at Deramore's town house, yet she had managed not only to ruin dinner, but also to anger the duke.

Well, her task did not always make her the most popular member of the household staff. This wasn't the first time an employer had questioned his own judgment in hiring her, but she wasn't overset. After all, Fiona wasn't called the Last Chance Governess for no reason.

As was most often the case, she had been hired in a final effort to rehabilitate a seemingly irredeemable wild child. That alone gave her some job security. She could afford to speak her mind and employ unorthodox methods because her employers were willing to try anything to get their children to behave. Which was a good thing, because Fiona suspected she was going to say a lot more to Lord Deramore that he didn't like before she completed her mission.

Closing her eyes, Fiona smiled. She truly liked her job. Her weariness was, in an odd way, comforting. Drifting off to sleep, she pictured little Alexander's face, all puffy lips and snapping eyes. By the time she finished with him, he would be as sweet and loving as a cherub.

A gentle rapping at her door startled her from her sleep.

"Who is it?" Fiona's feet slipped into woolen mules as she slid from the tall bed.

Alexander's voice answered from the other side of the door. " 'Tis me, Miss Plunkett."

Fiona cinched the sash of her robe, then opened the door. " 'Tis I," she corrected, blinking at the flickering taper held by Alexander.

"Have it your way." The child, clad in a white linen nightshirt that reached his ankles, slipped into the room. " 'Tis I, Alexander Fairhope Parmenas, Viscount Badwell. May I come in?"

"You already are, aren't you? What on earth are you doing awake at this hour? It must be after midnight! And why are you wandering the house in your nightshirt? Without slippers or a robe, for heaven's sake. Why, you'll catch your death of cold."

"I ain't cold," the child replied. "It's hot as blazes in my room!"

"You *are not* cold," Fiona said, wondering from whom Alexander had acquired such a colorful use of the vernacular. "And I doubt very seriously that your bedchamber is actually hot. Stuffy, perhaps, but that could be cured by opening a window. I shall speak with Mrs. Diggory about it first thing in the morning. In the meantime, we have to get you back to bed."

Alexander dodged the hand Fiona attempted to lay on his shoulder, crossed the room, and placed his candle on her night table. Hoisting one leg onto her bed, he pulled himself up and sat on the edge of the mattress. In the dim light, he patted the covers beside him. "Do you want to get beneath the covers while we talk?"

"No, thank you," she replied primly. "I'll stand. I don't think we're going to be talking that long anyway. Whatever you have on your mind, Alexander, I'm certain it can wait till the morning."

"But, this is very important. I thought it best to discuss it with you now."

Fiona started to fold her arms across her chest, then thought better of it. Troubled children were often extremely sensitive to an adult's nonverbal signals. "All right, Alexander, what is troubling you?"

"Father needs a wife. And I need a mother."

Resisting the urge to chuckle, Fiona said gently, "It's understandable that you would feel that way, dear. You must feel a great loss at not having a mother. But, it wouldn't be right if your father married a woman he didn't love. You see, he loved your mother very much. And he misses her, too. He is a wise man, and he will remarry if, and only if, he meets another woman that he loves."

"If he loved me, he would get me a mother."

"Oh, dear." Fiona sat on the edge of the bed, wrapping her arm protectively around the child's shoulder. Her years of experience as the Last Chance Governess hadn't prepared her to deal with the depth of this little boy's emotions.

Looking up at her, his gaze was full of hurt and anger and confusion. Somehow, he had got it in his head that he was being deprived of a mother's love because his father wouldn't remarry. Convincing him otherwise was going to be difficult.

"Alexander, your father loves you very much."

"Then, why doesn't he play with me?"

She stared into his limpid brown eyes. "He is a busy man," she said, her heart aching.

"You could marry him." Alexander nodded. "Yes, you could marry him and be my mother. You see, the others were too old."

"The other governesses?" Fiona drew back, clasping the child's shoulder. Studying him, she began to understand for the first time just how clever and grown-up he really was. Far too grown-up for his age. And far too concerned with matters beyond his control.

"Yes, that's why I had to get rid of them, don't you see? Father couldn't marry any of those stuffy old tabbies. He likes young women, pretty ones, like you."

She doubted very much that the duke favored women as boring and restrained as she. But that was hardly the tangent she should choose to discuss with six-year-old Alexander. "Are you saying you ran off those other governesses? On purpose?"

"It isn't that I didn't like them. And I'm awfully sorry old Mrs. Tavistock got such a shock when she found the snakes."

"Do you know what happened to Mrs. Tavistock?"

"She went to live with her sister in Dorset. That's what Bevis told me."

Thank heavens. "You gave her quite a scare, Alexander. You realize that, don't you? And you won't do anything of the sort again, will you?"

He said nothing.

"You wouldn't want someone to play a cruel trick on you, would you?"

"But I ain't afraid of snakes."

"You aren't afraid— Oh, that's not the point, dear. Mrs. Tavistock was deathly afraid of snakes, and I suspect you knew that. Which made your little prank all the more hurtful."

The child's gaze was downcast. "I didn't mean to hurt her."

She tipped up his chin. "I know you didn't. But let us try and be more aware of other people's feelings, shall we? Did you know that when you are nice to people, they are very often nice to you in return? Even if they aren't, there's a great reward in being pleasant and well-behaved. You'll see."

Though his answer was defiant, his eyes glistened with unshed tears. "I shan't be nice, and you can't make me. Father can't either. He doesn't even try."

With a sigh, Fiona wrapped her arms more tightly about the child. She felt like a detective who had just uncovered a meaningful clue in a mystery yet to be unraveled. "Your father loves you very much," she said softly, her cheek laid atop the child's head.

Snuggling against her, his tears stained her robe. The two sat on the edge of the bed for a long time, until Alexander's hiccups subsided and his little body relaxed. Only when heavy footsteps sounded on the stairs did Fiona release the child from her embrace.

He often visited Alexander's bedchamber late at night. Unable to sleep, haunted by regret, Lord Deramore frequently sneaked into his son's room in the dead of night. Sandy's gentle snores and peaceful expression never failed to reassure him. Standing by the child's bed, careful not to make a sound, the duke would hold up his glowing taper and watch his son sleep. Only when he had reassured himself that the boy was all right could he return to his own bed and drown his guilt in sleep.

His alarm at finding Sandy's bed empty was quickly replaced by a more disturbing thought. The child's history, after all, was rich with episodes of mischief, most of them involving one governess or another. What if the boy had decided to rid himself of Miss Plunkett's overlordship by some method more heinous than putting snakes in her bed? Swearing under his breath, Hugh quickly made his way up the stairs that led to the fourth floor and the governess's quarters.

Concern for Miss Plunkett quickened his pulse. Though Alexander had initially expressed approval of the lanky young woman—if wanting his father to marry her indicated *approval* and not bitter distaste—it didn't follow necessarily that the child wanted her to remain now. The scene at the dinner table might easily have changed everything. Sandy could have got it in his head that Miss Plunkett was as shrill an old tabby as Mrs. Tavistock. Spying a light shining in Miss Plunkett's room, the duke prayed that his suspicions were unfounded.

The door was ajar. When he pressed it, it swung open, revealing a most unexpected tableau: Miss Plunkett perched on the edge of the bed, her arm around Sandy's shoulder, the boy's head snuggled against the crook of her neck.

The hair on Hugh's neck stood on end. As he moved into the room, taking in the scene before him, he was assailed by guilt. *And longing.* His child's neediness reflected his own. Watching Alexander cling to Miss Plunkett, he was forced to confront his own needs. He found himself disturbed, rattled, and resentful toward Miss Plunkett's foray into what he considered intensely private and well-fortified territory.

"What is going on here?" His voice, more harsh than he'd intended, betrayed his disapprobation.

Miss Plunkett, perhaps in deference to the child's sensitivities, ignored his rude tone. "Alexander couldn't sleep. You know how little boys are. Perhaps a floorboard creaked, or the night crier wakened him. At any rate, he's all right now."

Hugh took a step closer. The light from two candles illuminated Miss Plunkett's disheveled hair, the expanse of creamy décolletage exposed by her cotton robe, the delicate pulse point at her throat. He met her gaze and held it. Physical awareness thickened the silence. An unspoken question seemed to pass between them.

"Father? Can I sleep with you?"

Startled from his erotic musing, Hugh addressed his son. "Not tonight, Sandy."

"What would it hurt?" Stroking Sandy's hair, Miss Plunkett slanted the duke a glance full of entreaty, gentle persuasion, perhaps even—unless the duke was imagining it—promise.

If she was attempting to draw out his emotions, then she was using Alexander as the bait. Deeply suspicious, Hugh noted his son's hopeful expression. "All right, then," he said, at length. "Go on, I'll be there in no time. That's right, take the candle. Be careful, now."

The child wriggled out of Miss Plunkett's arms and was gone.

Hugh remained, staring at the governess, a part of him wanting to be angry with her, a part of him wanting to sweep her into his arms. "In the future, Miss Plunkett, I'll thank you not to contradict me when I tell Alexander what he may or may not do. Wasn't it you who gave me a scathing admonition about the dire results of being wishy-washy when dealing with children?"

Amid the tousled bedclothes, she looked like a woman who had just been made love to. "One must be firm in administering discipline, my lord. When it comes to assuring a child you love him, I would suggest a bit more indulgence on your part. While I do not advocate allowing the child to sleep with you habitually, a night or two will do no harm. He loves you, Your Grace. And, in many ways, he is still a baby."

"He is a six-year-old boy, ma'am. When I was that age, I was not allowed to sleep with my parents. Nor was I allowed to cry. I most certainly was not permitted to hug the governess."

"He is not too big for a hug, my lord. No man is."

Startled, Hugh swallowed hard. *What the devil does she mean by that provocative remark?* "Take care, Miss Plunkett, that you do not start believing you know everything about children. Experts on any subject grow tedious when they are always right. In the short time since you've arrived, you've done nothing but correct, lecture and scold me concerning my lack of fatherly skills. To be frank, I am growing weary of it."

Her eyes flashed, betraying the fact that he had struck a nerve. "I never said I knew everything about raising children. No one can."

"Yet, you are called the Last Chance Governess." He deliberately raked his gaze over her. "I asked you before; now I'll ask you again. How did an unmarried woman such as yourself acquire such an expertise?"

"My eldest sister has children. Before her husband moved the family to Virginia, I helped her raise them."

"And you have never been married?"

"Is that question germane to my qualifications as a governess?"

"Perhaps." Even in the dim candlelight, Hugh could see that Miss Plunkett's color had deepened, and her expression had suddenly grown taut. Her agitation excited him. Suddenly, this lanky governess, whose half boots and high-necked dresses were as sturdy and no-nonsense as the air of Puritanism she wore, presented a mystery.

"I am widowed, Your Grace. My husband died at Badajoz."

"Ah, a war hero." After a beat, he said, "Children?"

"None."

"That must have been a great disappointment to you."

She turned her head, refusing to look at him. "Don't."

That single word, uttered so softly he wasn't certain he heard it, was like a cannonball fired through Hugh's middle. He had hurt her. His callous questions, his prurient disregard of her feelings, had wounded Miss Fiona Plunkett. Her unwillingness to meet his gaze put his heart into a panic.

"I am sorry." Wincing at the inadequacy of his own words, Hugh touched her shoulder.

When she looked at him, tears shimmered in her eyes. Her head tilted, her lips curved.

He cupped her cheek, soaking up the warmth of her skin.

Then, without stopping to think of the consequences, he leaned over and kissed her.

FIVE

Fiona stood before one of the tall windows of Alexander's schoolroom, watching the street below for signs of the duke's return. Given the unusual warmth of the afternoon, she had thrown open the shutters and pulled back the curtains. The cries of vendors hawking hot pies, coachmen shouting at everyone to get out of the way, and urchins begging for pennies wafted up from Curzon Street. But, at half past three o'clock, there was still no sign of the duke.

While Alexander practiced writing his alphabet, she waited. If the child was aware of her nervousness, he didn't show it. Seated at his little work desk, hunkered over a pad of paper, he dipped his pen in the inkwell and laboriously copied his letters.

Glancing at the wall clock, Fiona frowned. If the duke didn't appear soon, she would have to conclude he had ignored the summons she had issued at dinner. Which would only make for another lively confrontation at tonight's dinner table. And that would only enforce Alexander's perception that his father ignored him.

The rumble of carriage wheels drew her attention. Leaning over the windowsill, she watched the duke emerge from his equipage. When he glanced up, lifting a rakish summer hat woven of raffia, her heart skittered. Their eyes met, and he flashed her a roguish smile. So, he hadn't forgotten after all. And he knew she would be waiting for him.

When he entered the classroom, Alexander's face lit up. "Hello, Father!"

The duke made quite a show of inspecting his son's letters. "Why, I had no idea you could write so well. Very clever of you, old man. I was out of plus fours before I could do the entire alphabet."

"Would you like to see the picture I drew today?"

"Certainly!"

Fiona remained at the window, content to watch while Alexander proudly pointed out his artwork, his school books and primers, his collection of dried insects and a cage that contained two captured mice. It was obvious that the duke wasn't a regular visitor to the classroom. However, his exclamations of amazement seemed more than sincere.

Reluctantly, she reminded her charge that he had only got to J in the alphabet and had half an hour remaining in which to finish his work.

"Well, it seems you are doing an admirable job with the boy," said Lord Deramore, when Alexander resumed his letter writing.

"He has benefited from his previous tutors and teachers." Standing beside the open window, Fiona spoke in muted tones. "And he is an exceptionally bright child."

The duke, his skin brushed golden by the sun, shrugged negligently. "A trait he inherited from his mother, I'm sure."

In his snug breeches and crisp white shirt, Deramore was the very model of male elegance. Still, there was a sharp edge to his personality, a ruggedness about his emotional makeup that drew Fiona closer to him, yet warned her to stay away.

After all, he wasn't a wild child in need of rehabilitation. Introspective by nature, Fiona knew that she filled her inner emptiness, the bereavement over her barrenness, by caring for other people's children. But the Duke of Deramore wasn't a child. And he didn't need anyone to take care of him, hadn't asked for it, hadn't welcomed it. She had best guard her emotions and remember that she couldn't convince every man-child in the world he was loveable.

She would do well to keep her distance and forget about that silly kiss last night.

That kiss. Staring at the duke, as he stared absently out the window, Fiona felt a stirring. Her stomach flip-flopped, and her pulse galloped. For a moment, she was glad the duke wasn't paying her any attention. She would be mortified if he discovered how unsettling his presence, not to mention the memory of that impulsive kiss, was to her nerves.

It had been an act of impulse, she was certain. The duke had spoken rashly and hurt her feelings. In a moment of regret, he had unthinkingly leaned down and kissed her. The hour had been late; he had probably been in his cups. He hadn't meant a thing by it. Why, when he had realized what he had done, he had executed a French turn and fled the room as if the hounds of hell were behind him. Reminding him of his indiscretion would only embarrass them both, Fiona concluded. Pretending the kiss never happened, then, was the most charitable thing she could do.

His happy mood had vanished.

"Are you all right, my lord?"

Startled, he looked at her. "Forgive me. I was thinking about . . . something in the past. *Someone,* I should say. Being in the classroom with Alexander has made me inexplicably nostalgic."

"Were you thinking about Alexander's mother?"

His Adam's apple moved. "Yes."

She let a length of silence pass. "Tell me about her. I should like to know what the child's mother was like."

"Would you? Really?" He looked at her hard, as if he didn't quite trust her motivation.

"Why shouldn't I? Unless, of course, it pains you to speak of her."

"On the contrary. I should like to tell you about Hermoine. It's just that no one ever wants to listen."

"I'll listen."

He took a deep breath. Glancing at Alexander, he said, "Is his punishment almost over?"

She answered by clapping her hands and announcing the day's work was finished.

"Good, then," said the duke. "I'll direct Mrs. Diggory to serve the tea in the drawing room. We'll talk there." He ruffled his son's hair on the way out of the classroom. Then, as if remembering something, he pivoted at the threshold and returned. "I'm very proud of you, Sandy," he said, hugging the stunned child. He left the room again, this time more hurriedly, as if he had stunned himself also.

At the sideboard, Hugh poured himself a glass of brandy. Raising it to his lips, he paused. On second thought, perhaps he didn't want to numb his senses.

He had best keep his wits about him. He didn't want to make a fool of himself. Again.

His mind flashed on the scene in Miss Plunkett's bedchamber. It had happened so quickly, that seemingly innocent kiss that wasn't truly innocent at all. In fact, the duke had been miserable ever since, physically and emotionally. All night, as little Alexander squirmed beside him, he had struggled to put Miss Plunkett out of his mind.

Even as he took his noon meal at Watier's, Hugh was unable to forget the sensation of the governess's lips on his, the smell of her hair, the scent of her skin. At the whist table, he had been so distracted he lost fifty pounds in an hour. It was at that point he remembered he had a date in Alexander's classroom. On Curzon Street, he had been amazed to realize how pleased he was to see Miss Plunkett leaning from the upstairs window, waiting for him, smiling in return.

And here he was, opting for tea over brandy, and hoping he could muster enough sangfroid to avoid looking like a silly or plain schoolboy.

He stoppered the brandy bottle, then crossed the room.

Standing before the mantelpiece, he reflected on his actions the night before. Perhaps they were alcohol inspired. But, no. A few drinks might have lowered his inhibitions, but Hugh had kissed Miss Plunkett because he wanted to, because at that moment, sitting on the edge of her bed in her night rail and robe, she had looked so damned *kissable*.

A heavy, tingling sensation moved through his body. Just the thought of kissing Fiona Plunkett was now enough to heat his blood.

Mrs. Diggory appeared with a silver tray laden with teapot, cups and cookies. "Shall I stay and pour, yer lordship?"

"Thank you, no." Aware that the older woman was staring at him, the duke added, "Is there something else you wish to discuss with me, Mrs. Diggory?"

She wrung her raw-knuckled hands. "It's that governess, my lord."

Instantly alert, Hugh said, "What has Alexander done to her, Mrs. Diggory?"

"Nothing, Yer Grace. It's just that . . . well, I seen her at breakfast this morning. With Alexander. He's a high-spirited child, my lord. I've heard ye say so yerself. But, that governess, well, she wouldna' allow him to eat with his fingers, insisted on his usin' his knife and fork. Then, when the child asked me to bring him a cup of coffee, what do ye think she said?"

"I suspect she said he was too young to be drinking coffee," replied Hugh, half amused. "And she would have been correct, Mrs. Diggory."

The gray-haired servant gaped. "Well, Lord Deramore! He's just a little boy! And he ain't got no mother! He's always been permitted—"

"Perhaps that is the problem." Miss Plunkett's voice sounded from the open doors. Entering the room, she smiled pleasantly enough, but the tone of her voice clearly indicated she would brook no interference from Mrs. Diggory in the administration of her duties as governess.

Mrs. Diggory's face darkened, but she held the younger woman's gaze.

"You are quite right, Mrs. Diggory. The child *has* been permitted to do as he pleased. Unfortunately, an excessive amount of lenience has resulted in his being unruly, spoiled and defiant. That is precisely why Mr. Bevis retained me. So please, do not undercut my attempts to discipline the child."

"I'm sorry, Mrs. Diggory." Hugh smiled warmly. "I'm afraid I've been given my marching orders as well. Miss Plunkett is my general as well as yours, insofar as Alexander is concerned. After the debacle with Mrs. Tavistock, I have decided drastic measures are necessary. Otherwise, Alexander will be an outlaw before he is wearing long pants!"

"Yes, Yer Grace," mumbled Mrs. Diggory.

"Don't worry, Mrs. Diggory." Miss Plunkett's voice was kind, but firm. "I promise I won't break the child's spirit. I only want him to develop a sensitivity to the feelings of others. That is, after all, the essence of etiquette."

"Yes, ma'am." Mrs. Diggory looked unconvinced.

Miss Plunkett touched the older woman's arm. "One thing I should mention: I have been very impressed by the connections the child has made with you and Mr. Bevis. His affection for you both seems quite genuine. I attribute that to the kindness you have shown him. What I'm trying to say, Mrs. Diggory, is that Alexander really is a sweet little boy at heart. I believe you can take quite a bit of credit for that. And, when he learns to behave more gentlemanlike, you will find him even more of a joy to be around."

Hugh watched the sudden transformation of Mrs. Diggory's face. As a watery smile slid across her face, she sighed, apparently relieved of a great burden. When the two women embraced one another, the duke felt a tightening in his chest.

Uncomfortable in the face of so much feminine emotion, he cleared his throat. Taking the hint, the women released one another. Then, still dabbing her eyes with the edge of her apron, Mrs. Diggory quickly exited the drawing room.

"Please, sit." The duke poured tea with expert skill handing Miss Plunkett a cup as he said, "Are you surprised to see a man performing such a domestic ritual?"

Pushing back on the sofa, she chuckled. "I am impressed, Your Grace. Someone taught you well."

"Hermoine, I'm afraid." This time, the mention of his deceased wife's name did not make him sad. "She had rather strong opinions about roles traditionally played by husbands and wives. I'm afraid I would never have drunk a cup of tea if I waited on her to pour it for me. You see, she always had her head in a book and was too busy turning pages to do anything so menial as serve me. 'What's the matter, Hugh?' she would have said. 'Is your arm broken?' "

Fiona smiled. "She sounds like someone I would have liked."

"Yes, I think you would have."

"You must miss her terribly."

"I built my life around her. When she died, I fell apart."

"And now?"

"Now?" Now that he had kissed Miss Plunkett, he was aware of her physically. The mere arch of her brows captivated him.

"Have you put your life back together?" she asked him.

"It will never be the same. Nor will I."

"Are you happy, then? Have you recovered your equilibrium?" Tilting her head, she gazed at him in a concerned, thoughtful way.

"I know that I can never have what I once possessed," the duke replied, at length. Setting down his half-empty cup of tea, he looked at Miss Plunkett. Then he said something he had never said before, something that surprised even him. "Hermoine is gone. I loved her, true. Desperately. But perhaps I cling to my memories too tenaciously. I am so afraid of forgetting her, you see . . . so afraid of giving up the part of myself that she loved."

"Could it be because your memories of her are so closely connected with your youth?" Miss Plunkett said softly.

"I suppose I've idealized my marriage, romanticized it." The effort of beating back his emotion made him dizzy. The duke gripped the edge of the mantel and turned his face from Miss Plunkett, not wanting her to see the hurt in his expression. "Other women have befriended me. But I always compared them to Hermoine, always found flaws, always refused to see who they really were."

"How sad for you."

Suddenly, confiding in a woman not his wife, the duke's heart felt treasonous. "But, you see, Hermoine was everything to me."

Miss Plunkett nodded. "It would be hard for any other woman to compete with her memory, Your Grace. After all, Hermoine hasn't done anything wrong now for, what, six years?"

"And a half." Facing the governess, the duke saw that she was nothing like Hermoine. Pain knifed through him. He had been like a teapot, pouring out his troubled heart, and suddenly he was embarrassed that he should appear so weak and childish. Miss Plunkett thought him a fool; her cutting remark indicated as much. Well, he was a fool! And where had he thought this discussion would lead? What had he thought this heartfelt admission would accomplish?

It could only lead to his complete humiliation.

Violently, the duke suppressed his emotion and schooled his features into a mask of impassivity. Miss Plunkett, her expression warm and maternal, watched him. Inwardly, he shuddered, aware of her pity. When she looked at him, she saw a child, not a man. Perhaps she would bring him some warm milk, wrap him in her arms and tell him everything was going to be all right. Was that what the duke wanted from this woman? To be mothered? Consoled? *Rehabilitated?*

He stalked to the sideboard, poured himself a brandy, quaffed it, poured another, then returned to the mantelpiece. "Please forgive my ruminations, Miss Plunkett. I did very much enjoy sharing tea with you. Keep up the good work with Alexander, will you?" Noting her bewilderment, he added curtly, "You are dismissed now."

She left the room quickly, leaving behind a scent of her perfume and a lingering air of physical tension. Exhausted, Hugh slumped into a chair and sipped the rest of his drink. Loathing himself, he could only view Miss Plunkett's interest in him with suspicion. He had rattled on about his wife until the governess had no choice but to conclude he was fit for Bedlam, or worse, that he was a brokenhearted weakling who couldn't control his emotions. Which, given that Miss Plunkett was the Last Chance Governess, probably presented nothing more to her than a career challenge. She was going to rehabilitate him, just like she was going to rehabilitate Alexander.

Well, she could try, thought the duke, angrily pouring the last of his brandy down his throat. She could try. But he wasn't a child who needed to be coddled. He was a man firmly in charge of his life—despite the pity that he had seen glimmering in the Last Chance Governess's eyes.

SIX

He came through the front door just minutes before dinner was to be served.

Fiona, leaning against the curved balustrade, glanced at the long clock and forced a smile to her lips. "I am glad to see you arrived in time to dine with your son, Your Grace."

Her tone rankled. Did she expect him to conform to *her* schedule? Handing his hat and cane to Mr. Bevis, he gave her a cursory nod. "I am going back out as soon as dinner is finished. I'm going to see the fireworks in St. James Park."

Her brows lifted. "Yes, I have heard there is to be a great celebration."

"Well, getting rid of Boney is worthy of a celebration." The duke gestured toward the stairs, then followed Miss Plunkett toward the dining room. "Let us hope we have seen the end of him, at any rate."

Alexander, already seated, quickly removed his elbows from the table. "Hello, Father."

The duke studied his son for signs of subjugation. Could Mrs. Diggory have been right? Was the child's spirit being tested? Or was Alexander simply bending to the stronger will of Miss Plunkett? This governess was, after all, extraordinarily bossy.

During the consomme course, she said, "Guess where we are going this evening, Alexander?"

"Where?"

"To St. James Park, to see the fireworks display." She said it coolly, calmly, without a hint of facetiousness in her voice.

The duke's spoon clattered on the rim of his bowl. "What? Now, listen here! I did not invite you——"

But one look at his son's face told him he wasn't going to St. James Park alone.

Miss Plunkett's serene smile drew prickles of heat to the back of his neck.

An hour later, after the duke's carriage had pushed its way through the throng of traffic around Piccadilly, Fiona stood in the center of St. James Park, gaping at the night sky. Fireworks exploded in great blossoms of color, some with trailing stems of sparklers, some accompanied by frightening booms. It seemed all of London had turned out to celebrate the defeat of Napoleon. Aristocrats and commoners alike crowded the park, drinking and eating as if there were no tomorrow.

Alexander held tightly to both his father's and Miss Plunkett's hands. Between the adults, he leaned back on his heels, drinking in the sky, giddy with amazement.

In the bushes, uniformed men with blackened faces and bayonets crept about, reenacting the great battles of the Peninsular War. In a small wooden booth, puppets dramatized the Corsican's defeat by the Duke of Wellington. Vendors sold hot boiled peanuts and beer, while fortune-tellers conducted business at tables laden with crystal balls and cups of tea leaves.

Alexander, refusing to look anywhere but the sky, dragged his feet as the adults pulled him toward a little bridge. When they crossed the canal, the child forgot the fireworks, gazing instead at a seven-story, gas-lit Chinese pagoda. Lanterns strung in tree-tops bathed the park in a shimmering glow. In the distance, cannon fire sounded on the Serpentine as mock battleships enacted the Battle of Trafalgar.

"Isn't it magical?" Fiona said. Alexander's tiny fingers tightened around hers.

"Magical," the child repeated, awestruck.

Suddenly aware of the duke's gaze, she looked at him. He had been moody and remote since they had shared tea in the drawing room. Fiona attributed his darkened mood to the discussion about Hermoine. And, though she regretted that the duke was so entangled by his past that he couldn't enjoy the present, she considered it *his* deprivation. And Alexander's.

Fiona ruffled the boy's hair. The child deserved his father's love and attention, but as long as the duke was in mourning, he could never attend to his son the way he should.

It wasn't that the duke didn't love Alexander. On the contrary, Lord Deramore's expression was achingly poignant each time he saw or spoke of his son. His love for the boy was evident—to everyone but Alexander. The duke simply needed to let go of the past and focus on the blessings of the present. In Fiona's estimation, those blessings were substantial.

Alexander's body, bumping against hers, filled her with maternal longings. This was her life, she thought, meeting the duke's stare. What was the saying? *Always a bridesmaid, never a bride?* Well, that was the way she felt, only in her case it was: *Always a governess, never a mother.*

"Are you having a nice time?" He took her elbow, guiding her and Alexander toward the edge of the park.

"Lovely." His touch set her pulse to racing.

"I'm glad to see you left your prim little governess uniform at home."

Fiona's gown, conservative by the current fashion standards, was daringly low cut in her own estimation. A pale blue muslin confection, with cap sleeves and a high Empire waist, the dress was a gift from her previous employer. Prevented by pregnancy from wearing it, the lady had insisted Fiona have it. For months, the gown had remained in its tissue wrapping. Only when Fiona realized she was going to the park with Lord Deramore and Alexander, and that her ubiquitous dark blue dress lacked any degree of festivity, did she screw up sufficient courage to wear it.

The warm night air brushed the sensitive skin of her bare

decolletage. But the duke's heated gaze aroused goose bumps along her shoulders. A disturbing wave of liquid fire rolled through Fiona's body. Recalling her improbable ivory fan, also a gift from her previous employer, Fiona nervously unfurled it. Still, the slight breeze she created did nothing to cool her boiling skin.

"I'll be damned," he muttered.

She shot him a quizzical gaze. "Your Grace, don't forget that Alexander repeats everything he hears."

The duke, handsome in his dark blue coat and starkly white shirt, chuckled in a throaty way that made Fiona's knees wobbly. Still holding his son's hand, he leaned over and whispered against Fiona's neck. "I never would have believed it, Miss Plunkett."

"Believed what?"

"That you would lose control of your emotions, that you would lose that air of military discipline you are so famous for."

She fanned her neck furiously, nearly batting his nose. "Did you think I was such a cold, emotionless creature that I could not be *moved?*"

"I wasn't certain." He put his hand on top of Alexander's head, perhaps to prevent him from looking up, but the child's attention was firmly fastened on a pair of swans gliding across the lake. "Does this move you, Miss Plunkett?"

Nuzzling her neck, he wrapped his arm around her waist and drew her close to him.

She drew back, keenly aware of the child's presence, but not before she felt the duke's breath on her skin, his warm lips on her neck. Her heart boomed like a cannon; her senses spun crazily.

Pushing him away, she whispered, "What are you trying to do, Your Grace? Are you trifling with me? Are you mocking me?"

He stiffened; his expression lost all trace of levity. "Mocking you? Why would I do such a thing?"

"You said you didn't think I could ever lose control. Perhaps you thought it would be amusing to see if you could make me lose control."

"Good God, woman! Yes, I know Alexander can hear me! He's heard far worse, I assure you! What is so horrible about losing control?"

"What is so wonderful about it?" *It has kept me from falling prey to self-pity,* Fiona thought. Her firm discipline, her determination, her rock steadiness, those had kept her from losing her sense of worth when she discovered she would never have children of her own. They were what made her a good governess. But it clearly was not the key to success with men.

He clasped her upper arm and drew her to him again, crushing little Alexander between them.

"Are you going to kiss her, Father?"

"Watch the fireworks, son," the duke replied, perhaps in a more patient tone than even Fiona could have mustered.

"All right." The child turned his head. "I'm not looking now," he added optimistically.

"Don't—" Fiona started.

"You cannot control every aspect of your life, Miss Plunkett."

"Yes, I can."

"Nor can you control the conduct of all those around you."

"Only the children whose discipline is my responsibility. I don't see why that offends you so."

"Perhaps it offends me because I don't want to be told what to do. You see, Miss Plunkett, I am too old for the classroom and too stubborn to permit a woman to tell me what to do."

To keep her hands from fluttering, she clutched his lapels. But that was the wrong thing to do because it only drew him closer, so close that his lips were practically touching hers. "I'm-I'm sorry if I've offended you! Good heavens, I've been accused of being bossy before, most often by my charges, I must admit. But, if you find nothing about me which you can recommend, then why don't you leave me be, my lord? Why don't you release me? Please."

"Why don't I leave you alone?" He released her then, retreating a step. "Because I don't want to, Miss Plunkett. And because . . . I cannot."

There was a petulant tone in his voice that bordered on boyish. Fiona, though relieved to be released, could find no humor in the situation. Especially when her relief vanished. As soon as the duke's hand slid off her arm, she found to her horror that she sorely missed his touch.

"I think it is time to return to the carriage," she said briskly.

Alexander took the lead, skipping and pulling the adults behind him. He obviously thought Fiona couldn't hear him as he scrambled into the carriage ahead of his father. "You should have kissed her when you had the chance, Father."

But the governess's hearing was keen. And, though she nearly laughed out loud when she heard the child's whispered advice, she grudgingly wished the duke had followed it.

The duke entered his town house the next afternoon, hung over and ill-tempered.

"May I have a word with you, Your Grace?"

"Miss Plunkett, do you make a practice of loitering in the entrance hall, waiting for me to arrive home?"

Mr. Bevis, accepting his hat, coughed conspicuously. "Been waiting here an hour, my lordship," he said sotto voce.

"I heard that," Miss Plunkett snapped. "How else am I to speak with his lordship?"

"Ambush him, I suppose," the dour valet muttered.

Lord Deramore ushered Fiona into the drawing room. She stood while he poured himself a brandy at the sideboard.

"Haven't you had quite enough of that—"

His dark gaze silenced her. "Perhaps you didn't hear me last night, Miss Plunkett. I seem to recall informing you that I am not a child in need of supervision."

"Yes, my lord." Standing behind the sofa, she dug her nails into the soft chintz of the cushioned back. Watching him stalk across the room, she experienced a frisson of fear. Had she, indeed, lost control of her senses? In one moment, she thrilled at the sight of his long legs and broad shoulders. The next instant brought shivery apprehension and butterflies to her stomach.

Underneath all that confusion, however, lay one certainty. Fiona saw beneath the duke's steely exterior a sad little boy wanting to be loved. What truly frightened her was her own urge to be the one who loved him.

"I'm afraid I have some rather unpleasant news to share with you, Your Grace."

He frowned. "What has Alexander done?"

"Nothing. I mean, it isn't about the child. I am giving you my notice, Lord Deramore. I will be leaving Curzon Street as soon as you are able to make suitable arrangements for another nanny or governess to take my place."

His expression turned a darker shade of black. "Why?"

Feebly, she attempted a smile. "I never like to stay in one household too long.

"Why is that, Miss Plunkett?"

She bit her bottom lip. She knew why. It was because she feared growing attached to the children she cared for. That was why being the Last Chance Governess was such a perfect career. It was a ruse, really. She left whenever her little charges had learned their manners. That was what she always said. But, the truth was, she left whenever she felt she was falling in love. She left before she couldn't tear herself away. Simply put, she left because she was a coward.

How could she tell Lord Deramore that? Worse, how could she explain that this time it wasn't just her charge she had fallen in love with, but her employer as well?

"I like a challenge, my lord. When my duties are finished, I find another little boy or girl who needs me. It works out better that way."

"Poppycock. You've been here less than three days. I don't believe this gammon for a minute. Why don't you tell me what is truly the matter? Has Alexander put saltpeter in your bath salts?"

"No."

"Has he tied your boot laces together?"

"No."

"Short-sheeted you?"

"No, my lord."

The duke slammed his brandy glass on the mantelpiece. "Damme, then, what is it?" After an elongated silence, he said, "You are leaving because of me, aren't you?"

Her fingers twisted the edge of the cushion; her heart hammered painfully. "I am in a very precarious position here, my lord. Treated like a member of the family in some ways. Treated like a scullery wench in others. But, no matter my status, I am a woman—"

"I noticed."

"With feelings and emotions. Which I would do well to protect."

"Ah, that famous Fiona Plunkett restraint! Always be in control, Miss Plunkett. That is the thing!"

"You're mocking me."

"I am mocking your inhibitions, Fiona."

His deep, throaty voice and familiar tone stole her breath. Fiona. The sound of her name, spoken by him, was more seductive than a thousand kisses. Struggling to modulate her cracking voice, she replied, "Please. I must go. Before it is too late."

His jaw hardened. Turning his back, he gripped the mantelpiece. Then, in a voice that chilled her heart, he replied, "If you are going to leave, leave now. Before Alexander grows more attached to you than he already is."

It seemed to Fiona that the air had been sucked from the room. Unable to breathe, she left the drawing room. Packing her few belongings took no time. In less than an hour, she was standing on Curzon Street awaiting a hackney coach.

SEVEN

In the harsh light of day, Green Park looked like a *real* battlefield. Absent the sparkle of stars and the warm glow of the Chinese lanterns, the destruction of a week-long celebration of fireworks and drinking was evident. The grass was trampled, flower beds were demolished and trees were strewn with paper streamers.

Clutching the hands of the ten-year-old twins who were her new charges, Fiona leisurely strolled the grounds. With Polly and Anna Groblobbet in tow, she crossed the tiny bridge that she had crossed just a sennight earlier with Alexander and Lord Deramore. When she stood in the very spot where the duke had kissed her, a suffocating wave of loneliness engulfed Fiona.

Polly and Anna spied a pair of ducks paddling toward the bank of the lake. "May we feed them some biscuits?" one of the girls asked. "I've an entire bagful left from our trip to the pastry shop."

"Watch your fingers!" Fiona said, releasing the girls.

Standing alone, she watched them, identical in their capacity for mischief as well as their prettiness, as they raced toward the water's edge.

Though she had only been with the girls for a few days, Fiona had already developed a fondness for them. And Lady Groblobbet was pleased by the promising start Fiona had made. Just last night, the girls had got through dinner without one disruptive fit of giggles. At breakfast, they had shown superb manners. If their progress continued at this rate, Fiona might be searching for new employment within the month.

A deep male voice spun her around. "Fancy meeting you here."

Fiona's heart skipped a beat. Glancing around, she asked, "Where is Alexander?"

The duke smiled. "Do I detect a note of wistfulness in your voice?"

Fiona turned toward the water, redirecting her attention toward Polly and Anna. Embarrassed by the betraying eagerness in her voice, she beat back her emotions and tried to appear calm. "I must confess, I do miss the little thing."

"He misses you." The duke stood behind her, his shoulder brushing hers. Against her ear, he said silkily, "And so do I."

Disturbed by his nearness, Fiona took a little side step. "How on earth did you find me here?"

"I have been here every morning since you departed Curzon Street. For reasons of my own. To tell the truth, I didn't expect to find you here. I had hoped, however, you would send a letter in the post advising me of your whereabouts."

"I am living in Newhouse Road, Your Grace, with the Groblobbet family. Those two little girls, Polly and Anna, are my new charges. Aren't they pretty?"

"Charmers," replied the duke. "But what about your former assignment? What do you intend to do about Alexander? Can you really walk out and forget him? Go off, work for someone else, and never give the child a moment's thought?"

Pivoting, Fiona faced the duke with a scowl. "How dare you suggest I could ever forget about Alexander? Do you think I am such a cold-hearted creature? Good heavens, I think about him every minute of the day! And you, too, for that matter."

"Me?" Arching his brows, he touched his chest, feigning surprise. "And what do you think about me, Miss Plunkett?"

Fiona would have liked to slap the duke's handsome face, wipe the smug, knowing smile right off his lips, but she was— as the duke once pointed out—far too controlled a person to indulge in such a common display of emotion. Trembling with anger, she spoke through clenched teeth. "Do not mock me, my lord. You know that I cannot continue to work on Curzon Street, not given the events that transpired between us."

"Is it because I kissed you?"

"No. Yes." How could she explain? How could Fiona ever make the duke understand that a simple kiss had knocked her world off its axis? If he didn't understand already, he never would. If he knew what he had done to her, and didn't care, he was a cad. Either way, she was wise to disassociate herself from him.

As for Alexander . . . well, leaving him when she did was an act of pure self-defense. If she had stayed a day longer, she would never have been able to leave. She loved him that much. And missed him so deeply that her heart ached.

"Well, Fiona, which is it? Yes or no?"

"Oh, I hate you," she whispered. "Or, at least, I want to. Can't you understand? Don't you see why I cannot work for you? It would only cause me pain. In the end, when I finally left your employ, I would only be rewarded with a broken heart."

He clasped her wrist and drew her to him. "What are you afraid of, Fiona? Tell me."

"I should ask you the same thing. You are the one who lives in the past."

He flinched, as if he had taken a blow.

When he didn't respond, Fiona continued. "You as much as admitted it! You compare every woman you meet to her! You can't look at your son without missing her! Why, I'd be a fool to fall in love with a man like you. You've closed your heart to anyone else; you've latched on to your grief as if it were a crutch."

"How dare you," he breathed.

She met his blackening gaze. "How do I dare? Because I care for you, that's how. Perhaps you feel guilty, going on with your life after Hermoine's death. Is that it? It's like you're wearing a hair shirt, basking in your suffering in order to feel good about yourself. Well, that's a form of self-pity, Your Grace, an excuse, an escape!"

"I won't have you talk to me that way!" With his fingers tight around her wrist, he held her captive.

"You can't stop me! I'm not in your employ any longer!"

"No, you ran from me like a frightened child! 'Tis you who is afraid!"

"I'm not! But a woman must protect herself, and I am protecting myself from you."

They stood, staring at one another, silent, both of them trembling with emotion.

A splash, followed by a squeal, sounded from the lake. As the duke roughly released her, Fiona turned in time to see Anna's head bob to the surface of the water, her arms flailing, her eyes wide with fright.

"Hurry, Miss Plunkett. Anna cannot swim!" Polly cried.

"Oh, my stars! Neither can I!"

"I can." Stripping off his coat, the duke dashed toward the water. He dived in and swam toward the little girl. In no time, he had her on the bank of the lake where he turned her on her stomach and pressed the water from her lungs. As she spit and coughed, Fiona and Polly watched helplessly. After a few moments, she rolled over and sat up, clearly unconcerned that her gown was rucked about her knees and her frilly pantaloons were in plain view, torn, drenched and muddy.

Though she suffered little harm, she looked frightfully pathetic. Fiona's guilt at realizing she had neglected her charges plunged her into an even deeper state of agitation.

"Thank you, Your Grace," she said, helping Anna to her feet. "I am certain that Lord and Lady Groblobbet will be most appreciative for your efforts."

With a shiver, Anna said, "That water was monstrous cold, Sister! I'll teach you to push me in the lake!"

The duke touched the little girl's shoulder. "Well, see that you don't, young lady. You could have drowned in that lake if someone hadn't been around to rescue you."

"Yes, thank you," the child answered demurely. Turning to her sister, she burst out in girlish giggles.

"Time for us to go," Fiona announced. Guiding her charges toward the bridge, she said, "Thank you again, Your Grace. You were most heroic."

The duke looked down at his bedraggled clothes. "Wait a minute! My carriage is parked just on the other side of the park. Why don't you allow me to drive you and your charges home, Miss Plunkett? 'Tis the least I can do."

"You've done enough," Fiona replied crisply.

"But, Miss Plunkett, I'm cold!" cried Anna.

"And he is very handsome," added Polly in a whisper that seemed as loud as cannon shot to Fiona.

"Oh, all right." Fiona, mindful that her first duty was to her young charges, relented. What harm was there in sharing a carriage with the man, after all? What could he possibly do in the space of a ten-minute carriage ride that would threaten her resolve to forget him?

Climbing into his gleaming equipage, she contained her anger by biting hard on her lower lip. Her unexpected encounter with the duke had rattled her nerves. Anna's accident had destroyed her composure. But she would sooner jump in the lake herself before she'd let Hugh Parmenas know how deeply disturbing his presence was to her.

Perhaps he had been right to accuse her of being too tightly in control of herself. In reality, he had no inkling how much control she possessed, and how much restraint she exercised, as they rode the short distance to Newhouse Road. Staring at his long, lean legs, encased now in skin-tight, dripping-wet breeches, produced a wave of tingly desire that even the Last Chance Governess had no hope of disciplining.

Lady Groblobbet, surprisingly old to be the mother of ten-year-old twins, met them in the entrance hall. "What has happened to my poor Anna?" she cried, grabbing the child and pressing her between her ample breasts.

Fiona graciously described how the duke leapt into the lake, crediting him with saving Anna's life after the little girl gave chase to a mallard and dove into water much too deep for safety.

Gazing in astonishment at the equally sodden duke, Lady Groblobbet erupted in tears. Her twins, clearly distressed by their mother's show of emotion, clung to her tent-sized and incongruously frilly yellow morning gown.

"Don't cry, Mother," Anna pleaded. "I actually enjoyed my swim with the ducks."

"I don't think Sister was ever truly in danger," added Polly.

After dabbing her tears with a delicate handkerchief, then gathering up her girls in another bone crushing hug, the lady turned to Fiona. "And where were you when this crisis occurred?"

"Beg pardon, my lady, but I was right there."

"Do you mean to say you permitted Anna to dive into the lake?"

"Of course not." Fiona's cheeks darkened, but she held the lady's gaze.

Hugh, certain that he was responsible for Fiona's distraction, interjected. "Please don't be angry with Miss Plunkett. It wasn't her fault at all." Smiling warmly, he reached for the lady's hand, squeezing her plump fingers as he spoke. "You see, Miss Plunkett was recently in my employ, and when I ran into her in the park, I couldn't resist detaining her."

"Oh?" The lady actually blushed beneath the duke's handsome gaze. "You look too young to have a child, Your Grace."

Chuckling, he said, "My six-year-old, Alexander, was giving me quite a problem. Spirited chap, you know. Refused to eat his vegetables, go to sleep at a decent hour, that sort of thing."

"Yes, dear," she replied with a wink. "Know all about it."

"The other governesses couldn't do a thing with him."

"I went through at least twenty in two years before retaining Miss Plunkett."

"She did wonders with Alexander," said the duke, releasing the woman's hand. "My only regret is that I allowed her to go. My son and I miss her fiercely. So, you see it was I who distracted Miss Plunkett from her duties this morning. She only turned her back for a second, and that was when I pressed her to listen to my silly entreaty. As it was, she refused to consider leaving your employ."

"Oh?" The lady cut Fiona a quizzical glance. "Is that so?"

"On account of her being so devoted to you," concluded the duke. "And your lovely daughters. I hope I am not too bold in saying that it is obvious they inherited their beauty from you."

"Oh, Your Grace!" As she tittered, Lady Groblobbet's jowls quivered, and her eyes watered with pleasure. Eyeing the duke from head to toe, she said, "But, you're wringing wet yourself, Your Grace. We must get you into dry clothes before returning you home."

Retreating toward the door, Hugh shook his head. "My driver is waiting just outside, my lady. I'll be home and in dry breeches within the half hour."

"But, you'll catch your death of cold!" the lady protested.

"Not if I hurry home," returned the duke.

Fiona slanted the duke a conspiratorial smile. Picking up her skirts, she started up the stairs. "Thank you, again, Your Grace, for saving Anna. Please tell little Alexander hello for me. I do miss him."

With his hand on the brass knob behind him, Hugh stared at her. She paused, silently questioning him, appraising him with those big, unblinking eyes of hers. Had Lady Groblobbet not stood between them, he might have crossed the black-and-white-checkered floor and swept Fiona into his arms. His need for her suddenly overwhelmed him. His desire to love her suddenly consumed him.

He was, he realized with a jolt, in love with Fiona Plunkett. Her rigid self-control didn't fool him. He knew from experience that a person who feared losing control often lived inside a very orderly, insulated bubble of existence. It was Fiona's way of protecting her heart. He had protected his own these past few years by behaving like a wild Corinthian tomcat.

"Are you all right?" Lady Groblobbet asked him.

"Quite," he murmured, though he was far from it. For an instant, Hugh felt a twinge of regret. No, Fiona Plunkett was not Hermoine. But, when Fiona's lips curved in a smile, he saw only her, her no-nonsense beauty, her frankness, her refreshing openness. He saw her standing over Alexander in the classroom, gazing at the stars with wonder in her eyes, sitting on the edge of her bed in a flimsy night rail and robe, hugging Alexander to her breast. The duke saw her surprise when he kissed her, her desire when he drew her near to him.

Sighing, he knew that he would never relive the years he had with Hermoine. Like his innocence and his youth, that time was gone. But perhaps happiness could be his again. Perhaps it wasn't sacrilege to share his life with another woman. Loving Fiona in no way diminished the memory of Hermoine. His memories were precious, but if he didn't reach out to Fiona now, he might spend his future locked inside his own loneliness.

Lady Groblobbet started toward him. "Perhaps you've caught a chill. If you would only come into the drawing room, I'm sure we could find a pair of dry breeches—"

Opening the door, he backed through it. On the threshold, he said, "Thank you, my lady. But, might I ask another favor of you?"

"Certainly, Your Grace. You saved my Anna's life!"

"My son Alexander would love to see his former governess. I'm afraid he doesn't have many playmates, you see, and I was wondering if I could bring him here for a short visit. We won't stay long. And we will not detain Miss Plunkett from her responsibilities for more than half an hour, I promise."

The woman smiled, relieved, it seemed, to have happened upon a way in which she could repay the duke for his heroic deed. "Come tomorrow, Your Grace, around three o'clock.

We'll have tea in the drawing room, all of us. I'm certain Polly and Anna would love to meet your little Alexander."

Behind the lady's back, halfway up the stairs, Fiona froze. Lifting her brows, she shot the duke a frankly curious look. When he smiled broadly at her, she hurried up the winding steps and out of sight.

Hugh couldn't resist planting a wet kiss on Lady Groblobbet's plump cheek. As she giggled and cooed, he jumped into his waiting carriage. Laughing, he leaned out his open window and called out to his tiger, "Beautiful day, ain't it, boy? Want to ride inside with me?" Even the duke's driver turned and stared in amazement. Lord Deramore, it appeared, had suddenly gone mad.

In fact, he had never been more clearheaded. Today, he had launched a scheme that would ensure the swift return to Curzon Street of Fiona Plunkett. Leaning back against the leather squabs, he chafed his hands in mischievous glee. Tomorrow this time, the Last Chance Governess would be begging to return to his employ.

EIGHT

In the drawing room, Polly and Anna, seated on a pale pink, silk-covered sofa, made a deceptively prim appearance. Across from them, in a claw-footed club chair covered in a bright floral print, sat their mother, Lady Groblobbet.

"Lovely, lovely," she warbled, lavishing her gaze on the twins.

In response, they smiled back at her, two perfect little angels, sugar and spice personified.

Standing before the white marble hearth, Fiona regarded the scene. Something about it gave her the chills.

Perhaps it was the unrelieved femininity of the setting, she thought, twisting her fingers. Lady Groblobbet's morning gown, a lavender confection with puffy sleeves and a frilly hem, was more suited to a younger woman, not the overweight mother of ten-year-olds. And the twins' matching outfits, baby blue dresses with starched white pinafores, lent them an air of superficiality that made Fiona's hair stand on end.

When the door opened, however, and Alexander stepped tentatively across the threshold, all apprehension vanished. Fiona crossed the room, arms open wide.

He hugged her tightly about the neck, then offered her an unsolicited kiss on the cheek. "Hello, Miss Plunkett," he said, suddenly shy.

After kissing him back and hugging him as tightly as she dared, Fiona stood and offered the duke her hand. He squeezed her fingers, then, before she could protest, raised them to his lips.

The warmth of his skin brushing hers drew goose bumps to her skin. Fiona barely managed to murmur an appropriate greeting before following Alexander to the sofa.

Lady Groblobbet made introductions, and the children greeted one another with an exquisite show of manners. Pleased to see all her charges behaving civilly, Fiona released the breath she hadn't realized she had been holding. Perhaps this visit would come off without a hitch, after all.

Mindful of the duke's admonition that she was always too tightly in control, she resolved to relax and enjoy herself. After all, this was supposed to be a festive occasion. Alexander's desire to see her had made her happier than she would ever have guessed. And the duke's daring rescue of the Groblobbet twins had made him somewhat of a hero in the Newhouse Road abode.

"Do sit down, everyone," said Lady Groblobbet, moving to the sofa where she positioned herself between her twins. Alexander sat next to Fiona on a love seat, catty-cornered to the sofa. A maidservant delivered a tea tray, placing it on a lacquered table, then pouring expertly and passing a plate of sugary biscuits. The duke lowered himself into the chair vacated by Lady Groblobbet, directly across from Fiona and Alexander.

For a time, idle chatter about the goings-on in Vienna passed for conversation between the adults. At last, the duke turned to Polly, the twin seated nearest him, and said, "Tell me, young lady, did you have many governesses before Miss Plunkett arrived?"

"Oh, yes." She seemed to enjoy the duke's attention. "We had many governesses, but none so fine as Miss Plunkett. Isn't that right, Anna?"

"Quite right, Polly."

Lady Groblobbet beamed. "Miss Plunkett appears to be doing wonders with them. Of course, Miss Greenheath was doing well the first few weeks, too. And so was Miss Dodderingsham." Her smile wobbled. "Well, we shall see . . ."

"Oh, we like Miss Plunkett!" Polly assured her mother.

"I do hope so." To the duke, Lady Groblobbet remarked, "Twins are so demanding, you see. Double trouble, if you know what I mean. Most governesses don't have the energy or the patience to deal with Polly and Anna. But Miss Plunkett has excellent references."

The duke lifted his brows. "Yes, I know."

Fiona, desirous of changing the subject, turned to Alexander. "Have you a new governess, young man?"

"Not yet." He gave her a winning smile. "Mrs. Inchcape won't send any more to me, you know. Not since Mrs. Tavistock found the snakes and went to live with her sister in Dorset."

Replacing his cup and saucer on the table in front of him, the duke cleared his throat. "Not to worry, Sandy. We'll find you another governess. *Somewhere. Somehow.*"

His comment struck Fiona like a barbed arrow. Meeting the duke's gaze, she replied, "And in the meantime, I suppose you have been forced to curtail some of your, ah, *business*. How inconvenient for you."

"Yes, Father has been spending quite a bit of time at home of late," piped Alexander. "Last night we attended the circus. The night before we ate dinner in a chop house. Great fun, that was, wasn't it, Father? All the smoke and spilled beer and laughing women? Can we go again, Father?"

"Laughing women?" Fiona asked.

Lady Groblobbet, fidgeting on the sofa, averted her gaze.

"It was all very innocent," said the duke smoothly.

"Well, at least you are spending more time with Alexander," said Fiona, without the slightest trace of recrimination. She genuinely was glad that Lord Deramore was thawing in his attitude toward Alexander. Though she regretted having criticized the duke so harshly, perhaps her message had taken effect. Perhaps the duke realized how neglectful a father he had been and had taken steps to rectify the situation. If that was the case,

Fiona supposed it was good that she had left Curzon Street when she did.

A long glance passed between the duke and his son. Interpreting their unspoken communication as a positive sign, Fiona sipped her tea with a strange mixture of longing, happiness and envy. While she wanted only the best for Alexander and Lord Deramore, she couldn't help missing them both.

"Would you like to see my new pet?" Alexander suddenly asked the twins.

"Oh, yes!" they cried in unison, wriggling to the edge of the sofa cushion and putting down their tea.

Mildly curious, Fiona returned the duke's warm smile. Had Lord Deramore bought the child a puppy? As Alexander stood by the settee, she thought he intended to fetch the pet from the duke's carriage. Instead, he reached in his pocket and pulled out a frog, a very large frog, as big as a big man's fist.

"Ooh!" The little girls gathered around Alexander, reaching for the glistening toad.

Lady Groblobbet's cup and saucer clattered to the table. Clutching her throat, she slid down the length of the sofa, eager to distance herself from Alexander's pet. "Good heavens, a toad in my parlor! Polly, Anna, don't touch. You're liable to come away with warts, or God knows what else!"

Noting the duke's look of pure unconcern, a ribbon of apprehension slivered up Fiona's spine. "Alexander, darling, why don't you take the frog out to your father's carriage? I'm certain the tiger would be happy to watch over him while you're inside."

Ignoring her, Alexander handed the frog to Polly, who promptly squealed and dropped him to the floor. Two leaps later, the frog was under the sofa, and the children were on their knees, reaching for him. Lady Groblobbet cried, "Catch it! Catch it before it gets lost in the house or, worse, crushed underfoot on my Axminster carpets!"

Giggling uncontrollably, the twins crawled behind the sofa. The frog took off in the opposite direction, leading them on a merry chase around the room. Each time they nabbed the slippery creature in their hands, they squealed with horrified delight and let it loose again.

Alexander, in the meantime, stood beside the sofa, watching the scene with obvious relish.

"Aren't you going to help Polly and Anna catch the frog?" asked Fiona.

"Oh, they'll catch it when they want to," he replied calmly.

Fiona, suppressing her anger, spoke through gritted teeth. "Alexander, go and help the girls catch the frog. That is an order."

"No." He looked at her rather bashfully, Fiona thought with a strange presentiment. Then he glanced at his father and said, "Besides, I've got another pet."

"Another pet?" Lady Groblobbet asked. "Well, I for one don't care to see it, child. Lord Deramore, please. Tell the boy to keep his pets in his pockets."

The duke waved his hand dismissively. "I would, my lady, but he never listens to a word I say."

"That isn't true!" cried Fiona. "He's a good child! When I left your employment, his manners were greatly improved."

"So you said," drawled the duke.

A shriek erupted from Lady Groblobbet. Following her gaze, Fiona saw that Alexander had extracted a slender green garden snake from his other pocket. Holding it by the tail, he dangled it before Lady Groblobbet, grinning devilishly as she reared back and squirmed against the sofa cushions.

"Take that monster away from here this instant!" she screamed.

Servants, hearing the uproar in the parlor, streamed in. Quickly appraising the situation, two scullery maids joined the twins in their hunt for the frog. The butler and valet stood behind the sofa, warily eyeing the snake held aloft by Alexander.

"Someone grab it! Lord Deramore, do something!" Lady Groblobbet exclaimed, clearly offended by the duke's inaction.

The male servants exchanged looks, then skirted the end of

the sofa and approached the boy. Before they could snatch the snake from his fingers, he dropped it atop Lady Groblobbet's foot.

"Oh, my! I've let go my pet snake," he said, watching it wrap itself around her pudgy ankle.

It looked like a thin green ribbon embroidered on her delicate white stocking. A full-throttled yell escaped the lady's throat, and she kicked her legs in a vain attempt to rid herself of the snake. But the snake, probably more terrified than the lady, clung to the trunk of her leg like a bracelet of ivy. The valet and butler, unable to calm their mistress, could do no more than pluck ineffectively at her ankle as she flailed her limbs about in abject fear.

Sinking back into her chair, Fiona watched helplessly. Polly and Anna, suddenly bored with the frog, stood beside the sofa and watched their mother pass into a dead faint. At least now the butler and valet could retrieve the snake and return it to its rightful owner.

"I hope she didn't scare you too badly," Alexander said to the tiny creature as he tucked it back in his pocket. "Did you find my frog?" he asked Polly and Anna.

"No, but we will," one of them answered.

Slumped in her chair, Fiona covered her eyes with her hand. Whatever had possessed Alexander to instigate such chaos, she couldn't imagine, and she didn't want to see what was coming next. Exhausted, she shook her head and wondered what else could go wrong in her life.

A vial of hartshorn was waved beneath Lady Groblobbet's nose. Within seconds, she roused sufficiently to lift her head and intone, "Miss Plunkett?"

Fiona looked up.

"You are fired," said the lady, then collapsed amid the pillows again.

Standing, the duke held out his hand for Alexander. He cast Fiona a sympathetic stare, a look which sent chills up her spine, because it was full of amusement and totally devoid of contrition. He clucked his tongue and ruffled Alexander's hair. "Oh, dear. I suppose Sandy's behavior does reflect on your skills as a governess, doesn't it?"

"Oh, dear," the child aped, grinning.

"I am sorry," the duke continued. "Perhaps I should not have insisted on bringing Sandy for a visit. But, he does miss you so. And, truly, I never suspected he had a menagerie in his pockets."

"No, I am sure you had no idea." Fiona exercised Herculean strength in checking her acid tongue.

"I think we should go now," the duke said, pulling Alexander toward the door.

The child, scuffling his toes on the carpet, looked backward over his shoulder. " 'Bye, Miss Plunkett!" he called as he was dragged over the threshold. "Hope to see you soon!"

Fiona's heart lurched. Though she knew the duke wanted her back at Curzon Street, she was furious at his machinations. He had not, after all, disputed her accusation that he lived in the past. He had done nothing to persuade her that his flirtation with her was anything more than an overture for a dalliance.

She might very well succumb to her impulse and go back to Curzon Street—she would like to, after all. But just because the duke wanted her back as governess didn't mean she would escape a broken heart. He wanted to seduce her, that much she understood. But he could easily toss her out when he was weary of her charms. Fiona's yearning to be with the man and child she loved warred with her instinct for self-preservation.

Now the duke had caused her to lose her job, a ploy that fueled her resentment toward him, as well as her fear. What was she supposed to do? she thought, trudging up the stairs toward her tiny bedchamber. She wrote a note to Polly and Anna, urging them to be good girls, kind to their new governess and obedient to their mother. Then she quietly slipped out of the Groblobbet house. Her chest ached with sadness. Her heart told her to go to Curzon Street, but common sense told her to stay as far away from that place as she possibly could.

NINE

Two weeks passed. Two weeks in which Fiona interviewed a half dozen prospective employers. But the fiasco at Lady Grob-lobbet's house had become entertaining gossip in the drawing rooms of Mayfair. "You aren't the governess who worked for the Duke of Deramore, are you?" nervous mothers would ask her. When Fiona reluctantly nodded, the interviews inevitably ground to a screeching halt.

At last, Fiona realized the duke had completely sabotaged her prospects of gaining employment. As much as she dreaded it, she was going to have to visit Curzon Street and have it out with Lord Deramore.

She appeared at his house one sunny morning, dressed in her plain dark blue gown and sensible half boots. Though she was unexpected, Bevis smiled broadly when he opened the door. Even Mrs. Diggory emerged from the kitchen to give her a wink and a hug. Then Bevis led her into the drawing room, announced her, and pulled the doors shut as he departed.

Fiona and the duke exchanged mutual looks of surprise. For Fiona, it was the shock of seeing another woman in the drawing room that caused her stomach to flip-flop. *Evidently, the new governess,* she thought, forcing a smile to her lips.

Lord Deramore, standing at the mantelpiece, strode toward Fiona. Bending over her hand, he kissed her fingers. "Fiona."

Though he stared at her questioningly, she revealed nothing in her expression. "Permit me to introduce Mrs. Drusilla Tavistock. Mrs. Tavistock, this is Alexander's most recent governess, Miss Fiona Plunkett."

Fiona couldn't resist inspecting the woman from head to toe. Older and far more severe in her appearance and bearing than Fiona, Mrs. Tavistock looked as if she had just bit into a lemon. *Poor Alexander,* Fiona thought, sinking into a chair.

But the name Tavistock rang a bell.

Confused, Fiona returned the duke's questioning look.

"Mrs. Tavistock has come to discuss her sister, Lettie."

"Oh." Fiona met the woman's gaze. "I see."

Mrs. Tavistock pursed her thin lips. "Lettie was deathly afraid of snakes. Deathly. Do you understand?"

"Are you suggesting that Alexander's prank was the cause of your sister's demise?"

"I'm not suggesting anything, Miss Plunkett. I am telling you that my sister would still be alive today if it were not for that evil little boy, Alexander!"

"He is not evil, Mrs. Tavistock," Fiona replied. "That I assure you.

"How long did *you* remain in the duke's employ?" Mrs. Tavistock retorted. "You've returned, no doubt, for the same reason I have. To demand compensation for the injuries you've suffered at the hands of that monstrous little boy!"

"Monstrous?" The duke's tone was hushed and menacing. Crossing his arms over his chest, he stared at Mrs. Tavistock with darkening eyes.

Fiona was equally offended. "I was informed by Mr. Bevis, ma'am, that your sister had a history of poor health. Is that not true?"

The woman gave a little huff. "She was healthy when she got here, Miss Plunkett. She was dead when she left."

"What do you want from me?" the duke asked quietly.

A hostile tension thickened the silence. At length, Mrs. Tavistock, her spine as stiff as a board and her boney fingers clasped neatly in her lap, replied, "Five thousand pounds should do it, my lord. Five thousand pounds and you'll never hear from me again."

The duke's expression betrayed a frightening revulsion. Fiona thought if the man had trained that look on her, she would have collapsed.

The wiry Mrs. Tavistock stood up and squared her shoulders. "He's a bad seed, that one, Your Grace. I'm sorry to have to tell you this, you being his father and all. Parents don't like to think their children capable of such mayhem. But mark my words, that Alexander is going to be trouble. My dear sister Lettie would be here today if it weren't for that troublesome scamp."

"Get out of my house," the duke said.

"Five thousand pounds, my lordship. And you'll never see me again."

"That's extortion," said Fiona, standing.

A scrabbling at the drawing room doors startled the adults.

Fiona, thinking a servant had brought tea, went to the door. When she saw no one was there, she shrugged. When she returned to the room, Lord Deramore was bending over the tea table, signing his name on a bank draft. Straightening, he handed the slip of paper to Mrs. Tavistock.

"I am curious," Fiona said to the smug-faced woman. "Whom did your sister work for before she came to Curzon Street?"

"This was her first London assignment," the woman answered crisply.

"Where did she live before?"

"In Liverpool. What difference does it make?"

"Can you tell me the name of the family in Liverpool for whom she worked?" Fiona asked.

Suddenly, Mrs. Tavistock was eager to leave. Brushing aside Fiona's question, she tucked the bank draft in her reticule and headed for the open doors. "I'm sorry, I haven't time to chat."

When she was gone, Fiona turned to the duke. "Did Mrs. Inchcape send Lettie Tavistock to you?"

"Yes," replied the duke grimly. "That was before Mrs. Inchcape refused to furnish any more nannies or governesses to Alexander." At the sideboard, he poured himself a strong drink, consumed it in several large gulps, then poured another.

Fiona waited for him to return. Standing before the mantelpiece, they avoided one another's gaze, both of them unnerved by Mrs. Tavistock's visit.

At length, Fiona said, "I came to register an official complaint myself. But Mrs. Tavistock's accusations have quite taken the starch out of my sails, I'm afraid."

"Oh, never mind her. I am rid of Mrs. Tavistock; that's all that matters." The duke sipped his brandy. "I suppose you are angry with me for sabotaging your efforts to find employment. Well, I don't blame you. Go ahead, tell me what a disreputable scoundrel I am! I'm Alexander's father, aren't I? What did Mrs. Tavistock call him? A bad seed? I suppose that's fitting, isn't it? *The apple doesn't fall far from the tree.*"

Fiona struggled against the urge to reach out and touch him. Her heart squeezed at the sound of pain and frustration that rang so clearly in Lord Deramore's voice. "Alexander isn't a bad little boy, you know that. Good heavens, he hardly gave me a moment of trouble."

"That was because he handpicked you to be his mother," the duke growled. "He's hardly been such an angel since you were gone. Mrs. Diggory is on the verge of a nervous collapse, I tell you. Yesterday, he took it upon himself to roast my riding boots in the rotisserie. Nearly set the kitchen on fire. Had Cook and all the maids as angry as wet hens."

"I am sorry." Fiona hesitated. "Something has just occurred to me, my lord."

He sighed. "Hugh."

"Me?"

"No, Hugh! Call me Hugh, please." Turning, the duke slammed his glass on the mantel and reached for Fiona. Clasping her upper arms, he drew her close and, before she could utter a sound of protest, planted a kiss on her lips. A hard kiss, deep and passionate, redolent of brandy and as scorching hot.

When he released her, Fiona nearly stumbled backward. Touching her bruised lips, she could only stare in astonishment. A tiny, kittenish sound emerged from her throat. "Oh, Hugh!"

He swallowed hard, drew her into his embrace—more gently this time—and kissed her again. When Fiona finally opened her eyes, she saw her own surprise and confusion reflected in his gaze. For a long time, they clung to one another, their bodies pressed together, her fingers clutching his lapels, his hands exploring her neck and face.

Against her cheek, he whispered, "I love you, Fiona."

Waves of liquid warmth poured through her. Hardly able to breathe, she managed to reply, "I love you, too."

"Come back, then," he said, nibbling on her lip. "Come back and be my wife." A smile curved his lips. "We'll have more children, a houseful of them. Brothers and sisters for Alexander. He'll love it!"

She wanted to say yes. She wanted him. Nothing in her life had ever seemed as right or as wonderful. But, just as Hugh whispered he loved her, Captain Edward Plunkett's words rang in Fiona's ears. She couldn't have children of her own. What sort of wife and mother could she be to the duke?

Tearing herself away from the duke, she retreated. A sobering chill descended, and she hugged herself against a violent shudder.

"What is the matter?" The duke stepped toward her.

"I-I thought of something! I should have thought of it before!"

"What?" He reached for her, but she skittered away.

Before Fiona could answer, Mr. Bevis, his face ashen, appeared in the doorway. "Sorry, your lordship, but we've a terrible problem!"

"What is it?" the duke snarled.

" 'Tis little Lord Badwell," the older man replied. "I'm afraid Alexander has disappeared."

Behind him appeared Mrs. Diggory, her cheeks tear-stained, her hair in a frazzled mess. "Little chap came into the kitchen and said he was gonna run away. I didna' believe him! Half an hour later, I thought to look fer him, but it was too late. His little portmanteau is missin', and his coin purse, too! I'm sure he's run off somewhere, my lordship! I can feel it in me bones."

"Start looking!" the duke demanded. "We'll all look! And we won't stop until we find my son!"

The house was searched from top to bottom. The stables were inspected, the upper branches of trees were surveyed, beds were looked under, and even the fireplaces were peered into. After several hours, however, it was clear that Alexander was not in the house, nor had he taken refuge at the neighbors. For all the inquiries made up and down the street, no one had seen the little boy all morning.

Not since Mrs. Tavistock arrived, that was.

"Do you think the child—" In the drawing room, having downed a half glass of brandy herself, Fiona stood before the mantelpiece twisting her fingers. "Oh, no, that's impossible!"

Pacing the length of the carpet, the duke ran his hands through the thinning silver streaks at his temple. Abruptly, he whirled, facing Fiona with an expression of hope mingled with apprehension. "What is it? Spit it out! If you have any ideas, I'd like to hear them!"

She chewed her bottom lip. "Well, when Mrs. Tavistock was here, she said some very ugly things about Alexander. Do you suppose that he could have overheard the conversation?"

"I don't see how. The drawing room doors were shut."

"I heard a sound at the doors. I thought the maid had come with a tea tray and was unable to turn the knob. When I opened the door, no one was there."

The duke slammed his fist into his palm and swore colorfully. "Yes, that makes perfect sense. The child got it in his head he was responsible for Mrs. Lettie Tavistock's death. He must have been frightened to death. Good God, he must have felt terrible!"

A moment passed in which no one said anything. Then Fiona snapped her fingers. Lord Deramore stared quizzically as she ran to pull the bell cord. Bevis appeared in a flash, his eyes wide with terror.

"I've thought of something," Fiona said. "Bevis, did Mrs. Tavistock arrive in a rented carriage?"

"Yes, ma'am, it was a regular rented hackney. Black and dusty, like all the rest."

"What are you thinking?" The duke's presence, even in a crisis, affected Fiona in a disturbing way. Suppressing her attraction, she said to him, "Alexander was here just moments before Mrs. Tavistock left. Now he's gone. I think it quite possible he hopped inside the cab. Or latched on to the back, with the tiger, if there was one. For all we know, he clambered on top of the coach and held on to the luggage rails!"

"Why would he have gone off with Mrs. Drusilla Tavistock?" the duke asked. "After what that old witch said about him?"

"If he overheard her, he might have gone straight out the front door. The first carriage he saw was parked in front of the house. He leapt into it, not thinking that he was hitching a ride with Mrs. Tavistock. He's only six, after all."

"And a half," added Bevis.

The duke scratched his head. "I suppose that makes sense. But, as Bevis said, every hackney cab in London looks like all the others. How are earth are we going to find out where that one went?"

"You gave Mrs. Tavistock a bank draft, didn't you?"

"Yes."

Fiona smile wryly. "My guess is that she went straight to the bank. A woman as greedy as she wouldn't want to wait another hour to get her hands on that money."

"Right!" The duke flung himself into action. "Bevis, get my hat and send the driver round with my carriage. Now! I've got some banking to do."

"I'll go with you," Fiona said.

Minutes later, the gleaming carriage rumbled out of the alleyway. It had barely stopped before the duke opened the door for Fiona. Just as she set foot on the lower rung, another thought occurred to her. Pausing, she said over her shoulder, "Bevis, you must do one more thing."

"Anything, ma'am."

"Send a couple of Bow Street runners to the bank. Have them meet us there, will you? Tell them we are going to furnish them some real criminals!"

"Criminals, ma'am?" Bevis's face was smeared with dismay. "You ain't gonna turn over little Alex—"

"No, no, Bevis! I'm talking about the Tavistock sisters. *Both of them!"*

The traffic on Cheapside was miraculously light, and Deramore's coach made good time, heading east. Nearing the bank where he conducted business, the duke perched on the edge of the squabs, coiled to leap out and nab his quarry. Fiona had explained it all to him on the way over. If her theory was correct, and he had no doubt it was, the Tavistock sisters were con artists in the highest degree. They had probably pulled a similar caper in Liverpool, perhaps in other cities, as well.

"What an actress!"

"She only had to play dead long enough for her sister's driver to get her in the cab. My guess is, she's done it before!"

"Poor Alexander! Thinking he caused the old biddy to die!"

"The Tavistocks must have thought they'd hit pay dirt when they realized the child had an unfavorable history with nannies." Fiona shivered. "Ooh! I hope they get tossed in Newgate!"

The duke's blood coursed so violently through his veins, he could hardly hear the carriage wheels as they rumbled to a stop.

"There she is!" Fiona cried, pointing toward the bank.

Indeed, Drusilla Tavistock had just emerged from the building. Lord Deramore's feet hit the cobbled stones of the street just as she looked up. For an instant, the old lady froze, eyes wide with recognition. Then, as Hugh and Fiona started toward her, the governess's sister picked up her skirts and ran.

For an old lady, she was surprisingly agile. Clutching a large leather valise beneath her arm, she sprinted in the opposite direction. With Fiona at his heels, the duke gave chase for half a block, scattering pigeons and pedestrians alike.

"She's heading toward that cab," Fiona gasped.

A dusty hackney cab stood at the corner, its driver waiting, whip in hand. Suddenly, the door of the cab was flung open, and from inside, a terrible, squalling din escaped.

"Let me go!" Alexander's voice was loud and clear.

"I'm coming!" yelled Lord Deramore, increasing his speed.

A woman's face, familiar to the duke, flashed at the open door. Lettie Tavistock screamed, "You'll get him back when we get five thousand more pounds!"

Deramore swore pungently. "If that old witch harms a hair on Sandy's head—"

"So will I," managed Fiona, keeping pace beside him.

Quickly, but not quickly enough, Fiona and Hugh closed the distance between themselves and Drusilla Tavistock. As the old lady jumped into the cab, her sister yanked the door shut. The driver, evidently in cahoots with the sisters, slapped his horses' rumps with a whip and let out a holler. With a jolt, the carriage bounced forward just as Hugh and Fiona reached its side.

They pounded on the door, but it was firmly locked from inside. As the wheels of the cab rolled past, Hugh looked around desperately. He would jump onto the back, where the tiger usually rode, if he had to. There was no way he intended to allow the Tavistock sisters to get away, not as long as they had Alexander with them.

"Look, Hugh! The runners!" Fiona grabbed the duke's arm, preventing his leap onto the back of the cab. Then she ran into the middle of the street, waved her arms wildly and screamed, "Stop that cab! They have my child!"

Two burly men in dark blue uniforms pounded down the

street on horseback. Immediately taking stock of the situation, they drew their horses to a stop directly in front of the hackney's path. The cab's driver, cursing loudly, was forced to rein in his cattle. The dusty black equipage lurched to a halt.

Fiona, talking excitedly, explained as much to the runners as she could in ten seconds. Though there was no way they could absorb the full picture, they understood sufficiently to demand the Tavistock sisters to unlock the cab and exit peacefully.

From inside the carriage, a latch was thrown. The duke nearly tore the door off the hinges getting it open. When Alexander fell into his arms, Hugh backed away from the cab, holding his son tightly against his chest, smothering him with kisses.

After a moment, Fiona wrapped her arms around both of them. Vaguely aware that the runners had handcuffed the Tavistock sisters, she closed her eyes, sending up a silent prayer of thanks for Alexander's safe return.

Wriggling out of his father's arms, the child reached for Fiona's hand. She looked into Alexander's puffy, red-rimmed eyes.

"I thought I had killed her. But I didn't."

"No, dear. You are a good boy."

"Please," said the duke, his voice thick with emotion. "Don't ever run away again. I couldn't bear it if something happened to you, Sandy. I love you. More than you'll ever know."

As a smile replaced the little boy's worried look, Fiona's chest nearly caved in with the pressure of her emotions. Lord Deramore, his eyes wet, drew her toward him, crushing Alexander between them in the process. But no one protested, least of all Fiona.

"I couldn't bear it if you ran away, either," whispered Hugh. "Please say you'll marry me."

Terrified, she revealed her deepest shame. "There'll be no other children," she explained, too nervous to look at him. "I'm sorry I never told you."

"It is of no significance to me." He tipped her face up, forcing her to meet his gaze. "It's you I want, Fiona. It's you I want to marry. It's you I want to be Alexander's mother. Nothing else matters."

She clung to him as Alexander clung to her. The little boy's arms wound around her waist as the duke kissed her. A hundred emotions—amazement, relief, overwhelming love for Hugh and Alexander—swept over her.

Alexander tugged at her elbow. "You said, 'They've got my son.' You said it. I heard you. Does that mean—"

Fiona stared into the child's wide, questioning eyes. "Yes, I suppose it does, dear," she replied.

"Thank God," the duke whispered in her ear. "Thank God I found you."

The sun shone brightly on Fiona's face as she took one of Alexander's hands, and Hugh took the other. "Don't drag your toes, dear," she said as the three of them, a family now, returned to the duke's carriage.

"Mind your mother, Sandy," Hugh added, a smile in his voice.

"Yes, Father! Yes, Mother! Oh, I do like the sound of that!" Alexander cried, skipping between them.

Fiona liked it, too.

The Last Chance Governess was home. The duke was looking toward the future. And little Lord Badwell had found a mother's love, at last.

LOVE STORIES YOU'LL NEVER FORGET...
IN ONE FABULOUSLY ROMANTIC NEW LINE

BALLAD ROMANCES

Each month, four new historical series by both beloved and brand-new authors will begin or continue. These linked stories will introduce proud families, reveal ancient promises, and take us down the path to true love. In Ballad, the romance doesn't end with just one book . . .

COMING IN JULY
EVERYWHERE BOOKS ARE SOLD

The Wishing Well Trilogy:
CATHERINE'S WISH, by Joy Reed.
When a woman looks into the wishing well at Honeywell House, she sees the face of the man she will marry.

Titled Texans:
NOBILITY RANCH, by Cynthia Sterling
The three sons of an English earl come to Texas in the 1880s to find their fortunes . . . and lose their hearts.

Irish Blessing:
REILLY'S LAW, by Elizabeth Keys
For an Irish family of shipbuilders, an ancient gift allows them to "see" their perfect mate.

The Acadians:
EMILIE, by Cherie Claire
The daughters of an Acadian exile struggle for new lives in 18th-century Louisiana.